Two Months in Summer

Eleanor Michael

AVOCADO BOOKS

Avocadobooks.com

First published by Avocado Books in 2016

© Eleanor Michael

ISBN: 978-0-9935658-1-6

Cover artwork: Avocado Books

Author asserts the moral right to be
identified as the author of this work

A catalogue record of this book is
available from the British Library

To Pamela Oldfield - my inspiration, mentor and friend, who sadly passed away before I had finished this book.

Prologue

As the heavy Hercules transport plane lumbered into the air on take off from the British Air force base at Akrotiri on the island of Cyprus, the knuckles of my flight companion, frantically gripping the armrest, slowly relaxed.

"Thank God we're out of this place," she said, heaving a sigh of relief.

"Yes, we're safe," I said. "But what about all those poor people who didn't have the benefit of a foreign passport to get them away from the fighting?"

Looking down, as the plane banked away to the west, I could clearly make out the rugged coastline where the legendry Goddess of Love Aphrodite had been washed ashore in a spray of frothy spume.

I'd spent many happy hours with my husband on that same deserted beach before this terrible tragedy had occurred. This beautiful island of Aphrodite had produced a people who were considered to be the friendliest and most hospitable in the whole of the Mediterranean. Now their lives were in ruins.

They had just lived through a catastrophic upheaval.

Whole communities, both Greek and Turkish Cypriots, had been displaced during a war that lasted only one month but had changed the course of everyone's lives forever.

The political pot had been simmering for a long

time but it came abruptly to the boil when a plot to assassinate the President was discovered. This thwarted plot led to a coup and another hasty attempt by the corrupt military Junta in Greece to kill him. But he escaped and left the island.

He was replaced by a notorious killer, who had annihilated Turkish Cypriot villages and murdered British soldiers.

Within a few days Turkey had sent an invasion force to the north coast to protect their Turkish Cypriot citizens - steadily fighting their way east and west. They were ripping this beautiful friendly island apart and making tens of thousands of the population refugees. Killing and raping in their wake, until almost half the country was in their hands, despite international condemnation. These events made world headlines.

My involvement in this story would only have made a short entry in a police report. Yet, that one incident was the catalyst that started this dreadful chain of events.

It was I who discovered the plot to assassinate the President.

This is how it happened.

1

Nicosia, Monday 28th June, 1974

The peace of our quiet afternoon was shattered by an impatient banging at the front door. We both jumped, startled by the noise.

"Who the hell's that?" Ann exclaimed angrily. "Why don't they ring the bell? Don't they realise it's siesta time?"

The banging became more insistent as she hurried into the hall and pulled open the front door.

"Sally," she called to me, startled. "There are three policemen here."

"Make sure they show you their identity cards," I called back to her from the kitchen where I was about to put the kettle on for tea.

"I don't think I'll bother," I heard her exclaim. "They've got guns. That's enough identification for me."

The curtains in the kitchen were tightly closed, to keep out the scorching heat of the summer sun. But, peeping through, I saw that three floors below, the building was surrounded by police vehicles. Quickly I joined Ann in the hall.

"We were told that a Miss Andrulla Mousaris is the caretaker of the building and lives in this flat. Is that correct?" the police sergeant standing at the front door demanded.

Ann bristled. Normally gentle and well mannered, she certainly wasn't a snob, but she wasn't happy to be described as a 'caretaker'. Her shoulders lifted as she pulled herself up to her full five foot six height. Her rich, deep voice had a haughty edge as she replied. "Yes, I am Andrulla Mousaris. My family own the block and I live here."

The sergeant was a bit taken aback but never the less he barked: "We have orders to search the building. We would like to start here and then work through the rest of the block."

"In that case," Ann retaliated. "Perhaps you should show me your identification. I've heard that there have been armed men up to no good, posing as policemen recently."

The sergeant scowled, but grudgingly produced his papers.

Ann studied them intently, though I knew she hadn't a clue what she should be looking for.

"You'd better come in and take a look then," she said, handing them back.

The sergeant and one of his constables followed her as she led the way through her flat. I waited in the living room while the third policeman stood in the doorway.

"What's going on?" I asked curiously, but he ignored me.

Soon Ann and the searchers returned.

"Could you tell me your name please, madam?" said the sergeant, turning abruptly to me.

"Mrs Sally Lytras."

"Do you live here too?"

"No, I just called in on my way back to work. But what are you looking for?"

This time it was the sergeant who ignored me.

Turning back to Ann, he barked: "Do you know all the people who live in this block?"

She nodded. "Yes. My parents have a flat on the ground floor which they use for their holidays. This flat belongs to me, and the others are rented."

"Do you have keys to all the flats?"

"Yes, of course I do," she snapped back. "I look after the administration of the building. I have to let repair men in when tenants are at work.

The sergeant glanced again round the room then nodded to his constables.

"We've finished here; now let's look at the rest of the building. Please bring the keys to open up if necessary."

Ann stubbed out her cigarette and gathered up a large bundle of keys from the hall table. "I'll be back in a minute," she said to me. "Help yourself to tea. You know where everything is."

Ann and I had known each other almost from the time I arrived in Cyprus five years ago.

Though our temperaments and looks were completely different - she was tall and slim with a quiet, shy manner, while I was shorter, excitable and chatty, with a positive attitude - we complemented each other and were more like sisters than just good friends. Next month would be her 29th birthday, but she was still single. I had already been married for three years. We saw each other almost every day so, over the years, we had learned all each other's hopes, fears and secrets.

Her Cypriot parents had moved to England before she was born and she became part of the large extended family already settled there. Despite being brought up in the UK, rules for Cypriot girls were very strict and protective. She always had to be accompanied by a family member when she went out and even then it was usually only to visit someone within the family circle. But one day she rebelled at her restricted life and eventually she was allowed to find her roots in Cyprus.

Once there, living in her own flat, she had more freedom, though she was still under the protective eye of various aunts.

Returning to the kitchen, under the watchful eye of the corporal, I smiled to myself as I poured boiling water into the tea pot. My Cypriot husband, Alecos, who was in Germany on business till the end of the week, always pulled my leg about the fact that, being British, I drank tea with milk every afternoon, even during the intense heat of a Cyprus summer.

I carried the tray into the living room, wondering why the police wanted to search this building. I knew from the newspapers that there had been trouble brewing for quite some time. Several police posts had been raided and guns and equipment stolen. Now there were roadblocks in unexpected places. I'd been stopped and searched once when I was on the way to visit friends in the country.

The rumour was that General Grivas had secretly returned after being exiled as a dangerous agitator some years earlier. He was reputed to be leading the newly formed 'National Association of Cyprus Fighters' EOKA B, a rebel group intent on overthrowing the government.

Some months earlier the President's helicopter had been shot at while taking off. Fortunately he'd escaped, but now there was a feeling of unease hanging over the island.

But why did the police want to search a modern

block in a quiet upmarket suburb of Nicosia? These EOKA B rebels were based far away from here, hidden somewhere in the mountains. It was puzzling!

As I settled down to enjoy my tea, an announcement in the corner of the front page of the national English language newspaper caught my eye...

On Sunday 7th July at the Kiko Seminary in Strovolos, Archbishop Makarios will attend the Ceremony for the Inauguration of five novices into the priesthood of the Greek Orthodox Church of Cyprus.

"Ahh! That's the reason the police are here," I murmured. "This block is next door to the seminary. The police must be doing a routine check of the neighbourhood before Makarios comes on Sunday."

Ann returned, as the sound of police vehicles leaving the area, reverberated on the quiet afternoon air.

"Did you find out what they were looking for?" I asked, as she flopped down onto the settee grabbing a cup of tea.

She shook her head. "No. They just made a note of everyone's name and had a quick look around but they didn't seem very concerned about doing a thorough search."

"It's probably something to do with this," I said, handing her the newspaper. Glancing at it she nodded. "Yes. It must be," she agreed. "If Makarios is coming, hordes of people will be here on Sunday. At least a bus load of family for each novice, all dressed in their Sunday best, carrying huge bags of food."

"Yes," I nodded. "But it's considered an honour to have a relative in the church. Archbishop Makarios was the son of a shepherd, yet he became head of the Greek Orthodox Church and the President of Cyprus too. If it could happen to him, I'm sure they all hope it could happen to one of their sons as well!"

"Perhaps!" shrugged Ann, scornfully. "But I remember the last time there was an inauguration; the whole place was swarming with people having picnics after the ceremony."

I smiled as I imagined the scene. Hundreds of bodies squashed together trying to shelter in the shade of the few scrawny olive trees in the field outside.

"Oh, damn," she grumbled. "I was supposed to go to my aunt's for lunch on Sunday but the garage entrance will be block by parked cars and I won't be able to get out."

"Why don't you come and stay with us in Kyrenia for the weekend?" I suggested. "Alecos will be home from Germany on Friday."

"No, not this time," she grinned. "I don't want to be a gooseberry. You and Alecos will have a lot of catching up to do after two weeks apart!"

It was true. We hadn't been apart since we were married and Alecos was very demonstrative. Ann knew he would be all over me when he got back from his business trip. Alecos and I had met when I accepted the job as his personal assistant in his rapidly expanding cosmetic company. At first he was very formal. But as he came to appreciate and understand my sense of humour, his manner relaxed, allowing his mischievous personality to bubble up. I found his uninhibited southern warmth very flattering and appealing after the more restrained behaviour of most Northern Europeans. Before long we were together and were now happily married

As I was about to leave for the office I smelt

something burning.

"Have you left anything in the oven, Ann?" I asked, sniffing the air.

"No, I haven't been cooking this afternoon!"

We followed our noses in the direction of the smell. It became stronger as we opened the front door. It seemed to be coming from the flat across the hallway.

"Someone must be cooking over there," I said, indicating the other flat.

"It can't be," Ann looked agitated. "That flat's been empty for ages. I told the police it was unoccupied so they didn't bother to look inside."

"That's strange," I said as I walked across the hall to the door of the flat. "It smells like burning paper! Have you got the key, Ann? We'd better go in and take a look."

Ann sorted through the bundle of keys she'd dropped onto the hall table when the police left. "I gave it to Mr Dimitri downstairs some time ago. He wanted to show the flat to a friend. I can't remember if he gave it back."

The keys jangled noisily as she sorted through them. "Oh hell, I can't find it, but take these, something might fit," she said, thrusting a bunch into my hand.

Crossing the hall I tried various keys in the lock. Suddenly, I heard a loud thump followed by a strangled cry from behind the door. The hairs prickled on the back of my neck as I jumped back, startled.

"My God!" I shrieked. "There's somebody in there! Call the police quick, Ann."

She gasped and ran back into the living room. I could hear her dialling frantically as she tried to get through to the police station.

Suddenly, the door opened and a man stumbled out.

2

Discovery

The face of the man standing in front of me was grey with fear and pouring with sweat. His eyes darted frantically from left to right like a cornered animal.

A scream started in my throat but turned into a strangled gurgle, as terrified, I backed away. He stared blindly at me for a moment then, in a trembling voice, he mumbled something. I shook my head, too scared to speak. He moved towards me and as he raised his arm I smelled his acid sweat. Afraid he was going to hit me I moved back further, till I was pinned like a fly to the cold wall behind me.

"Help me, I need a car," he pleaded, his voice croaking with fear.

I shook my head. "I don't speak Greek," I lied, playing for time.

With an agonised groan he stumbled across the hallway and rushed head-long down the stairs.

I dashed back into Ann's flat, slamming the door hard behind me. With knees like jelly, I collapsed into a chair. My whole body was shaking and my teeth chattering with terror. I was nearly in tears.

Ann stared at me in amazement. "What on earth's the matter? What happened? You look as though you've seen a ghost!"

With a shuddering sob, I buried my face in my hands.

"Sally, what is it?" she demanded. "Tell me!"

Eventually the panic subsided and in a ragged voice I told her about the man.

Her mouth dropped open in shocked silence.

Soon, a new team of police arrived. After giving them a garbled explanation, they marched across the hall, removing the pistols from their holsters as they went.

We crept behind them.

On the floor, just behind the door, lay a revolver. I recoiled in horror as I realised that if the man hadn't dropped it in his panic, he might have shot me instead! A clammy shiver ran down my back.

Once inside the front door the flat was in darkness. A policeman snapped on the light in the kitchen as not a chink of daylight penetrated the tightly closed curtains.

Flies buzzed around the congealed food left on the dirty plates piled in the sink. An oily fish smell came from a couple of empty sardine tins next to a half eaten loaf, its crumbs strewn across the Formica table. On the stove was a small coffee pot, thick with recently brewed coffee grounds, but there was nothing burning anywhere in the kitchen.

The living room was a squalid mess too. Newspapers were strewn over the floor. Piles of spent matches were scattered next to candles in wax encrusted bottles stuck to saucers. The predominant smell in this room was nicotine. Mountains of cigarette butts spilled out of every ashtray. But nothing was burning in this room either.

As the police entered the bedroom, we peered after them through the doorway.

The room smelt stale and musty. The sheets on the bed were crumpled and soiled and a pile of dirty laundry was in a corner. A policeman flicked it apart with the toe of his boot and a sour smell wafted up from the heap.

Following the policemen down the hall to the bathroom, the burning smell hit us. The bath was black, full of burnt paper. Pieces were still smouldering, their edges glowing as they slowly curled over. A policeman grabbed a glass and threw water over the burning papers. They smoked and sizzled as they were smothered.

The floor was covered in official stamped documents and letters, while more spilled out of black plastic dustbin sacks. The man in the flat must have tried to destroy them when he heard the commotion of the police arriving outside.

The sergeant snapped an order to one of his assistants who began to gather them up.

As the remaining team moved on towards the second bedroom, we followed.

The sergeant tried the door but it was locked. He stood to one side with his pistol cocked as the young constable smashed the butt of his automatic rifle several times against the lock. It snapped apart with a loud crack. He kicked the door with his heavy boot and jumped away from the open space as the door crashed back against the wall.

"My God!" I breathed, as we saw what was inside.

The wardrobe was crammed with weapons. Automatic rifles, pistols, revolvers, shotguns, and huge piles of gun clips and cartridges, all packed together so tightly there was hardly room enough to get a matchstick between them. There were more boxes piled on the floor.

The room was an arsenal. From a hook on the wall hung a long black robe and a black pillbox hat worn by priests of the Greek Orthodox Church.

The sergeant's eyes bulged and a low whistle escaped his lips.

At that point, he realised that Ann and I were behind him staring into the room. He snapped an order to his constables as he hurriedly herded us back into Ann's living room.

Turning abruptly to me, he barked, "Did you see the man in the flat?"

"Yes," I said, "but only for a moment before he ran down the stairs."

"Did you recognise him?"

"No, I've never seen him before. But he was short, fat and terrified," I said in a rush. "He was even more terrified than I was," I added.

He glowered at me, not amused. Then turning to Ann he started to bombard her with questions. Why had she said the flat was empty? Why hadn't she given the key to the police? Hadn't she seen any lights or movement from that flat? How could someone be living there without her knowing? The questions were coming so fast I could almost see her head start to spin.

She became hesitant and muddled. As she caught my eye, I gave her a reassuring nod. Her mouth twitched in a grateful smile not quite hiding her discomfort, nor her fear of the bullying man towering above her. She fumbled for a cigarette and inhaled deeply.

"I don't believe you didn't know anyone was there? You women always know everybody else's business," the sergeant sneered.

"Wait a minute," I shouted angrily. "Do you think we would be so stupid to call you again, if we'd been involved with this nasty business? We were just having a siesta like everyone else when that bunch of policemen came hammering on the door. If they'd asked to look inside the flat they'd have known that Ann had lent the key to one of the tenants. Why don't you ask him about it instead of yelling at us?"

The sergeant's aggressive expression changed. He raised his eyebrows in surprise.

"Did you give the key to a tenant?" he asked Ann in a quieter voice.

"Yes," she said breathing deeply to regain her composure. "I gave it to Mr Dimitri in flat 6 downstairs."

"Why did you do that?"

"He said his friend wanted to rent a flat in Nicosia."

"Don't you show the new tenants the flats yourself?"

"Yes, but, the only day his friend was in town, I was working, so, I let Mr Dimitri show him."

"How long ago was that?" the sergeant asked.

"About three weeks, I think."

"Right," the sergeant said, moving swiftly to the door. "We're going downstairs to see this Mr Dimitri. You two stay here for the moment, but you'll have to come back to the police station to make an official statement. You stay with them," he added, turning to one of the constables. "Make sure they don't use the phone!"

They left and we collapsed onto the sofa, exhausted after the unbelievable events of the afternoon. Eventually breaking the tense atmosphere, I said: "I think I could do with a cold, strong gin and tonic."

"Good idea," Ann agreed, relieved to focus her mind on a mundane task. "Can I get you one, too?" she asked, turning to the constable..

He shook his head regretfully. "No thanks, I'm still on duty."

As Ann handed me my drink, I held the frosted glass to my cheek to enjoy its coolness. Then as the cold liquid ran down my parched throat, I felt myself beginning to unwind. My mind turned to the consequences of our innocent discovery. Would these rebels harm us because we'd found their cache? And how would we recognise a rebel? The frightened man looked just like anyone you'd pass on the street. Mr Dimitri from downstairs, with his bald head and glasses, had always been polite and friendly when I met him in the lift. He didn't look suspicious either. These two certainly didn't look like the tough and fierce men one would think of as rebels!

And that first bunch of policemen? Why hadn't they searched the empty flat? Did they know someone was there?

If all those papers in the bathroom were anything to go by, it seemed that half the country could be involved with these rebels. Maybe even some of our friends were connected with them too. There was nothing to distinguish them so there no way of knowing who we could trust.

What had we got ourselves into? Our quiet Monday afternoon tea time had turned into a terrifying nightmare.

3

Police HQ, early evening

When we arrived at the police headquarters the air stank of cigarettes and garlic.

They separated us and I was taken to a small room near the canteen, from where the additional greasy smell of cooked lamb wafted in.

From two small windows high up near the ceiling a faint glimmer of light came through the dirty glass. Hanging from a frayed wire in the middle of the room a bare bulb illuminated a small metal table with an uncomfortable looking wooden chair next to it. The room had once been whitewashed, but certainly not recently.

The bleakness of the room however, was relieved by the standard issue framed photograph of President Makarios, in his sombre black Archbishop's robes. Only the large gold cross hanging from the heavy ornate gold chains of office round his neck relieved the blackness. But, the twinkle in the dark eyes and a slight smile on the lips hinted that the man was not as forbidding as the funereal robes suggested.

A large bluebottle slammed itself repeatedly against the glass as it flew an erratic course between the two windows. In the confined space its buzzing sounded noisy and angry, adding the final touch of gloom to the already depressing room.

The constable indicated that I should sit. Then placing a large, unwieldy book onto the table in front of me, he said: "Have a look through that. See if you can spot anyone you recognise."

The book had photographs on each page, showing a full face and profile of men or occasionally a woman, with a number printed underneath each picture.

Many were photos of young men, doing their compulsory national service in the Cyprus National Guard. One of the conditions imposed by the three guarantor powers, Greece, Turkey and Britain at the signing of the Cyprus Treaty of Independence in 1960, was that mainland Greek officers should control the Cyprus National Guard army. Now the government of Greece had been taken over by a corrupt Military Dictatorship, the Greek Officers were being replaced by a more militant anti–Makarios contingent. It was commonly assumed that they were backing the EOKA B rebels to destabilise the Cyprus government. So it was easy for these mainland Greeks to influence the young Cypriot conscripts under their command.

I hadn't realised though, that so many police were now EOKA B rebel supporters too.

It seemed more than possible, in the circumstances, that some of the policemen, who came to the flat today, were involved with these rebels too.

The constable chatted away while I leafed through the book. He talked about his family and asked about my husband and his business. He also asked about Ann and it was obvious from his questions that she was still under suspicion.

She had never been the type who listened to local gossip. It was enough for her that her tenants paid the rent and didn't wreck the place. The comings and goings of her neighbours was none of her business. But the police didn't know that or even believe it was possible for a woman not to enjoy a gossip. Cyprus was still a very chauvinistic society.

I was angry and worried and was sure they were giving her a rough time.

Getting to the end of the book, I shook my head. I didn't recognise anyone. Another book was produced, then another. I was thirsty, my eyes hurt and after being shut up in this miserable room for more than an hour, every picture had begun to look the same.

Suddenly the door flew open. A tall, distinguished looking man, with a commanding aura, strode in to the room. The policeman hastily pulled himself away from the wall where he had been slouching, snapped to attention and saluted smartly.

"Good evening. Mrs Lytras. I am Commissioner Marco," the tall man said. "I would like to speak to you in my office. Would you come with me please?"

My heart sank. I knew this man to be the most important police officer in the country and although he was polite, his request sounded ominous.

As I entered his air-conditioned office, I shivered both from the cold and the fear of what might happen.

He indicated a couple of arm chairs next to a low coffee table. I sank gratefully into the softly upholstered leather, my back aching from sitting so long on the hard wooden chair downstairs. The curtains were already pulled as it was now past eight and dark outside.

"Can I offer you some refreshment?" he asked, courteously.

"I'd love a coffee and a glass of water, please. It was so hot and stuffy in that room downstairs."

A slight smile twitched at the corner of his mouth

as he phoned the canteen.

Running his fingers through thick grey hair, combed straight back from a square jawed face, I glimpsed a jagged scar on his left temple. His steel rimmed glasses on a prominent nose gave him a severe look. For such a tall man his movements were graceful and constrained, but I was sure he could be very tough, if pushed.

Sitting opposite me he leaned forward and offered me a cigarette.

"No, thank you, I don't smoke," I said.

He raised an eyebrow in surprise. "Would it disturb you if I do?" he asked.

"No, not at all, I'm used to it. My husband smokes."

"It's quite unusual to meet someone who doesn't smoke these days," he remarked.

I laughed. "Yes, that's true, but my father was old fashioned and didn't like to see a woman smoking. So when I asked him if I could try, he promised he would give me twenty one pounds on my twenty first birthday, as long as I didn't smoke till then. I was only eleven at the time and it sounded like a fortune so I agreed!" I gabbled nervously.

He smiled. "I wish I'd thought of that when my daughter was growing up. It would have saved me a lot of money!" As his eyes twinkled behind his glasses, he seemed less intimidating and I began to relax.

The coffee arrived and as he lit his cigarette I sipped the cold water and looked around the office. On the wall behind the desk were several framed photographs as well as the obligatory picture of the President that I'd seen in the interrogation room, though in the Commissioner's elegant office the portrait was surrounded by a heavy antique gold frame. Files and papers on the polished mahogany desk suggested he was a busy man, not someone in an exalted position who just gave orders.

Commissioner Marco sat back and crossed one long leg over the other. "I don't want you to be nervous," he said, as he eyed my hands clenched tightly in my lap. "I just want you to tell me everything you can remember about this afternoon."

Oh, here we go again! I sighed to myself.

Then, to my surprise, he asked, "Would you prefer to speak in English or Greek?"

Maybe he wasn't so formidable after all? Then I |realised it wasn't so unusual. Since Cyprus had once been a British Colony, every government official was obliged to speak English.

"English, if you don't mind. My Greek isnt bad, but in a difficult situation like this I can think more spontaneously in English."

He nodded. "Go ahead," he said. "Just forget I'm here and tell me what happened. Say whatever comes into your head."

I rested my head on the back of the armchair and returned my thoughts to the afternoon.

I explained again how Ann and I had smelt burning from the empty flat and the frightened man appearing at the door.

The Commissioner nodded and wrote something on the pad on his lap.

"Had you ever seen the man before?"

I shook my head. "No."

"What exactly do you remember about him?" he asked softly.

Closing my eyes I let my thoughts drift back. "He wasn't very tall. When he came out of the door and stared at me, our eyes were almost on a level. I'm five foot three and in these shoes...," I said, looking down at my wedge heeled sandals, "...I must be a couple of inches taller. So maybe about five foot seven. He was a bit on the fat side. He had a Pier Cardin logo on the pocket of his shirt but his clothes looked slept in."

"Was he wearing glasses?" the Commissioner asked quietly.

I shook my head. "Not when he came out of the flat, but I think he normally did, because there were pinch marks either side of his nose."

"Do you remember the colour of his eyes?"

"Oh yes. When he stared at me, I noticed that they were pale brown."

"Was he carrying anything when you saw him?"

I thought for a moment. "Yes, it looked like a black leather document case. It banged against the rail as he ran down the stairs...and...," I said, as small details started to return, "...he was wearing expensive leather shoes. I remember hearing them clatter on the stairs."

The commissioner sat perfectly still as I searched back in my memory for more details. "Despite the fact he was unshaven, he certainly didn't look like a villain," I said. "His complexion was pale...as though he spent most of his time indoors."

The Commissioner nodded absently. He stared unfocused at the wall behind my head. Deep in thought he ran his long forefinger slowly up and down the side of his nose. The room was completely silent. My stomach turned over. My instinct told me that by the time this conversation was over I was going to be in big trouble.

Eventually, his eyes returned to the pad on his knee. "You didn't tell me the colour of his hair."

"My God. That's it!" I spluttered, sitting bolt

upright in my chair. "I knew there was something odd about him. My mind was so focused on his face I completely forgot about his hair. He was wearing a wig!"

"A wig?" exclaimed the startled Commissioner. "How do you know it was a wig?" he demanded, his hand unconsciously touching his own thick hair.

"My husband's company supplies hair cosmetics. Wigs and hair pieces are used to test our hair tints and perming solutions. In the Mediterranean, most hair is so thick, wigs are unusual, but this man was wearing a full wig so he must have been practically bald," I said.

The Commissioner, deep in thought, took off his glasses and rubbed his eyes.

Suddenly he jumped up and in three long strides reached the far wall. He unhooked one of the photographs. Handing it to me, he switched on the lamp by my chair.

In the picture President Makarios was shaking hands with General Gizikis, the military president of Greece. The Commissioner was standing next to Makarios and behind the Greek president were several figures, slightly out of focus.

"Does anyone there look familiar?" the Commissioner asked.

I moved the photo directly under the light and stared hard.

I pointed to one of the men in the background. "That could be him! Yes, I think it is! Who is he?"

The Commissioner sighed loudly but didn't reply. Walking back to his desk he dropped heavily on to his swivel chair. My mouth felt dry with fear. I took a sip of the bitter, black coffee then drained the rest of the water in one gulp.

Eventually, the Commissioner spoke. "You must be

very careful who you talk to. You could be in danger."

My stomach turned over again. "I don't understand. Why should I be in danger?" my voice squeaked. "I don't know who that man is."

The Commissioner came over and sat opposite me again. He stared at me for a long time, then he seemed to come to a decision.

Leaning forward, his arms resting on his knees, he looked directly at me. Then, he said in a voice that chilled me. "You are the only person who has seen this man here in Cyprus. That's why you are in danger."

"But I don't know who he is. How can I be in danger?" I demanded.

"The people behind him don't know that so they will try to stop you saying anything."

I felt sick. He could see just how scared I was becoming.

"I'm sorry, Mrs Lytras" he began. "I know this must be frightening for you but you appear to be an observant and intelligent woman. The more informed you are about the situation, the better you will be able to protect yourself!"

Unable to speak from fear, I nodded limply.

"This man is George Kallis," the Commissioner said, obviously expecting some reaction.

The name meant nothing. I shook my head.

The Commissioner continued: "He is an administrator for the dictatorship in Athens and close to Demetrios Ioannidis. I'm sure you know he is one of the most ruthless and callous members of the military junta in Athens. Ioannidis was behind the shooting down of President Makarios helicopter, but as the assassination attempt failed, the junta then smuggled the expelled General Grivas back to Cyprus, in order to set up a new 'Union with Greece EOKA B' group.

"So the rumours are true that Grivas returned to Cyprus?" I said.

"Yes, they are. Although he died recently, Grivas was originally a patriotic fighter against the British in the fifties. This time round though, his targets were Cypriots loyal to President Makarios. Many of the present EOKA B supporters are respectable members of society, politicians, lawyers, teachers. People you might know."

My eyebrows raised in disbelief. "But why should they be against Makarios now? They were all behind him when he was fighting to get the British out."

"That's correct. He was in the forefront then, when they were fighting for enosis, union with Greece. But now many people have turned away from him when it became obvious that enosis was no longer at the top of his agenda.

"I'm sure your husband must have told you about the constitution, Mrs Lytras?"

"Yes, bits and pieces."

"Well, then I'll try to explain briefly so you'll understand better what you are up against."

He settled back in his chair. Resting his hands comfortably in his lap, he cleared his throat, and began.

"During the British occupation in Cyprus, Enosis which, as you know, translates into 'union with Greece', became the Cypriot rallying cry. We Greek Cypriots felt we were fighting to be part of the Greek motherland and its heroic traditions. We shared the same religion, the same language, the same flag. We've had ties with Hellenism since the Trojan wars."

Thoughtfully touching the deep scar on his forehead, he added: "We put up a furious fight to get rid of the British colonial rulers during the 'fifties struggle."

He continued: "Until then, both Greek and Turkish Cypriots had lived more or less in harmony as neighbours and friends. But bitterness grew against the Turks when the British called on the Turkish community to help them keep law and order. The Greek Cypriots resentment against the British became more militant and violent. Consequently, as Britain finally agreed to leave Cyprus, the government in Ankara, in lieu of the part played by the Turkish minority living in Cyprus, insisted that no final settlement could be made without the full approval of Turkey."

He reached across and took a cigarette. Inhaling deeply, he explained: "If we, the Greek Cypriots, hadn't agreed to this condition, there would have been no end to the harsh emergency rule by British troops. Makarios, as the figurehead of the insurgents, had been deported to the Seychelles by then and would never have been allowed to return to Cyprus. There would have been no possibility of self government. So, the choice was either to agree to allow Turkey to approve the final draft of the constitution or to have even more unacceptable conditions foisted on us by the British."

The Commissioner paused, stubbed out his cigarette and immediately lit another before continuing.

"The Cyprus Constitution was signed in 1960 by the governments of Britain, Greece and Turkey. The Cypriots were hardly consulted. Makarios on his return to Cyprus, stood by his undertaking and attempted to make the unfair settlement work despite his misgivings about the feasibility of the agreement," he said.

The commissioner sat forward in his chair, exhaling a great plume of smoke with a sigh.

"But that was more than ten years ago," I said, surprised. "Since then Cyprus has boomed under Makarios' leadership."

"Yes," he agreed. "He has performed an economic miracle, opening up expansion of every kind of trade and encouraging the growth in tourism, but many people feel he has gone back on his promises and is standing in the way of union with Greece, which, after all, was what we fought for originally. But I can't understand why any intelligent Cypriot would want union with those thugs in power in Athens now," he added bitterly, angrily grinding his cigarette in the ashtray.

"So you can understand why, in the present circumstances, Makarios doesn't feel it is in the best interests of the peoples of Cyprus to have union with Greece."

I nodded. "But how does all this affect me?" I asked.

"If it were proven that Kallis is here undercover, it would confirm that the Greek Junta, backed, as they are, by the CIA, is behind the rebels that are trying to overthrow the Cyprus government. That could obviously lead to international repercussions."

I was horrified. "You mean we're up against Cypriot terrorists, corrupt Greek military thugs and the CIA? I can't believe it!"

Gravely he nodded. "Yes, now you understand why you must be very careful. The fewer people who know you saw Kallis, the safer it will be for you. Let's keep this strictly between ourselves. Don't even say anything to your friend, Miss Mousaris."

I sat there with my mouth open, stunned by what he'd told me.

Finally he broke the silence. "Now, just one last thing. If anything unusual happens, day or night, call me immediately. This is my private number here at headquarters, my home number," he said, scribbling on the back of his card and handing it to me.

Tucking it safely into my bag, I couldn't believe that I would ever have to use it. But it still felt reassuring to have it.

Suddenly the Commissioner's grave expression changed. He smiled. "Now I think you should go home. You know all there is to know. You've had a long day and look very tired."

And scared stiff too, I thought, as I shakily stood up to leave.

When I got downstairs, Ann was sitting on a wooden bench in the entrance hall, cigarette held tensely between her fingers and exhaustion written all over her face.

I knew she'd have been quite unprepared for the bullying and pressure from the police and she'd have been absolutely devastated that no one would believe that she knew nothing about the existence of the man in the flat next door,

As we were leaving, there was a commotion at the main doors. Mr Dimitri was being roughly escorted into the police station by two burly policemen. As he saw us, his upper lip curled in a snarl and his eyes became hard slits.

"You interfering bitches!" he spat. "You'll pay for this!"

We were shocked. What was he talking about?

Then I realised that it must have been Mr Dimitri who was hiding Kallis and feeding him. Then I remembered seeing his wife hanging around on the stairs when the first lot of police left. She must have been making sure that Kallis was safe. Mr Dimitri also had a younger brother who was a priest. Perhaps the robe in the flat belonged to him! My mind whirled. It seemed we had been innocently sitting on a hornet's nest.

Supposing the constable, who was driving us home, was a rebel too and would kidnap us on the way. I was becoming paranoid!

But this whole drama wasn't something that just happens in a Frederick Forsyth thriller. It was real, and, it was happening to us.

4

Late evening

We stopped at Ann's flat on the way home to pick up her car and pack a small case for a few nights stay with me, as neither of us wanted to be alone after our scary ordeal.

Our stay at the police HQ had been very long and now we were starving.

So while Ann settled into the guest room, I searched around in the kitchen for something to eat.

While Alecos was away, I hadn't bothered to shop, just making do with what I had in the house. This now turned out to be half a loaf of bread, a few eggs, a couple of onions and some shrivelled potatoes. All of which ended up as a Spanish omelette with toast. Once the food was on the table we fell on it like vultures.

We hardly spoke, as we were still in a state of shock, but by the time our meagre supper was finished we felt better and ready to put the afternoons events behind us.

Carrying our coffee outside to the spacious terrace that wrapped around two sides of the apartment, we settled ourselves comfortably into softly cushioned easy chairs. Lighting her usual 'after dinner' cigarette, Ann exhaled contentedly as the smoke wafted gently upwards into the warm night air. The sky was like blue velvet shot through with tiny points of silver thread. The lights of Nicosia sparkled like diamonds across the city, getting smaller and fewer till finally disappearing as they neared the top of the distant mountain range.

The balmy night air washed over us, relaxing our frazzled nerves. The large measure of Metaxas brandy that I'd poured for us helped too!

"I don't think we should say anything to anyone about what happened today," I suggested to Ann. "You know how people love to gossip here."

"Yes, you're right," she agreed. "Everyone knows that if you blow your nose loudly in Nicosia, you're sure to meet someone in Limassol who's heard you had a cold."

I laughed. "That's the trouble with living on a small island, everyone knows everything. But seriously, if, by any chance, someone does say anything, just be vague, don't mention about the man in the flat or what we saw there. The less we appear to know the better."

Ann was very open and trusting. She could, in all innocence, let something slip, so I was trying to get the Commissioner's warning across to her without having to explain further. "In fact," I said. "I'm not even going to say anything to Alecos. There's nothing he can do and he'd be worried stiff."

Alecos phoned me every evening while he was away. He'd probably tried earlier and would already be concerned that I wasn't at home.

I was desperate to tell him what had happened, but I knew it was impossible. He was so protective. He would be on the next plane home regardless of how close he was to finalising his negotiations.

As I sipped my brandy, my thoughts wandered back to a Friday night some time after I'd started to work for him. By then, I had moved in with Ann who was much calmer and quieter than me, so we had agreed I spend the weekends at my family's holiday house on the north coast, to give her a bit of peace and distance from my noisier exuberant personality.

On that particular Friday night there was a tremendous electric storm. As the thunder rumbled overhead, all the doors, windows, pots and pans rattled and shook. A pot of geraniums that I'd watered earlier toppled off the window sill in the kitchen and smashing to the ground, it spilled out over the floor, filling the room with the pungent smell of damp earth.

From the small terrace on the roof of the house I could see the full extent of the storm. Sheet lightning bathed the sky in one direction and at the same instant the jagged edge of forked lightning ripped across from another. The light illuminated the heavy purple clouds which boiled and churned in the wind: yet there was not a single drop of rain.

I was amazed. I had never seen anything so magnificently furious before.

The craggy peaks of the mountains behind were black silhouettes against the stark white light which etched the outline of every tree, bush and building on the slopes.

The sea at the back of the house heaved and roared and I could taste the salty spray from the silver waves crashing against the cliffs. The air was so charged with electricity, the tiny hairs on my arms bristled with energy and excitement. It was exhilarating.

As the fury of the storm slowly lessened, the darkness was lit by headlights coming into the driveway.

A car door slammed and Alecos leapt out, banging frantically on the front door. Thinking something terrible must have happened, I rushed downstairs.

As I opened the door, Alecos threw his arms around me, holding me so tightly I could hardly breathe.

I was astonished. Until that moment he had always been friendly and polite in the office, but had given me no indication that he felt we were anything more than working partners.

"Are you all right, Sally mou?" he asked, adding an affectionate endearment to my name, which he'd never done before. "I was so worried about you. I came here as fast as I could."

"What's the matter?" I spluttered as I freed myself. "What's happened? Why were you worried about me? I'm perfectly all right."

"Thank God," he said, breathing a sigh of relief. "I saw the storm from Nicosia and rushed to Kyrenia because I thought you would be terrified as you were alone."

My mouth dropped open in amazement. No one had ever been so concerned about me before. It was so touching and romantic; it brought a lump to my throat.

"I was watching the storm from the roof," I confessed. "It was awe-inspiring."

The expression on Alecos face changed from surprise to indignation. Then, he let out a great laugh. "I can't believe it! Do you mean to say, you weren't the least bit nervous? And I've rushed all this way for nothing?"

I gave an apologetic shrug. "I'm sorry," I said quietly. "I didn't realise that you would be worried about me."

"It doesn't matter, I should have realised. You British, with your 'stiff upper lip', you're a tough lot. Most Cypriot women would be cowering in a corner in a storm like that!" He grinned and added: "Anyway, at least it gave me an excuse to come here and see where you live. So now I'm here, what about giving me a drink before I go on my way?"

I smiled, regaining my composure. "Yes, of course, come in. I'll even make you something to eat."

That was the first of many weekends we spent together in Kyrenia and, even now, having been married for almost three years, Alecos was still as protective and concerned as ever, despite my strong independent streak.

This time though, it wasn't just a case of being scared of lightning. I really was in serious danger. If he knew what had happened today, I'd never be able to persuade him to stay on in Germany and finish his negotiations. He'd worked so long and hard to get this prestigious hair colouring contract. It could be the turning point of his business career.

Anyway, I tried to convince myself, crossing my fingers behind my back, by the end of the week when he got home, it could all have blown over!

Looking at my watch, I realised he would be phoning any minute. "I think I'm about ready for bed. It's nearly eleven and we've both had a terrible day."

Ann nodded. "Yes, I've had enough of today. It hasn't been very nice."

Just then the doorbell rang. The shrill noise made us jump.

"It's a bit late for visitors, isn't it?" I exclaimed nervously, remembering the Commissioner's warning.

Peering through the spy hole I made out the distorted shape of a man.

"Who's there?" I called tensely.

"Is me, Spiros."

I relaxed as I opened the door. "Good evening, Spiros. Come in."

"*Kalispera* Sally. Sorry I call so late," he said, coming into the hall. "But I want ask Alecos question about new production. I see lights as was passing so come to leave message for him."

"You're in luck. He hasn't called yet," I told him. "I'll make you a coffee and you can talk to him yourself. He should be phoning any minute."

Spiros was Alecos' step-brother and the production manager of the company.

He was a wizard with machinery. It was a skill he had inherited from his late father who had been the chief mechanic at the Amiendos asbestos mines in the hills behind Limassol.

Like his hot headed father, Spiros was a heavy drinker and in the local bar, *Kafeneon*, he would inevitably get into noisy drunken political arguments lasting well into the night. Still, the skill of his stubby nicotine stained fingers never seemed to be effected the next day, by his nightly drinking.

Spiros was five years older than Alecos, but his stocky build and close cropped, grey flecked hair, made him look well into his forties.

He and Alecos had grown up together when Alecos' widowed father had employed Spiros' mother as a housekeeper.

The boys had barely tolerated each other then, but when their respective parents got married, the tolerance lapsed into open dislike.

Spiros was jealous of the younger, brighter Alecos and bullied him unmercifully. But, when some years later, Alecos inherited a small wholesale shampoo

company from his uncle, Alecos suggested that
Spiros, with his genius for machinery, join the
company. Today the original small business was now
a successful, thriving cosmetic company.

From the kitchen, I could hear Spiros' gruff voice
talking to Ann in the next room. She sounded guarded
and ill at ease. Though she was easy going and only
saw the good in most people she'd always disliked
Spiros.

"I hear was police search by you today," he said
to her, as I appeared with the coffee.

"Humm, yes, we..." she began.

I shot her a look to keep quiet and before she
could finish I interrupted. "Yes, they turned up while
we were having tea. They were in and out in no time.
Goodness knows what they were looking for."

Spiros gave me a doubtful look as I handed him
his coffee. So to get him off the subject of the police,
I asked: "How are Stella and the boys? Did they do
well with their exams?"

Still looking at me suspiciously, he nodded. "They
all well and Vagi, he third in class," he said proudly.
"I take all family to mountains at weekend; they stay
with mother of Stella for summer."

This was a common occurrence. Many families, in
Cyprus moved up to the mountains for the long summer school holiday period, when the temperature in
Nicosia could rise to over one hundred degrees.
Consequently, the foot-loose husbands flocked to the
night clubs, cabarets and bars in the cities. To my
northern upbringing, it seemed very chauvinistic and
dissolute. But, it was a very Middle Eastern tradition.

The wives were very aware of this annual pastime
but seemed to turn a blind eye to it as long as the

husbands dutifully showed up at the mountain resorts at the weekends. Spiros, I knew, would certainly spend much of his time in the cabarets.

At that moment the phone rang. "That must be Alec now," I said, as I snatched it up.

"Sally mou, where have you been? I called you earlier but there was no reply." The line was so clear, he sounded like he was in the next room so I could hear the worried note in his voice.

"Alec, I'm sorry. I was with Ann," I said, as an excuse. "I popped in on my way home from the office. We lost track of time."

"Is everything all right?" he asked with concern.

Hastily, I remembered how quickly he could pick up the nuances of my mood, so as cheerfully as I could, I replied: "Yes, everything's fine here." Then changing the subject, I asked: "How about you? Have you signed the contract yet?"

His voice became animated as he told me about his successful day. "But, Sally, I need a few details to add to the contract. They're in a file in my desk. I need them before I leave the hotel in the morning so I'll phone you in the office at 9.30 tomorrow morning Cyprus time.'

"Ok, I'll be there by 9.30. I was going to the supermarket first but I'll do that later. By the way, Spiros is here. He wants to talk to you," I said, handing him the phone.

While they talked, I finished the washing up. Then Spiros handed the phone back to me and went out to the terrace as I continued my conversation with Alecos. "Oh Alec, I miss you so much," I said.

He must have heard the strain in my voice as he asked anxiously again: "Sally, are you sure you're all right? You sound worried."

"No, it's nothing. I'm tired, and it's been a very hot day. I can't wait for you to get home."

"I miss you too, my lovely, but it's only four more days. Then we'll spend the whole weekend in bed to make up for lost time," he added, gently. "I'll say goodnight now. It's late. I love you and I'll speak to you in the morning. Sleep well, Sally mou. Take care."

"I love you too," I whispered as the line went dead. I stared at the silent phone in my hand, feeling very lonely. I thought about his last words. If he'd realised just how significant his "take care" was, all his excitement and enthusiasm for the project would have disappeared.

Looking up, Spiros was watching me from the doorway. He still had that odd look in his eye but I was too tired to be concerned about Spiros and his moody ways.

"I go now. I sort all things with Alecos. *Kalinikta,* Sally," he said.

"Yes, ok," I said distractedly. "Goodnight, see you tomorrow."

By now it was almost midnight. I was ready for bed. Feeling grubby and noticing the greasy lamb smell from the police canteen on my skin, I ran a shower. Staring at my reflection in the bathroom mirror, I saw that the small frown lines between my eyebrows seemed much deeper; my face looked drawn and tired.

It's a good thing that phones don't have screens, I thought. Alec would never have been fooled if he'd been able to see my face!

Suddenly, I felt very afraid.

Tomorrow it will all seem like a bad dream. I tried to convince myself, but my sixth sense told me that there was trouble ahead.

42

5

Next morning, 29th June

I hadn't expected to sleep well, but I didn't stir till the alarm woke me with a start at eight the next morning. I lay for some minutes thinking over the extraordinary events of the previous day and the grim warning of Commissioner Marco.

After I've been to the office to get the information for Alecos I'd decided to take his advice and stay home out of harm's way, though I felt sure he was exaggerating.

Ann obviously hadn't slept well. Her eyes looked dark and heavy when I woke her. But she soon revived after a coffee, a slice of toast and her inevitable cigarette. Then we left the flat together to drive to our separate offices.

The cars were parked in the space under the flats on the ground floor. I smiled with pride and pleasure as I looked at my lovely shiny new white Ford Capri.

The Ford Motor Company had recently chosen to come to Cyprus to make the promotional film of their latest model, the Capri. I had been invited to drive one of the show cars during the filming. I'd fallen in love with its sporty lines and powerful engine, so in anticipation of the impending boom in business, Alecos had bought me the new model as a celebration present. It was the first Capri on the island.

As I drove out of the car port I noticed a dilapidated blue van filling up at the petrol station alongside the building. It was unusual to see such an old vehicle still on the roads. Over the past few years, the economy of the island had boomed and almost everybody now was able to own a car. It wasn't unusual to come alongside the latest luxury car, only to see it driven by someone who didn't look as though they could afford a bike, let alone a new BMW or Mercedes!

The new premises of The Cyprus Cosmetics Company was a short drive out of the city towards the airport.

We had moved in to our custom built air-conditioned offices only a few months earlier. Everything was under one roof, with plenty of parking space outside the glass fronted entrance. It was pure luxury after our previous cramped offices, tucked away in the rabbit warren of narrow streets, within the Venetian walls of the old city.

Precisely at nine thirty Alecos rang as arranged and I gave him the information he needed.

As I was about to leave, I remembered I needed to pick up a couple of things from the store. I ran down to the basement stock room and took a large bottle of Badedas Gelle which we'd recently added to our agency list. While I was at it, I choose a bottle of my favourite Roger Gallet toilet water. Alecos loved the spicy scent of carnations. So, I intended to splash myself liberally with it for his homecoming.

"Kalimera, Sally," Spiros gravelly voice growled, making me jump as he came into the store room. "You talk with Alecos now?"

"Good morning, Spiros. Yes. I've given him the

information he needed so they should be signing the contract today. I'm going home now as I've got lots to do before he comes back. I've signed for the bath gel and perfume," I said, indicating the stock book.

I was particularly careful not to take advantage of my position as Alecos' wife, especially with Spiros.

Since the day I'd started work with the company, he'd been antagonistic towards me.

His father had been killed in the riots against the British in the fifties when the Governors residence had been burned down, and Spiros had been very anti-British since that time. He was also very chauvinistic!

I tried not to provoke him in any way and be as pleasant and considerate as possible, but it wasn't easy. He was moody and abrupt, and hardly ever smiled.

He followed me upstairs and, as I left the building, he raised his hand appearing to wave me goodbye.

That's strange, I thought, as I entered the car. He's not usually so friendly, but he's such an unpleasant character I never know what he's going to do next.

His wife wasn't one of my favourite people either. She put up with his drinking and womanising in order to have her big house and the latest gadgets in the kitchen so she could show off to her village friends. She was so full of her own importance and always very scornful that I still hadn't produced any children for Alecos. I kept out of their way, whenever I could.

Then, I completely forgot about Spiros and his peculiar behaviour. There, on the forecourt of the car showroom opposite, was the blue van I'd seen earlier.

I laughed aloud at the thought that the owner had finally decided to exchange his old heap for a new model. It certainly wasn't before time. It looked as if it would fall to pieces in the middle of the road if it were driven much longer.

I drove happily along to the newly opened Sofroniou supermarket. It was the mecca for every foreign resident in Nicosia. Its shelves bulged with imported goods, in complete contrast to the small, dark cluttered grocery shops we were used to in the walled city. Inevitably, I would meet someone I knew and stop for a coffee, but today wasn't a day to chat, so I quickly collected the bits I needed to replenish my empty larder.

As I left the cool air-conditioned building and stepped into the heat outside, it was like a blast of hot air from the open oven door on baking day. Local myth claimed it was possible to fry an egg on the pavement in the heat of a Nicosia summer. I could well believe it, but I'd never tried it!

Crossing the service road to my parked car, the blue van came hurtling into the road. I jumped back just in time as the wing clipped my shopping basket.

"You bloody idiot," I shouted, shaking my fist as it shot away. "You'd better learn to drive before you get a new car."

Making sure the eggs were still intact in my basket, I climbed into my car and pulled out into Grivas Diginis Avenue.

The road was wide and at that time in the morning, not too busy. I drove steadily with the hot air cooled by the breeze from the open windows. I loved driving. My reflexes were quick, allowing me the thrill of driving fast. Friends, who regularly competed in the two day Cyprus International car rally, had taught me to handle a car at speed.

I would like to have driven in the rally too but

Alecos wouldn't hear of it.

Switching on the radio, the sexy orgasmic sounds of Donna Summer singing *Love To Love You Baby* made me wriggle in my seat, my body ached for Alecos.

I'd heard the song for the first time a few days earlier and had to pull onto the verge to listen properly to the words. I couldn't believe that the censor for the BBC World Service would allow such an erotic song to be broadcast. I'd heard we'd had the Swinging Sixties. Now I suppose, we were in the Sexy Seventies.

As Donna Summer finished her song, I glanced in my rear view mirror to make sure the police weren't on my tail. Instead, the old blue Ford was speeding along behind me.

"I can't believe it," I said aloud. "There's that idiot again. What's he up to this time? He'll shake himself to bits if he tries to overtake me at this speed!"

I took my foot off the accelerator and pulled over to let him pass. As he started to overtake, the van suddenly swerved sharply towards me, every part of its chassis rocking dangerously.

I slammed my foot down hard on the brake. The van straightened and shot away, spewing stinking black fumes from the exhaust as the engine roared. I wrestled desperately with the steering wheel as my car skidded towards the parapet of the bridge over the dry river bed ten feet below. The wheels screeched as they clung to the edge of the deep storm drain that ran alongside the road, I wrenched the nose round and the car veered towards the central reservation. I smelled burning rubber as I frantically spun the wheels back to the left to avoid a red Mini that was coming up fast on the outside lane behind me.

Shooting across the junction of a side road, I just missed the nose of a Rover that was edging out onto the main highway. My front wheels hit the paving slab opposite with a shuddering jolt, knocking the breath out of me. My head flew forward, narrowly missing the steering wheel as the car jumped the pavement, hurtled past the heavy trunk of a palm tree and came to rest in the middle of waste ground at the other side.

It had all happened so quickly I hadn't had time to be frightened, but now I started to shake. "God!" I said aloud. "That was close."

Even though I drove fast, I was still a careful driver and had never had an accident. The perspiration dripped into my eyes and my hair stuck to the back of my neck. Gulping for breath, I rested my sweating forehead against the steering wheel. I sat unmoving for what seemed like hours, but could only have been a few seconds. Suddenly I jumped as the man of the Rover poked his head into the open window.

"Are you all right?" he asked in concern. "You're not hurt, are you?"

"No," I replied shakily. "I'm ok, but it was close. That idiot was going much too fast."

"You were lucky you didn't crash through barrier of the bridge. You'd have broken your neck if you'd hit the river bottom. It was the van driver's fault and from where I was, it looked as though he'd tried to push you off the road on purpose."

I laughed mirthlessly. "I doubt it. I think he was just a very bad driver. He must have come in from the country and wasn't used to driving in traffic."

"Unfortunately," he apologised. "I didn't get the

number, but if you're sure you're ok and there's nothing I can do, I'll be off."

After thanking him for his concern, I watched him drive away and sat for a moment longer to let my heart slow down to normal. Then, cautiously, I backed the car out of the dry stubble and pulled on to the road, hoping I'd seen the last of the battered van and its lunatic driver.

By the time I got home I'd put the incident out of my mind as I busily planned how I would fill the next few days while I was confined to the apartment.

6

Late that night

The rest of the day passed productively. There were plenty of jobs to tackle that were well overdue, so I set too and the time flew by. When Ann came home, we ate a light supper, then sat in front of the television to watch the latest revelations about President Nixon and the Watergate scandal. Then we went to bed.

I had already fallen into a heavy sleep when the phone rang. The illuminated dial of the bedside clock showed two thirty. Fumbling around for the light switch, I knew it wouldn't be Alecos, as he'd phoned earlier.

"Hello," I snapped, angrily snatching up the phone.

Silence.

"Hello, who is it?" I demanded, furious that someone was playing silly games at that time of night.

"Sally Letras?" a man's voice asked.

"Yes, who's that? What do you want?"

"You got away this morning, but next time you won't be so lucky." The man spoke in Greek. It sounded familiar, but muffled, like someone speaking through a handkerchief.

"Who's that?" I asked again. "I don't understand

what you're talking about."

I shook the receiver, trying to clear the sound. There was a sharp click as the line went dead.

I stared at the phone in my hand. What a peculiar message! What on earth was he talking about? It sounded like a line from a Humphrey Bogart movie. It was nonsense. Someone had obviously dialled the wrong number.

I replaced the receiver and settled down again to sleep.

Suddenly the hairs on the back of my neck stood on end and I broke out in a cold sweat.

It wasn't a wrong number! It was meant for me! He knew my name.

Until that moment I'd forgotten about the car incident earlier in the day. Now, I realised it hadn't been an accident after all. Someone had deliberately tried to kill me!

The delayed shock of the car incident and now the phone call caught up with me and my whole body began to tremble. Stumbling into the bathroom, my knees feeling like jelly, I hung on to the edge of the basin to stop myself falling over and threw up.

Breathing deeply, the retching eventually stopped. Rinsing the foul taste from my mouth, I splashed cold water onto my face and pushing aside my hair, now clammy with sweat, I pressed a damp flannel to the back of my neck till the shaking stopped.

The Commissioner had warned that I would be considered a threat by the terrorist but I hadn't believed him.

"Someone had really tried to kill me this morning!" my brain screamed in horror.

"God, what am I going to do now?"

All at once I remembered the Commissioners card

He said I could call him anytime. Snatching my handbag from the dressing table, I tipped everything on to the bed and scrambled for the card. Grabbing the phone I dialled his number, even though it was almost three in the morning.

His sleepy voice answered on the second ring.

"It's Sally Letras. I've just had a phone call. They said they'd tried to kill me this morning but they wouldn't miss next time," I babbled.

Through the phone, I heard heaving noises as he struggled to sit up, but when he spoke, his voice was completely alert.

"Calm down, Mrs Lytras," he ordered. "I don't understand what you're talking about. Tell me slowly what happened."

My voice trembled as I tried to explain clearly. It probably didn't make much sense but he listened patiently and seemed to catch the drift of my muddled story.

"What should I do now?" I almost screamed.

"Take an aspirin and some hot milk and try to get some sleep. I'll be over first thing in the morning," he reassured me.

I had expected a more positive remedy for an attempted murder, but I took the aspirin and hot milk as he suggested. Needless to say, it didn't help. I tried reading, but my mind kept imagining my car falling into the river bed.

Eventually I must have dozed off, because when morning came, the book had fallen to the floor and the twisted sheets looked as though I'd spent the night thrashing about in terror.

It was still very early but I couldn't get back to sleep. Not wanting to wake Ann, I reached for my robe and padded quietly into the bathroom.

I hardly recognised the face staring back at me in the mirror. The eyes were dull and hollow like black holes; the hair hung lankly round the face which had turned from a healthy tan to a awful shade of grey. It was as though I'd aged twenty years. It looked as ghastly as I felt.

I scrubbed my teeth vigorously to get rid of the foul taste that still lingered. Then, dousing my face in icy cold water to relieve the puffiness, I ran a brush through my hair; it made a slight improvement and I felt a little better.

I crept into the kitchen and made myself a strong black coffee. As the powerful brew started to make me feel human again, Ann poked her head round the door.

"Good morning," she said brightly. "Oh dear! On second thoughts, it doesn't look like such a good morning for you. What on earth's the matter? You look awful?"

I told her about the near accident I'd had the day before.

She shrugged dismissively. "You know how chauvinistic Cypriots are about woman drivers. He probably got annoyed when you overtook him. It's a good thing your reflexes are so quick though. If it had been me, in my little Beetle, I'd have gone into the river!"

"No, Ann!" I said, my voice breaking with emotion. "Somebody deliberately tried to kill me."

"Oh, come on, Sally. You're overreacting, she said impatiently. "You're letting this whole terrorist business get you down. We're not involved anymore."

"No, it's true," I insisted. "In the middle of the night a man phoned. He said I'd escaped in the morning but I wouldn't get away next time."

Her dark eyes widened in disbelief. "But why?" she asked in amazement.

"I don't know," I lied. "But I'm scared. I called the Commissioner and he's coming over this morning."

She was still too stunned to question how I'd been able to get hold of the Commissioner in the middle of the night. Unlike me, she didn't have a suspicious mind. She accepted things at face value.

We finished our coffee in silence. Shaking her head in disbelief, Ann eventually sighed as though it was all too much to take in.

Looking up at the kitchen clock, she said: "I'd better get ready or I'll be late for work. We seem to be in enough trouble without the boss having a go at me too. Will you be all right alone, Sally, or shall I phone in and say I'm ill?"

"Don't worry, you go. The Commissioner will be here soon so I'd better hurry up and get dressed too."

When the Commissioner arrived, he strode into the living room with his usual reassuring air of confidence and authority. His eyes took in the comfortably furnished room with its marble floor covered in colourful rugs and the white walls hung with paintings.

He nodded approvingly. He then strolled across to the large north facing French windows and stared for some minutes out over Nicosia's Venetian walls, and across the plain to the ever changing colours of the Kyrenia mountain range thirty miles away. The early morning sun tipped their crests with a golden glow which contrasted vividly with the clear blue of the sky.

"You have a wonderful view from here," he murmured, appreciatively.

I nodded absently. It was frustrating that he seemed more interested in the view than my terrifying situation. But, despite his lack of concern, I concealed my impatience and offered him a coffee.

Dropping comfortably into the soft leather couch facing the window, he lit a cigarette. Sipping his coffee he said: "Now tell me again about the accident and the phone call."

This time I repeated clearly what I'd told him the previous night.

He was thoughtful for some moment, then leaning towards me he asked: "Did you tell anyone what time you were going to the office yesterday?"

"No," I replied, shaking my head. "Normally, I arrive at ten thirty but I was earlier yesterday because Alecos wanted some information by ten. Then I left and popped into the supermarket on my way home. It certainly wasn't my usual routine."

"Um!" he muttered, tapping his cigarette on the ashtray. "Did you tell Miss Ann you were going in early?"

"She's been here since Monday evening. She would have heard the conversation when I spoke to Alecos. We left together in the morning."

"Is she staying with you till your husband returns?"

"Yes, but she's working all this week so she's only here in the evening."

"You must stay in the flat. I don't want you to go out at all. Do you have everything you need for a few days?"

"Oh, yes. I can always phone the office if I need anything."

He shook his head. "No, I don't want you to do even that. The fewer people who know where you are, the safer you will be. I'll send someone round to keep an eye open. I presume Miss Ann has a key?"

"Yes, she does."

"Good. Don't open the door to anyone."

He stood up. "Now I'd better get off to my office. Don't worry, you'll be all right."

"Well!" I said aloud when he left. "I'd better keep myself busy and hope that I can stay out of trouble!"

I decided to make a start on the linen cupboard. Opening the windows to air the spare room, I waved to old Mrs Paniotis sitting in her usual place by the French window in the parallel block next to ours. Sometimes, her daughter-in-law took her down the road to the nearby park, but mostly she sat in her wheelchair by the window. It seemed like she sat there day and night watching the traffic and the people going in and out of the government offices across the Avenue.

The time passed as I became absorbed in sorting and tidying the sheets and towels.

Suddenly I heard the doorbell ring. It startled me and I quickly moved to answer it, but then I remembered the Commissioner's warning. Who could it be? It rang again, this time more insistently. I slipped off my shoes and crept silently into the hallway. Peeping through the spy hole, I made out the shape of two big men standing by the door.

I pulled back, stifling a scream, the hairs on the back of my neck standing on end. I stood stock still as the bell rang again. I was really scared. If I opened the door even a fraction they would push their way in and goodness knows what would happen next. Eventually the ringing stopped. I heard footsteps going down the stairs.

I quickly double locked the door and scurrying back to the bedroom I fell on the bed in terror, my breath coming in short panicky gasps. They soon gave way to tears of fear, confusion, desperation and loneliness. The last time I'd cried like this was five years ago when my long term boyfriend left me for my best friend. It was then I decided to start a new life in Cyprus to get away from all the places and people that held so many memories.

Eventually I stopped crying and apart from feeling foolish, the cry had done me good. The tension had obviously been bubbling up over the last few days and now the tears had released it and I felt better for it. I grabbed a tissue, blew my nose and went into the kitchen to put the kettle on; carefully looking through the window to see if anyone was hanging around outside.

Generally I was practical and logical; I didn't panic or make a fuss when something unexpected happened. But being threatened by gangsters obviously wasn't a situation I'd had to deal with before! Keep calm, don't let your imagination run away with you. I told myself, after all, nothing happened. Nevertheless, I still felt vulnerable and afraid.

I was alone and needing to talk to someone who would understand. The Commissioner was the obvious answer.

But, I asked myself, suppose he was playing a double game? After all, he was the only person who knew I could identify the man from the flat. He'd made a point of telling me not to mention it to anyone, or to let anyone know where I was. Looking at it that way, it did seem rather suspicious. Could I really trust him?

He's Ok my woman's intuition answered back. You remind him of his daughter. He's on your side. But, could I trust my own intuition anymore? I'd never been in a criminal situation like this before!

Should I call him yet again and tell him about the men at the door? He'd probably think I was becoming hysterical and dramatising every small incident.

But, it might be important, I argued with myself.

To hell with it, I'll risk his disapproval. Why should I worry if he thinks I'm hysterical? I'm entitled to be. Nobody has ever tried to kill me before!

So once again I picked up the phone to call him. This time there was no reply on his private office number. I wandered listlessly around the flat. Even doing my embroidery, which always relaxed me, had no effect. I wasn't able to settle to anything. Darting between the veranda, the kitchen and the bedroom windows, to see if anyone was lurking outside, the panic rose as my imagination conjured up new and more lurid incidents that could happen to me.

Eventually I could stand the waiting no longer. I snatched up the phone and tried the Commissioner's number again. To my relief, this time he answered.

As unemotionally as possible, I told him about the two men I'd seen at the door.

"What time did this happen?" he asked.

"About 11.30."

"What did they look like?"

"I didn't see their faces because they had their backs to me but they looked tough."

"What were they wearing?"

"I think one was wearing a blue checked shirt."

There was a pause at the end of the line. Suddenly,

the Commissioner laughed.

"Why are you laughing?" I asked, indignantly. "I was really scared."

"I'm sorry, Mrs Lytras," he replied, still with a hint of amusement in his voice. "Those two toughs, as you call them, are the plain clothes officers I sent to protect you. They were not there to harm you."

"But why did they come to the door?" I asked sharply.

He sighed. "I'm sure you can appreciate that, although I gave them a description of you, it is better to see the person they have to protect," he said, rather sarcastically. "They called me to say you didn't answer the door and perhaps you'd gone out. After the warning I'd given you, I thought it very irresponsible of you," he added, sounding exactly like my father when he was angry with me.

Now it was my turn to justify my actions. I explained that I was too scared to open the door because he had told me not too.

He sounded a little less annoyed as he replied: "They will be around to see you again within fifteen minutes. Their names are Petros and George. Please tell them anything they need to know. They will be watching the block from now on. You won't see them, but I can assure you they will be there. They are good men. And please, Mrs Lytras, don't leave the flat until you go to the airport to meet your husband on Friday."

"Thank you," I said. "I'm sorry I made such a fuss."

I hung up feeling sheepish, but relieved. My shoulders which had been bunched into a hard knot of tension, softened and relaxed.

Within a few minutes Petros and George, my two

minders, were at the door again.

Over coffee they asked me various things they needed to know. They were friendly, alert men and looked even bigger close too. We agreed they would call in at nine o'clock each morning after Ann had left for work, to make sure everything was Ok. And I gave them a spare key, for any emergency! They were good guys and I certainly felt more secure knowing they were around to protect me.

7

The following Friday, 2nd July

The rest of the week passed uneventfully. I felt secure in the knowledge that Petros and George were some-where outside watching the comings and goings around the block. By the end of the week, the whole flat sparkled. All the surfaces were dusted and polished, the books tidy on the shelves, the linen folded and stacked neatly. As for the kitchen, I now knew what had been tucked away at the back of the cupboards.

I was proud of what I'd achieved. After all my efforts at cleaning, tidying and sorting, I felt my enforced time at home had been put to very good use.

Friday morning arrived and I woke early. The unease and fear I'd felt over the last few mornings seemed to have fallen away and now I was alive and excited. Today, at last, Alecos would be home and I would be safe with him by my side.

Throwing back the sheet, I padded barefoot to the window. Pulling back the curtains, the top branches of the slender eucalyptus trees in front of the build-ing, made a lacy screen at the level of my bedroom window. The grey green leaves turned a soft pink in the early morning sun and their clean antiseptic smell wafted into the room.

It was amazing to realise that the original seeds planted to drain the malarial swamps at the end of the last century, had turned the land surrounding the ancient walled city of Nicosia, into a rich fertile plain supplying the city with an abundance of vegetables and fruits of which the melon and figs were what we was about to eat for our breakfast.

All my senses seemed heightened by my excitement, so, humming contentedly, I knocked on Ann's door, on my way to the kitchen to prepare breakfast.

"Why did you wake me so early?" she asked indignantly, her eyes still heavy from sleep. "And, you sound so cheerful. I can't stand it, so early in the morning!"

"I'm sorry, I should have let you sleep longer," I apologised. "But I'm so excited, I can't wait for this afternoon. I hope the plane isn't delayed."

She smiled understandingly but her eyes were tinged with yearning. She'd rarely experienced the thrill of looking forward to being with someone special.

I knew she was no longer a virgin. She'd spent a very tearful evening telling me about a handsome Australian UN policeman she'd met. After some time together, she'd nervously agreed to spend the night with him. It was her first time and it should have been a romantic experience for her. Instead, she was devastated by his indifference once he'd had his satisfaction.

Men were attracted to her initially, as her warm, sympathetic personality flattered their egos, but the heavy drinking, 'have- fun' men of the UN forces always lost interest if sex wasn't immediate. She needed a man with a more gentle temperament. She'd had a heady affair with an Austrian doctor who would have been perfect for her, but he was married and before long had been posted elsewhere.

One day perhaps she would meet her 'Mr Right' but for the moment, he was nowhere in sight.

"Let's hear what's happening to President Nixon today," I said, switching on the radio. "I wonder if the Supreme Court judges have decided to hand over the tapes from the Watergate break in?"

"Shh, shut up and listen to this," she hissed as the clear tones of the BBC World Service news reader filled the kitchen.

"In an outspoken six page letter to the President of Greece, President Makarios has openly accused the Athens regime of conspiring to seize power and destabilize the Cyprus government by plotting to assassinate him. He demands the immediate withdrawal of all 650 Greek army officers who control the National Guard. The letter goes on to say that there is irrefutable documentary evidence to link the Greek officers based in Cyprus to the activities of the EOKA B terrorist group."

"My god, those must be the documents we found in the flat," Ann said in amazement.

"Hooray!" I whooped, pushing back my chair and dancing round the kitchen. "It's public knowledge now. It won't matter anymore about identifying Kallis."

"What are you talking about? Who's Kallis?"

"That man in the flat! He's the administrator for Ioannidis. I was the only one who could identify him, so it would have directly implicated the Greek government. But now, Makarios public letter shows clearly they are involved so they don't have to shut me up anymore."

I plopped down on to the chair again, weak with relief.

Ann stared hard at me, trying to fit things together. Slowly she realised what I was talking about.

"So that's why they tried to kill you...you knew all the time. No wonder you were so scared. I thought you were just over- reacting! Why didn't you tell me?"

"I couldn't. The Commissioner told me not to tell anyone, for my own safety."

She nodded, now understanding all the strange happenings.

After a pause she said excitedly: "It'll be safe for me to go home too, they'll leave us both alone now!"

She gave me a hug as she left. "Thank goodness that scary business is over. Sometimes I think life in Cyprus is a bit dull and predictable, but after these last few days, I think I prefer it dull!"

I nodded. "You're right. I've had enough upset in the last four days to last me a life time. Nothing could ever get any worse!"

Soon after Ann left I phoned the Commissioner to get his reaction to the letter .

"At last the Greek government has been exposed," he announced, jubilantly. "That letter from Makarios was quite specific in its accusations that the Greek military regime was behind the activities of the terrorists in Cyprus. At last we can get rid of those arrogant Greek officers who are corrupting our soldiers," he added, emphatically.

"You should have no more trouble either," he told me. "But I'll keep Petros and George with you until Alecos is finally home."

Several hours later, most of my wardrobe was strewn over the bed and on the floor in my frenzy to find the perfect outfit to wear for Alecos homecom-ing. Eventually I was satisfied with the result, but it was impossible to sit around at home. I was too fidgety and excited.

Leaving early, I drove at a sedate speed, still feeling apprehensive whenever anything blue appeared in my rear view mirror.

Arriving at the airport with plenty of time to spare, I parked the car and walked across the wide arrival area to the main entrance. A constant breeze blew round the airport perimeter, and the shady fronds of the palm trees made a dry rasping noise as they swayed in the wind. A taxi driver watched intently in anticipation, as the breeze tugged at the hem of my dress.

The insistent breeze reminded me of another time that I'd been meeting a glamorous friend and her new husband arriving for their honeymoon in Cyprus. Leaving the airport building, a gust of wind threatened to remove his very expensive hair piece. Grabbing at it with both hands, he nearly knocked himself out with his Louis Vuitton brief case. After that unfortunate experience, I noticed that his hair piece had probably been assigned to the suitcase and he'd bought himself a hat.

Thinking of hair pieces, I gave an involuntary shudder as my mind turned to the man in the flat and the subsequent events..

As I entered the airport, the text of Makarios outspoken letter was the main headline on all the papers on the newsstands in the building. Snatching one up, I immersed myself in the report, amazed that our unexpected discovery had led to such a monumental political situation. It was unnerving to think that we unknowingly had been instrumental in making history.

Eventually the voice over the loudspeaker

announced the arrival of the Lufthansa flight from Frankfurt. With any luck Alecos' plane would have touched down and, with the skill of long practice, he would be through in no time.

Hastily pushing the newspaper into my bag I went to the arrival gate. Unexpectedly, the first passengers through the gates were a gaggle of tired looking British holiday makers from a long overdue British Airways flight.

Tourism in Cyprus consisted almost entirely of visitors from Britain. Some years previously the Labour government of Harold Wilson had imposed a fifty pound exchange control for visits to all countries outside the Sterling area. Cyprus, was one of the few places people could use any amount of their pounds without restriction.

Once the British discovered the warm seas, sandy beaches, good food and the legendary hospitality of its people, they returned in droves, making tourism now a major industry of the island.

The tourists streamed through the barrier, and were whisked off to their holiday destinations in the picturesque coves around Kyrenia or the wide sandy beaches of Famagusta.

As the holiday makers drifted away, the Lufthansa passengers came through. First came the middle aged business men travelling first class with their fashionably dressed wives who, with their air of elegant sophistication, were destined for the opulence and glamour of the recently opened Nicosia Hilton Hotel.

But where is Alecos, why hasn't he come through yet?

Suddenly there he was. His dark hair curled around his head like a Greek God. His tall, lean, body enhanced by a silver grey mohair business suit, made me gasp in delight. He looked gorgeous. His deep blue eyes, searching the crowd, lit up as he saw me.

He grinned with delight, exposing a set of perfect white teeth. In two long strides he was through the barrier. Dropping his flight bag to the floor he hugged me tightly, lifting me off the ground in his strong arms as he held me close.

"Sally, my lovely, you feel so wonderful," he whispered, kissing me.

As he put me down I noticed a leggy blond ogling him. I smiled proudly, tucking my arm comfortably into his, as we strolled out into the balmy warmth of the early evening.

"It's so good to be home again," he sighed with relief, settling himself comfortably behind the wheel of my car. He pulled me to him and this time our kiss was long and lingering. "Now tell me what you've been up to since I've been away," he said.

I hadn't intended to tell him about the recent events until we got there but, the relief of being with him again brought tears to my eyes and the words tumble out in a torrent. "Oh Alec, it's been terrible. I've been so frightened."

He looked startled as my voice dropped almost to a whisper. "We discovered a terrorist hide out so they tried to kill me!" Sniffing, I grabbed a tissue from my bag to wipe my running nose.

"Sally mou, please don't cry," he begged. "Start from the beginning. I don't know what you're talking about."

I gulped back another sob and taking a deep breath, began again. We drove home slowly, Alecos listening in horror to my story. As soon as he'd switched off the engine I thrust the newspaper into his hand and he quickly read the report.

"My God!" he exclaimed in amazement. "That's terrible. Why didn't you tell me? I thought there was something wrong when I phoned on Monday, but I never imagined it was anything like this. Thank God you're safe. He drew me to him, holding me protectively.

"It seems I can't leave you for a day without you getting into trouble. But I'm home now to take care of you," he sighed in relief.

"I don't know how I managed without having a nervous breakdown," I said.

He laughed gently. "Sally mou, you're beautiful, you're sexy and you're smart. But under that shiny mane of hair, you're as capable and tough as any man," he finished seriously.

As we entered the building, Petros and George drove away. George raised his hand in a farewell salute as I caught his eye. They'd done their job. Now they were leaving me in the capable hands of my husband.

Dropping his bags in the hallway, Alecos walked into the living room now bathed in the golden light of the evening sunset. He looked around as though everything in the room was new to him.

"It's so good to be home again," he sighed. "There is so much light here. Everything in Germany looks grey and flat. I missed the sun, but most of all I missed you," he breathed hungrily as he shrugged off his jacket and loosened his tie. Casting both on the nearest chair, he moved purposefully towards me. I felt the warmth of his hands through the thin silk of my dress. "I've been aching for you," he whispered huskily, as his mouth came down on mine in a long lingering kiss.

The movement of his hands sent shivers of desire

through me. Responding at once, I pressed my hips against his. Without interrupting the kiss he kept one hand on my breast while the other undid the zip and slipped the dress off my shoulders. It slithered to the ground around my feet, the wispy bra soon followed. His cupped palms replaced the lace of the bra as his thumbs drew light spirals round the dark rosettes of my nipples.

"I love these nipples, they're like dark, ripe cherries and taste just as delicious," he murmured as he bent his head to kiss each one, sending more exquisite shivers down my back. The movement of his tongue made me tremble, becoming soft and moist and aching to have him inside me. We sank to the ground and made love in the final shaft of the setting sun which slanted across the silk rug of the living room floor.

Later, when the mutual need of our lovemaking had left our bodies satisfied and content, I picked up our discarded clothes, dressed again and brushed my tangled hair while Alecos took a shower.

Earlier in the day I'd laid the table on the terrace and prepared a chicken so now I just had to pop it in the oven and do the finishing touches

"Everything looks beautiful, Sally mou, and you're using your best lace tablecloth. It must be a special occasion," Alecos said, coming up behind me.

"Yes, of course it is. You're home. Do you remember the day we went to Lefkara to buy that cloth? They told us that Leonardo De Vinci had visited the famous village and bought some of their exquisite lace for the altar cloth in Milan Cathedral."

"Mm!" he muttered, not listening. Pulling me to him, I could feel he was again ready for me. As he nibbled my ear I felt myself beginning to melt too.

"Shall we have a drink or do we have time to make love before dinner?" he whispered playfully

Reluctantly wriggling out of his arms, I said: "No, dinner is almost ready and I've got a couple of bottles of your favourite Arsinoe in the fridge."

As Alecos poured the dry white wine, the glasses immediately frosted in the warm night air. Snuggling up to him on the hammock, tucking my bare feet under me, our raised glasses, chimed like a crystal bell as they touched.

"To the success of 'Silhouette' in Cyprus," I toasted him.

"To 'Silhouette'," he replied, crossing his fingers.

Savouring the wine, I marvelled that almost everything in Cyprus had a history. It had been my favourite subject at school and now, here I was living it in almost everything I touched or saw. First, the tablecloth, now the wine. Julius Caesar had bequeathed the Island to the Egyptian king Ptolemy who had named a city after his sister Arsinoe. Today, this small picturesque town, now known as Polis, sat amongst flourishing citrus groves, far to the west of the island. We had two hairdressing customers there who would be delighted that the Silhouette colour range would be produced in Cyprus; not only would it cost less but it would be readily available to them when they needed it.

Over our leisurely dinner, we talked excitedly about the new venture. Alecos enthusiasm was catching, so for the first time, I completely forgot about the worries of the past week.

Eventually I left the table to make coffee. When I returned, his eyes had clouded over and he looked preoccupied and worried.

"What's the matter?" I asked in surprise. He shook

his head. "Nothing," he said unconvincingly.

"Come on Alec, tell me," I insisted.

"I'm sorry, agapi mou, I don't want to spoil our lovely evening but I keep thinking about what happened to you. It makes my blood run cold. Thank God your troubles are over, but the political repercussions could be disastrous."

"How do you mean?" I asked, a cold shiver running through me.

He took a sip of brandy, then putting down his glass, rested his elbows on the table. "Cyprus is just a pawn in the international game. The Americans are paranoid about anything that suggests the Left. That's why they got rid of the socialist government in Greece and backed the corrupt right-wing colonels. They will never forgive Makarios for joining the non-aligned countries of Africa and the Eastern bloc, but what option did he have after they ignored his requests for help."

A worried frown crossed his face. "I want to make an appointment to see the Commissioner. There are a lot of questions I need to ask him." He paused thoughtfully. "I think the political situation will get a lot worse before it gets better. That could make a great difference to the business," he sighed unhappily. "Just as I thought everything was going our way, it now looks as though we could be in for a lot of trouble."

8

Next day

The Commissioner agreed to see us early next morning. The city had hardly begun to stir when we arrived. We were immediately shown into his office and after shaking hands with Alecos he indicated that we should sit down and ordered coffee.

After thanking him for helping me, Alecos said: "I'm still worried about the consequences of Sally's discovery. How will Cyprus be affected by the demands Makarios has made to the Greek government?"

The Commissioner replied firmly: "The documents the ladies discovered enabled President Makarios to foil yet another attempt to assassinate him."

He chuckled unexpectedly, his eyes twinkling behind his glasses. "God certainly protects his own! This has been proven once again," he said with a smile. "His open letter showed the whole world the colonel's intentions. It could panic them into doing something even more rash and clumsy, but in my opinion, it is more likely that the Americans, who are well aware of what the Junta is up to, will call them off, for the time being."

The coffee arrived and offering Alecos a cigarette, the Commissioner continued: "The Americans regard

Makarios as a pest. They have never forgiven him for turning down the hurriedly concocted Acheson plan in 1964.

Alecos nodded in agreement as he puffed at his cigarette.

"I'm sorry, I'm not familiar with the Acheson plan you mentioned," I interrupted. "I only came to live on the island in '69, so I'm a bit vague as to what happened before that."

The Commissioner nodded understandingly. "In that case, I'll have to go back a few years to put you in the picture."

He settled back on the sofa and placing his fingertips together, forming a steeple under his nose, he began his explanation.

"The conditions of the so called independence in 1960 were so biased against the Greek Cypriots. They were a two thirds majority of the population, but were given only a 50% share of the voting power. Eventually, President Makarios prepared a revision of the constitution so that voting would become more proportionate between the Turkish and Greek Cypriots communities, but the Turkish minority were not willing to accept it."

The Commissioner paused while he tapped the ash from his cigarette. "Fighting broke out with some of the most disgusting acts of arson and sadism carried out against Turkish Cypriots," he said with shame. "So for their own protection the Turkish Cypriots established an enclave on the north coast."

He rubbed the side of his nose, an unconscious gesture I'd noticed before when he was being thoughtful. "Then the foreign powers started to interfere. We already had Turkish forces in the enclave in the north and Greek forces in the south.

The British were in the middle on the 'Green line' in Nicosia, to keep the two communities apart, but that became impossible so they called in the UN as a neutral peace keeping force. The United Nations forces were made up of Swedes, Irish, Danes, Australians and Canadians. 'But despite this foreign intervention, the unrest continued. Cyprus became like a fruit cake of foreigners!"

I smiled at his description. Even today it was still the same.

"Eventually, Makarios was unjustly accused by his enemies and the foreign press of trying to starve out the Turkish Cypriot population in the northern enclave."

"Yes, I remember that," I interrupted. "When I was in my late teens, the British press depicted Makarios as a monster and the news pictures made him look cruel and menacing. My mother called him the 'Black Devil', but from what I've learned of Makarios since then, he has the best interest of both communities at heart. Though it must be difficult for outsiders to appreciate that, if the press is manipulating the situation."

"Yes, it was nonsense," Alecos said indignantly. "I've had two Turkish salesmen working for me for years and some of my best customers are Turkish Cypriots. When I was a boy growing up in Limassol I had lots of Turkish friends. The two communities mixed quite happily in most of the island."

The Commissioner nodded in agreement. "As the Turkish Cypriots were still being harassed the Turkish government held the Greek minority living in Turkey hostage. They confiscated all their property and expelled all the Greek population from Istanbul."

"I'm sure the Greek government must have reacted to that?" I said

"No. This time there was no tit-for-tat reaction. Instead the Americans, concerned about the crisis that was brewing between two NATO allies, sent Dean Acheson, the former Secretary of State, to Cyprus to report on the trouble."

"Ah, now you've come full circle," I said. "I understand why he was here, so now you'll have to explain what the Acheson plan was," I reminded him.

"I'm getting hoarse," he chuckled. "I think we should have another coffee. It will give me strength to continue with this history lesson!"

"I'm sorry," I apologised. "You've been very patient and we have taken up so much of your time already. Alecos can explain it to me later,"

"It's no problem," the Commissioner said. "You're so much like my daughter." He indicated the photo on his desk that I'd noticed on my previous visit. "She has an inquiring mind too."

He strode across to his desk to phone the canteen. Almost immediately more coffee arrived.

"Where were we?" the Commissioner continued. "Ah yes! 'The Acheson plan'. It basically proposed that most of Cyprus would belong to Greece, while part of the north coast would become a military base and canton of Turkey. By giving both countries a slice of the cake, the quarrel within NATO could be averted and the "Cassocked Castro of the Mediterranean", as the Americans called Makarios, would have his power neutralised. Once again, the Cypriots themselves were completely disregarded in the plan."

"But wasn't the union with Greece what the Greek Cypriots wanted when they fought to get the British out?" I asked, puzzled.

"Correct," the Commissioner replied. "But by then, we had experienced the heady freedom of independence under Makarios so the majority of the Greek Cypriots rejected the plan."

He removed his glasses and rubbing his eyes, he commented: "The Americans, of course, were furious and from then on Makarios was considered a danger-ous nuisance."

"But how does this effect today's situation?" Alecos asked.

"Ah well, General Grivas, the original leader of the EOKA rebels fighting against the British in the fifties, was an ardent supporter of the Acheson plan. As I told Sally previously, he was recently smuggled back to Cyprus by the Greek Colonels. And until his death earlier this year he had been leading the EOKA rebels who have been trying to destabilize Makarios independent government and get union with Greece. Now that their headquarters were discovered by you and your friend," he said, turning to me. "There is undeniable proof that EOKA is backed by the Greek Junta. As Henry Kissinger is a firm supporter of that right wing mob in Athens, it means, by default, it is backed by the government of the USA."

"My goodness," I exclaimed in amazement. "Our discovery had even wider implications than I imagined."

"Yes, my dear, but I didn't want you to have a heart attack by letting you know that you were up against the CIA too.

"My poor Sally," Alecos said, affectionately squeezing my hand. "It's a good thing I had no idea what was going on. I would have had a heart attack too."

The Commissioner smiled at us. "Yes, she's safe

now; I'd be surprised if after Makarios' accusations the Americans would want to be seen flirting with the most corrupt government in Western Europe. They will probably tell the Colonels to back off until things calm down."

Alecos sat forward in his chair. Letting out a sigh of relief he asked: "So you think Cyprus will have a stable period for a while?"

"Logically, yes," the Commissioner replied. "But when you are dealing with those arrogant Greek maniacs one can never rely on logic."

We left his office feeling reassured and happy in the belief that the Commissioner's assessment of the situation made sense and that after yet another political upheaval in its turbulent history Cyprus would again be peaceful and stable.

Our lives could return to normal and we could continue with the daily effort of building a successful business.

In that confident mood, we returned home to pack a bag and spend a peaceful weekend in Paphos, our favourite place on the island.

9

Journey to Paphos

Alecos had decided that a weekend in Paphos would be the best therapy for me after my frightening experiences of the past week.

Situated on the south west coast of Cyprus, it was a place where time seemed to stand still. The whole area was imbued with legends and remains of ancient shrines and temples attributed to Aphrodite, Goddess of Beauty, Love and Desire. Pilgrims came from all over the then known world to pay homage to the most worshiped goddesses of antiquity.

On the way there we passed Petra tou Romiou, the wild and beautiful setting of the legendry birthplace of Aphrodite.

"Alec, stop the car, please," I begged. "Let's get out for a while. I love it here. I can quite understand why the goddess would choose to be born in this place. It's so peaceful and unspoiled," I murmured, gazing at the deep sapphire blue sea beyond the huge rock, which had supposedly been hurled there, many centuries later by a legendry Byzantine frontier guard against the invading Saracens.

"Yes, whenever I'm here, I imagine the Botticelli painting, 'The Birth of Venus'," Alecos said.

"You mean the picture of a beautiful woman with

long hair swirling round her naked body?"

"Yes, that's the one. She's standing on a huge shell, riding in on the foam and her hand-maiden is holding a richly embroidered cloth to cover her nakedness."

'It's a very voluptuous painting, but why did he paint her as a fully grown woman?" I wondered, curiously.

"According to Greek mythology, the God Uranus was castrated by his son Cronus, who then threw the testicles into the sea and, from the foam, Aphrodite, or Venus, as the Romans called her, was born, as a young woman, hence love and desire."

"Umm! The foam does have a creamy richness here," I remarked. "It might have some bearing on the story."

Alecos laughed, his white teeth a perfect contrast against his tanned skin. "You're too gullible. It's a legend. The creamy colour is due to the disintegration of marine organisms, not the richness of male organs!"

"Don't spoil my illusions. I prefer the mythological version. It's more romantic."

Scrambling down to the sandy beach I kicked off my sandals. The warm breeze lifted my hair which rippled out behind me. Gazing at the creamy foam swirling around my feet a feeling of sheer delight wafted over me.

Suddenly, behind me, Alecos was reciting in his lyrical voice, the homage to the goddess.

"Laughter loving Aphrodite went to Cyprus, to Paphos, where is her realm and fragrant alter..."

The words were carried on the wind over the soft

sigh of the waves as they gently broke on the shore.

"In case you don't know, that's from Homer's Odyssey," he said, as he came down to the water's edge to stand behind me. "As a classical Greek scholar, I had to learn the whole poem, pages and pages of it," he said, nuzzling my neck and putting his arms round my waist.

"I'm very impressed," I replied mockingly.

"But you, my lovely..." he added, ignoring my playful sarcasm. "...are my goddess of beauty and desire. My own Aphrodite! Come on let's get to Paphos. I want to spend the afternoon in bed. It must be something to do with the spirit of love here because I'm hungry for you again."

Looking playfully up at him I put my arms around his neck and looked into his strong face.

"Why don't we make love on the beach?" I suggested, knowing full well that Alecos hated sand.

He shook his head. "I desire you, but the thought of sand all over me puts a damper on my ardour so I'll have to wait a little longer. Come on, we're leaving."

I gazed around wistfully, not wanting to leave such an untouched, beautiful spot. It was idyllic, just the huge rock, the silvery beach and the foamy blue sea.

"My God, wouldn't it be awful if one day someone built a 'Goddess of Love' or 'Aphrodite Beach' restaurant here, with a car park, beach umbrellas and pedalos," I said, aghast. Alecos grabbed my hand impatiently, dragging me back to the car. "Don't worry it will never happen!" he assured me.

Paphos was an area full of ancient sites; many were thousands of years old. It held a magical charm for me. But, the magic stopped as we approached the

Paphos Beach Hotel. It was built in the latest style of low maintenance, grey, fair face concrete, quite out of keeping with the marble columns and granite ruins of the ancient town.

"This hotel is so ugly," I grumbled. "It looks like an airport hangar."

"Maybe you think it looks like a hangar," Alecos replied. "But the people of Paphos are very proud of it. It's the most modern architecturally designed building in the whole of Cyprus. It's their five star shrine to sixties' modernity. But don't worry," he added with a grin. "We're not staying in this echoing concrete block. I've booked one of their beach bungalows for the weekend.'

The bungalow apartments were luxurious. Spacious, beautifully furnished and with an enormous comfortable bed and of course, full room service. They were scattered amongst palm trees, in gardens stretching almost to the edge of the sea. Only the breeze whispering through the palm fronds and the gentle sound of waves breaking on the shore disturbed the peace, lulling one into a gentle sleep at night.

Dropping our bags, we threw on our swimsuits and ran across the shady lawns to dive into the sparkling, warm Mediterranean.

At dusk, sipping the cool sparkling Bellapais wine, we watched from our terrace as the sky turned from deep blue to rose pink through to misty violet, as the sun set over the sea.

The peace and serenity of Paphos had much to do with the fact that it was the least visited area of the island. The pleasant, sleepy market town stood on a high rocky plateau, which had protected it in ancient times from Arab marauder attacks from the sea.

Our favourite spot was at the bottom of the hill, down by the tiny harbour of Kato Paphos where the colourful fishing boats, tied up at the jetty, rose and dipped as if some ancient under water god was breathing gently beneath the calm water.

On the west side a small Venetian fort overlooked the port, while at the edge of the harbour wall were two 'tavernas', their pavement tables covered in green and white checked cloths and illuminated at night by light bulbs strung from metal frames holding faded striped awnings. In the cool of the evening, dinner here, by the edge of the sea, had a special charm.

At our chosen tavern, Aristos, the owner, welcomed us like long lost friends. He insisted we share a glass of wine with him. Paphian hospitality was legendary, even in a country renowned for its hospitality.

"You know, my lady," Aristos boomed at me, "Here in Cyprus, we never drink alcohol without a small delicacy to eat with it, he said, producing a small plate of grilled Halloumi, the delicious goat's cheese only found in Cyprus and another dish of paper thin slices of the smoked ham of the island, 'Lounza'.

"The stronger the alcohol, the more food we serve. No man ever got drunk on a full stomach," he roared, patting his own ample belly.

The talk turned to politics, the favorite subject of all Cypriots and naturally to the open letter sent by President Makarios to the Greek leader. The people of Paphos were very pro-Makarios. They felt he was one of their own as he had been born in a small village nearby.

"That Makarios is a brave fellow," Aristos said

proudly. "He doesn't believe in silky diplomatic words. He told them straight. He sent one of those documents they found to that Greek bastard, Gizikis, as proof that he'd ordered the assassination. He won't be able to wriggle out of that!"

Aristos banged his glass down on the table, the red wine splashing onto the tablecloth.

"And what about those bastard Greek officers controlling the National Guard? It was them who supplied equipment to the rebels. Those arrogant pigs," he continued. "They think we Cypriots are peasants. It's a good thing Makarios demanded that the whole lot of them leave immediately. Good riddance! They should all be gone in two weeks." he bellowed, this time banging his hand on the table. "With them gone and Grivas dead, things should calm down and we can get on with our lives." He took a gulp of wine and filled our glasses again, almost to overflowing.

Alecos threw a warning glance at me to say nothing. How Aristos would have feted us if he'd known it was me who'd found those documents. I gave an involuntary shudder as I remembered that terrible day.

Eventually, as more customers began to arrive, Aristos went into the kitchen and returned with a large tray.

"What would you like? He asked holding the platter of shining fish in front of us. "Red Mullet, Sea Bream, Squid, Swordfish and Snapper, all fresh out of the sea from my brother's boat this morning," he said proudly.

Each fish looked better than the one before, it was difficult to decide, but eventually I settled for the Red Mullet. The bony pink fish with its distinct flavor held no qualms for me since the day Alecos, after watching me struggling with the bones, taught me how to properly fillet a fish. Alecos chose the swordfish and Aristo prepared our order on the open grill beside the taverna. With the delicious aroma rising from the charcoal cooked fish, I realise how hungry our lazy afternoon of love making had made me.

Soon the food was ready. Squeezing lemon juice over the warm fish and dribbling rich green olive oil on the salad of juicy tomatoes, sweet onions, olives and tangy Feta cheese, we tucked into our dinner. The fish was so fresh it tasted of the sea.

Aristos brought us a carafe of white wine, made from grapes grown in his own vineyard and its dry, fruity, cool taste was the perfect complement to the delicious fish.

While we ate, we were entertained by the antics of two pelicans that had been rescued during a storm and now lived on the harbour. Washing their plumage at the water's edge they shuffled around clacking their long-pouched beaks. They were used to humans, so they waited around for tit-bits, which quickly disappeared in lumpy ripples, down their long necks.

We sat back, full and content. But Aristos would not let us finish.

"Grown in the rich soil and ripened in the hot sun of Paphos," he proclaimed, placing before us huge slices of sugar melon, juicy and sweet as honey.

Then with our coffee he brought Alecos a large brandy. "And for you, beautiful lady, Commanderia," he said, holding the sweet dessert wine up against the light to admire its rich ruby color. "On the house," he generously insisted.

Commanderia, the oldest named wine in the world, was reportedly served at the wedding of the crusader King Richard Coeur de Lion to Berengaria of Navarre when she arrived in Cyprus for her marriage to Richard, subsequently becoming Queen of England after her coronation in Limassol, in 1191. History was all around me, I loved it!

Suddenly, I heard a familiar voice. "Hello Sally, how are you?"

A tall man in uniform stood behind me. The sky blue beret and cravat tucked into the open neck of a sand colored safari jacket, made his blond, sun bleached hair and blue eyes look amazing. Whoever had designed the uniform for the United Nations peace keeping force, certainly knew a thing about colour. No man could fail to look attractive wearing this combination.

"David! What a surprise! How lovely to see you," I exclaimed. "What are you doing in Paphos? I heard you'd left the island."

"Yes, but now I'm back at the BritCon camp, down the road."

"And you've been promoted too," I remarked, noticing the golden crowns on his epaulettes.

He nodded proudly. "Major David Hamilton at your service," he saluted smartly.

Alecos frowned.

"Oh, I'm sorry. Alec, this is David. David, this is my husband, Alecos Lytras."

Both men were of similar height and though they smiled politely as they shook hands, they eyed each other warily.

"Perhaps you would like to join us for a drink?" Alecos invited. His manners were always impeccable, but his voice betrayed a note of antagonism.

"Thank you, but no. I'm meeting some friends next door," David apologized, indicating the other taverna. "It's good to see you, Sal. You look absolutely marvellous. Obviously married life agrees with you," he said, with a touch of irony in his voice.

"Goodnight," he nodded towards Alecos "It was a pleasure meeting you," he aded before striding off with a straight military bearing.

Alecos stared after him in silence. The fun and mischief in his face, from only a few moments ago, had gone. My heart plummeted. He called to Aristos to bring the bill and silently finished his brandy.

"Good night, lovely lady," Aristos said. "I see you eat fish like a Cypriot. You know the sweetest meat is in the head. You teach her well," he said turning to Alecos, who nodded and smiled absently. I could tell he was angry. Although he was good looking, successful and generous to a fault, his one failing was his underlying vulnerability that made him jealous and possessive.

He enjoyed the fact that other men admired me as we walked into a room together but, he didn't like to be reminded that he wasn't the first man in my life.

In Cyprus, it was still generally expected, that a woman would go to her marriage bed knowing only one man, her new husband. Alecos was modern and sophisticated enough not to expect that, but the old ideas were still ingrained in his Mediterranean psyche. Though he was well aware that in northern Europe we were already in the promiscuous days of the seventies, it would probably have been clear that the way David looked at me we had been more than just friends!

As we drove slowly back to the hotel, Alecos was quiet and preoccupied. I sighed. The day that had been so perfect was now turning sour over a chance encounter.

10

Later that evening

As we entered the apartment I put my arms around him. I could feel the tension in his body. "Please Alec," I pleaded, "I've been so happy since you came home, don't let anything spoil our perfect evening."

"I don't like to think of you with anyone else, Sally mou. It reminds me of Inga and how she cheated on me. I studied so hard at the university so that I would be able, eventually, to give her everything she wanted, but she couldn't wait, she wanted the high life straight away." He paused. I could see from the pain in his eyes that the memories he'd suppressed for so long, were flooding back.

"It was agony when she left me. And for what? A flashy car salesman! He didn't even own his own car. For years after, I avoided any serious involvements. Instead, I worked hard and made my uncle proud that he'd handed his business over to me, and now I've built it into one of the biggest beauty product companies in Cyprus!"

"But Alec," I interrupted. "I'm not Inga. I'm never going to leave you. Since we've been together, you're all I ever wanted. David was just someone I met when I arrived in Cyprus. As far as I was concerned he was good company and we went around together and had fun but it happened before I met you," I insisted, stretching the truth slightly, not wanting to hurt him more. His piercing blue eyes peered deeply into mine. I could see he was fighting with his jealousy and wanted to believe me. What he wanted from me was love and emotional security. We needed each other and being needed was almost as important as being in love.

"I love you, Alec. That's all that should matter now, not something that happened in the past before we met." I could feel his body slowly relaxing. He held my face between his hands. "I'm sorry, my lovely," he said tenderly. "I'm being stupid and unfair, but I can't bear the thought of being without you."

"Don't worry. That will never happen," I assured him, holding him tightly to reassure him. Then, pulling gently away, I said: "Come on, let's forget about it and have a midnight swim. It'll make us both feel better."

His mouth slowly broke into a grin and the mischief returned to his eyes. "Good idea, I'll race you." He quickly shrugged off his clothes and sprinted down to the water.

At thirty four, he was in good shape. He still played tennis regularly so, his tall frame was lean and muscled. Even his naked bottom, illuminated by the moon light had definition. I was full of love and admiration for him.

Swimming out to where he floated in a shaft of silver from the moon, I caught his outstretched hand and pulling myself close to him, planted a kiss on his cheek. "Don't ever think about us being apart. Just enjoy every moment that we are together."

He nodded and holding hands, we floated peace-fully looking up at the million stars flickering in the black velvet sky overhead.

Waking with the early morning sunlight filtering through the shutters and the sound of the waves breaking on the shore, I sat up gently.

My heart turned over with love as I looked down at Alecos' peaceful sleeping face. He was asleep on his back, one arm flung across the pillow. He looked innocent and contented, his jealousy forgotten after our tender lovemaking of the night before. His dark lashes fanned his cheek and his breathing was soft and regular.

"I missed you so much. I never want to be without you again," I whispered.

Staring at him enviously, I marveled at how men managed to sleep so deeply. They had the gift of switching to oblivion as easily as turning off the light.

Easing myself out of bed, I quietly ordered breakfast from room service, knowing it would take about half an hour to arrive. By then Alecos would be awake.

I crept outside and sitting in a shaft of morning sun, I watched it sparkle on the sea and listened to the gulls as they swooped and dived around the fishing boats plowing through the water to unload their early morning catch at the little harbour. It was magical!

I heard Alecos stir and go into the bathroom. He came out to the terrace running his hand through his thick damp hair, drops of water still clinging to his eyelashes.

"What are you doing out here? I need you in bed, as you can probably notice." Grinning, he pulled me to my feet but at that moment there was a knock on the door.

"Room Service," a voice called. Alecos reluctantly let me go and grabbing a towel, wrapped it round his waist and opened the door. The waiter, eyes unseeing, placed the brimming tray on the veranda table and left.

"Uhm, that looks good. I think I'll eat first and finish the other business later!" Alecos chuckled, settling down to a breakfast of sweet melon and warm croissants, oozing with butter and apricot jam.

As he sipped his coffee he buried his nose in the newspaper. I leaned over his shoulder to read the headlines, the ruffled front of my robe falling open to reveal the inner curve of my breasts. He turned his head and planted a kiss between them. Then, lifting my hand that rested on his shoulder to his lips, I felt his teeth nibbling gently on my knuckles and saw the glint in his eye. The sensation in my stomach flipped like an aircraft hitting a pocket of turbulence. The breakfast and newspaper forgotten, he hooked an arm around my waist and drew me back to the bed.

Later, languid with love, I sat up and looked at my watch on the bedside table.

"Alec, don't we have to check out soon?"

"Yes, my lovely. Don't worry. I know you want to go to Fontana Amoroso. But we've plenty of time to shower and get ready, then we can go straight there."

The shower was large, with more than enough room for two. In a couple of seconds we wereengulfed by a stream of warm water. Alecos reached out for the sponge and a bar of creamy soap and began to wash my back. It felt very sensual being systematically lathered all over. He was very thorough, making me hold onto his shoulders for balance while he picked up each foot and soaped between the toes. When he came to the top of my thighs I pressed them together trying to resist his questioning fingers. His knee nudged between them as his soapy hand stroked gently. Almost at once I discovered that although my desire had been dampened just a short time ago, it was quick to revive. The two weeks while Alecos had been away had been a long time and my body seemed to want to catch up. He pulled me into his arms. Soon his fingers were sending ripples of pleasure down the inside of my thighs. Closing my eyes, feeling jets of water cascading down the back of my legs, my body relaxed against his supporting arm. My hands rested lightly on his shoulders until as the lovely sensation grew stronger, my fingers tightened and clung. The pleasure was overwhelming, making me gasp and tremble until a piercing implosion of feeling made me shudder and cry out.

A moment passed before he was inside me, my arms around his neck and my legs clasped around his hips. He moved rhythmically, without hesitation. Suddenly, his movements became faster almost desperate. A half cry rose from his throat and with a heaving shudder he became still, the warm water spilling over us like a waterfall.

Lowering my legs I leant against him feeling almost too weak to stand unsupported. Slowly, my strength returned.

"I must dry my hair otherwise it will be damp all day," I murmured, pulling away and turning off the shower.

"I'm exhausted," Alecos groaned, following me from the shower and flopping onto the bed. "Why do you want to drive another fifty miles to Aphrodite's baths at Fontana Amarosa just to see a pool of dirty water?"

"You know I'm fascinated by the cult of

Aphrodite. After all, Cyprus is known as Aphrodite's Realm and people come from all over the world to worship her here. I wanted to stop yesterday and look at the ruins of her temple at Kouklia, but I knew you were eager to get to Paphos."

"But that's just another pile of stones. There's nothing to see. Nobody goes there now."

"The trouble with you is that you grew up with these legends and ancient sites all around you, so you take them all for granted, but for a cold blooded northerner this worship of female beauty and love is exciting and romantic."

"I'd never call you cold blooded," he said, winking wickedly. "There's plenty of Mediterranean fire in you from your Italian ancestors. But 'Fontana Amarosa', the Fountain of Love, why?"

"The legend says: If you drink the water there you'll fall in love."

"But I thought you were already in love with me! So I can't see the point?"

"Yes, of course I'm in love with you, but that's not the reason I want to go there. It's supposed to be an enchanted place with a crystal pool at the base of an overhanging cliff, with butterflies fluttering in the ancient fig trees."

"Yes I remember it from my schooldays. There's a knobbley old tree, growing from a lump of rock and hanging over a dark mucky-looking pool," he said, sarcastically.

"Well, my friend Lula, told me it was where Aphrodite bathed and now, when a woman bathes there she becomes pregnant. She said it happened to her."

Alecos left eyebrow raised in disbelief. He desperately wanted to be a father, though he'd never said anything specific. He loved children and they were all entranced by him. They seemed to realise he was just a big kid himself! I knew he was surprised and a little worried that I hadn't already conceived.

I watched him turning the idea over in his mind, then, he shrugged his shoulders.

"I can't imagine you bathing in that pool," he said. "But I suppose you could splash water over yourself. Why not? What's there to lose? We might as well give it a try."

11

Next week, David's warning

First thing on Monday morning after our romantic weekend in Paphos, Alecos gathered the whole company together in our new showrooms to drink a toast to the success of the new Silhouette Products. Everyone was as excited as the next to be part of the big new venture. We then all trooped down to the machinery room where in no time Spiros had all the machinery humming in harmony as hair tints from golden blond to blue black came spurting out of the machine nozzles into the tubes.

The following days were spent in a whirl of activity. It was a heady and exciting time. Now that President Makarios had the rebels under control, the political situation appeared to be stable, so there seemed nothing to stop us becoming the leading hair colouring supplier in Cyprus and, if we were lucky, perhaps in time, the whole of the Eastern Mediterranean.

There had been no time for my usual tea and gossip with Ann, but on Monday of the next week. she phoned. Her beautifully modulated dark brown voice purred into my ear.

"Hello, stranger. I've missed you. You must be going frantic with the new production?"

"Yes, you're right. We don't know if we're coming

or going. Alec gets so excited when there's a new project. He's running around like a cat chasing its tail."

"Is he with you at the moment?"

"No, he's down in the store. Why?"

"I heard you met David in Paphos. How did Alec react?"

"Not too well. He turned jealous and moody but I managed to persuade him that there had been nothing between David and me. But how do you know about it?"

"Ha! You know how gossip travels in Cyprus!" she laughed. "But seriously, Sal, David came to the flat. He wants to meet you. He says it's important."

"Oh, my God. I hope he doesn't think I'm going to see him again. I know he was pretty devastated when we broke up but he knows I'm married now."

"I don't know what he has in mind but he seems very concerned. I think you'd better meet him just once to find out. He has leave on Wednesday afternoon and says he'll meet you here if I give him the OK. Can you make it? It would be like old times," she said, with a wicked laugh in her voice.

"Oh, Ann, don't joke about it...Alec is really so insecure, though no one would ever imagine it. You know what trouble I'd be in if he found out. He'll get into a frantic rage, then clam up for days.

"Don't worry, there's no reason he should find out if you only intend to see David this once.

"I hope you're right. I've already had more than my share of trouble these last few weeks and now David turns up to rock the boat. Life just isn't fair!" I complained. "But OK, tell David I'll be there."

Although I'd managed to convince Alecos in Paphos that there had been nothing between David and me, it wasn't true. I'd arrived in Cyprus, five years ago, after the break up with my long-standing boyfriend in England.

I'd met David soon after I'd moved into the family holiday home, which my father had bought several years earlier. It was just outside the picturesque harbor town of Kyrenia on the north coast of the island. There was a UN contingent of Canadian police based in the Coeur de Lion hotel in the town. They soon noticed that an unattached female had arrived, so it wasn't long before I was invited to their parties and social occasions. It was at one of these parties that I was introduced to Lieutenant David Hamilton of the UN British Contingent based in Paphos.

He was very attractive and attentive and we began to see each other whenever he had leave. Maybe it was because I was feeling vulnerable after my unhappy breakup. but in the romantic environment of dinners under the stars dancing the night away, barbecues on secluded beaches or skiing in the mountains, we had fun together and we became more seriously involved than I'd expected. Before long, he hinted that he'd like to get married. The suggestion was very flattering and helped to restore my shattered confidence, but marriage was never on my mind. So though I certainly didn't encourage the idea, I didn't dissuade him either.

Eventually the lazy, hedonistic life began to feel unreal. So needing to earn a living, I answered an advert in the Cyprus Mail for an English speaking, personal assistant to the director of the Cyprus Cosmetics Company in Nicosia. I got the job and Alecos Lytras was the owner and managing direc-tor. We hit it off straight away and I settled in happily as the work was very interesting and enjoyable.

Ann then suggested I move in with her during my working week in Nicosia, but for the weekends I went home to Kyrenia.

I'd met Ann soon after I'd arrived on the island, so when I was invited to the Canadian UN parties she was invited too. She soon overcame her shyness about mixing with strangers and really enjoyed herself. David would meet me at Ann's flat when he had leave and often he'd bring along another officer and we'd go out as a foursome.

Then, several months later, after the night of the terrific electric storm, when Alecos had arrived so unexpectedly in Kyrenia, we became close. Before long, I realised I was falling in love with Alecos and I would have to end my relationship with David.

It came to a head when David said he wanted to announce our engagement at an important regimental dinner. I couldn't let it happen and consequently we had a very painful parting. But, from that day until our unexpected meeting in Paphos, I'd never seen avid again.

Now here he was, wanting to meet me. I knew it wasn't a good idea and could probably lead to trouble but we'd been so very close I did want to see him once more.

David was already at Ann's flat when I arrived.

"Sally, you look even lovelier than you did in Paphos." It was obvious that he was longing to take me in his arms but he held back, not sure how I'd react.

Instead, putting my arms around him I kissed him lightly on the cheek.

"David, it's good to see you too. Let me look at you properly." I held him at arm's length, my eyes travelling over him approvingly. "With your new pips you look even more impressive," I said. He really was a good looking man!

Ann coughed in the background. "Can I get you something to drink?" she asked, edging discreetly out of the room.

"Yes please, Ann. I'd love a cup of tea," I said.

"And if I remember rightly,"Ann said. "You're a tea drinker too, David!"

"Thanks, Ann, you've got a good memory," he said, dragging his eyes away from me.

The instant she was out of the room David sighed: "I missed you, Sal. If I hadn't been posted to Egypt soon after we broke up, I'd never have let you get away. I'd have gone mad here without you."

"I'm sorry, David. I know how hard it was for you. We had such wonderful times together but after meeting Alecos, I realised I wasn't in love with you.

The pain was visible in his eyes as he replied. "At the time I could happily have killed you both. But now I wish you every happiness and hope he will always be good to you."

"Thank you, David. You're still as kind and considerate as you always were, despite me letting you down." I reached up and kissed him gently.

Before he could respond I stepped back. "But you didn't come all this way to tell me that, did you?" I asked curiously.

"I would have been more than happy to. But no, you're right, I didn't."

"Ann said it was something important."

"Yes, Sal, it is. I came to tell you that you should leave Cyprus."

"Why?" I asked, my eyebrows rising in amazement.

"Seeing you the other day brought all the old

feelings back and I realise I still care about you. I shouldn't be telling you what I know, but I don't want anything to happen to you."

"Yes David but why should I leave?" I asked urgently.

He hesitated for a moment. "We've had a report that a coup is imminent and this time Makarios will be out once and for all."

"But surely that can't happen now!" I exclaimed. "The Greek officers are due to leave next Monday on the 20th of July so there will be nobody left to lead another coup. Now Makarios knows the people who are involved with the terrorists so he must be keeping an eye on them."

"Yes, that could well be the situation but something is definitely being planned according to what we've heard through our various sources."

"But if you've heard about it, then so must he. He's always managed to out manoeuver his enemies. A coup would disrupt the economy of the whole island. It would set us back ten years. Both tourism and International business would suffer. Makarios would never allow it to happen. He's built Cyprus into a prosperous country. Even the differences between the Greek and Turkish communities are becoming much easier. Everyone is benefiting!"

"Yes, Sal, I agree with all that. But that's what we've heard through the grapevine. If you were my wife I'd want you safely out of the country till we could see how things worked out."

"But it's only a couple of weeks since the last attempt failed. Surely another attempt couldn't be planned so quickly even with the CIA behind it. Nothing could happen for months."

"I hope you're right, Sally. I just felt I should warn

you because I still care about you. You must make your own decision about leaving."

Leaning forward I laid a hand on his arm as he sat opposite me. Even though my rejection had made him suffer, he still worried about me.

"But, Sal, please don't breathe a word about what I've told you. I could be court-marshalled if anyone found out that the information came from me."

"Don't worry, David, I'll keep it to myself. But here comes Ann with the tea. She'll want to know what your visit was all about. I'll have to think of something to tell her.

As we drank our tea Ann and David chatted about the good times we'd all had together. Listening with only half an ear, I was distracted by David's warning, not wanting to believe that anything more could happen. Then a comment from Ann brought me back to the conversation.

"Do you remember that wonderful lunch on the beach that November?" she asked me.

"Oh, yes," I said. "We were all sitting in our swimming costumes round that huge table. The damask cloth was piled high with regimental silver and waiters in dress uniform hovered around serving us from silver platters. It felt like a scene from *Alice in Wonderland*. It was really quite bizarre!"

"Yes, that's the one. I was sitting next to someone called Stephen. He made me laugh with his stories. We were going to meet up, but I never saw him again. Did he get posted?" she asked David.

"Yes," he replied. "He went back to England soon after the party. I think there was some family trouble.

"That beach lunch was really impressive," I said in awe. "So much silver, I could hardly believe my eyes."

"Yes, the more prestigious the regiment, the more elaborate the silver!" David laughed. "Those were good days," he commented, looking at me regretfully.

We reminisced about all our times together but eventually David looked at his watch.

"Goodness, I have to be back in camp by seven," he said, jumping up. "The time has just flown; it was like old times seeing you both again," he said wistfully.

Leading him into the hall and giving his hand a squeeze, I reached up and gave him a light kiss. "Thank you for being concerned enough to warn me, David."

"I'm sorry that's the only thing I can do for you now Sally. But remember, if you ever need help, just give me a call and I'll be there."

Nodding, I smiled my thanks. He was a good man and would make someone a wonderful husband one day, I thought, closing the door.

Ann had a questioning look on her face when I returned. "Well, what was that all about?"

"He wanted to be sure that I was happy with Alecos and that if I ever needed help he would still be there for me," I replied. Ann nodded, quite willing to believe it. She knew how thoughtful David had always been.

Later, back at the office, watching the bustling activity, a sinking feeling descended into my stomach. If there was trouble, all this would come to a grinding halt. The dream that Alecos had worked so hard for would become a nightmare. The economy would crash and the bank would call in the loan for the new machinery and supplies. He'd be ruined.

Should I tell him? But what could he do about it? He'd want to know where the information came from.

Eventually, my relationship with David all those years ago would come out. Alecos would feel humiliated and furious that even though we had been together almost permanently at that time, I had been seeing David behind his back. He'd know then that I'd lied to him in Paphos after our evening at the harbour.

Knowing how emotional he was, he wouldn't be able to cope with the idea that he'd been cheated for a second time. He would be shattered and his Mediterranean ego and pride would probably force him to leave me.

But, what if there really was a coup? What then?

If things did get bad, at least we'd live through them together and salvage what we could. Hopefully, we could eventually start again.

No, I decided. For both our sakes I'd have to ignore the warning. President Makarios had withstood every political and physical attempt to depose him up till now. Next time, whenever that would be, he would manage to do it again!

For the next few days, I listened intently to every news broadcast on the Radio and TV, scanning the newspapers for anything that might lend substance to David's warning. Alecos was surprised at my sudden interest in the political situation, but presumed it was due to my recent frightening involvement in the intrigues of Cyprus.

So, for the next couple of weeks, everything seemed to be running smoothly. David's warning appeared to have been unfounded. Thankfully, I hadn't allowed myself to be panicked into saying anything to Alecos. It was very probable that the Greek colonels would eventually make another attempt to overthrow Makarios, especially since he had humiliated them internationally by exposing their plot. But, it seemed that by the time they got organised again, our new business would be established and we would be able to weather the storm.

12

The coup, Monday 15th July

Almost two weeks after David's warning, on Monday
15th July, I left the flat for my weekly tennis lesson,
at the legendary colonial style Ledra Palace Hotel.
My only concern, that early in the morning, was how
I could improve my backhand.

This luxury hotel was famous in the Mediterranean area as 'one of the great watering holes of the
world' by international journalists covering stories in
the Middle East. No matter what time of night or day
there were always at least one or two bleary-eyed
reporters propping up the bar or sitting outside in the
shade of the jasmine covered terrace, sipping Brandy
Sours. This cocktail, was a concoction of local
Constantino Brandy, Angostura bitter and lemon
juice, created by the barman of the hotel. It had now
become famous and was included in every good
barman's repertoire the world over.

The hotel, set in extensive grounds, was only a
few yards from a heavily sandbagged checkpoint. The
thick barbed wire fence known as the Green Line
separated the Greek part of the island from the
Turkish sector of Nicosia. It was set up in 1964 by
the first United Nations peace-keeping contingent to
arrive in Cyprus.

Finishing my lesson just after eight and driving

past the municipal gardens on my way home, I heard a commotion. Looking across the road, I saw, to my astonishment, Commissioner Marco being forcibly escorted from his house by the military police of the National Guard.

Almost immediately, dull thuds could be heard coming from the direction of the radio station and behind me I heard a strange rumbling noise like muted thunder. Glancing back down the road, I was horrified to see a line of tanks and armored cars bearing down on me.

At that moment, a deafening wail erupted from the air-raid siren on the roof of the main prison.

My heart gave a sickening jolt as the significance of all these incidents struck me. David's warning was coming true. This was the start of a military coup to oust and kill the President!

The tanks rumbling up the main avenue were obviously on their way to bombard the Presidential Palace.

It was common knowledge that every Monday at eight in the morning President Makarios returned from his weekend retreat in the mountains and drove straight to his office in the Palace.

I was terrified and my heart was pumping as I raced at breakneck speed up the avenue in front of the tanks and skidded into the carport of our apartment. Flying up the stairs, not bothering to wait for the lift, I burst into the flat. Alecos, appearing from the bathroom looked worried.

"What's happening out there?" he asked urgently.

"Quick, get dressed," I yelled. "I saw Commissioner Marcos being arrested and there are tanks coming up the road towards the palace. I think a coup has started."

Dashing into the kitchen, which overlooked the main avenue, I peered out of the window but the eucalyptus trees blocked the view, so charging up another three flights of stairs I reached the flat roof of the building.

Hearing the rumble of the tanks passing in the road below me I ran towards the parapet to look over.

As I got to the edge I was grabbed from behind. My knees scraped against the wall as I was roughly pulled to the ground by a heavy man I hadn't noticed in my rush. Wriggling into a sitting position as the man's weight moved off me, I saw the face of George, my ex-bodyguard, glaring at me.

"Keep down," he growled. "You'll be shot if you put your head over the top."

"What's happening?" I asked, as my breath returned.

"The tanks are going to destroy the presidential palace and kill Makarios."

"Well, what are you doing here then? Why aren't you at the palace protecting the President?"

"We only have pistols. What good would they be against tanks?" George hissed in frustration and anger. "If he is at the palace, his bodyguards will protect him and get him away," Petros added, as he crawled out from behind the bank of water tanks located on the roof.

"I just came from the Ledra Palace hotel. I saw the Commissioner being taken away by the National Guard!" I told them breathlessly.

"Yes, we got there too late to help him. All important Makarios supports are being arrested. You'll be on their list too. You caused them too much trouble and they will want to get even."

"Oh my God! I never thought of that!" I exclaimed

in horror.

"You should get out of Nicosia. Go to the house in Kyrenia you told us about. It will be safer there for the moment. Go quickly while you have the chance," George said urgently.

Without another word, crouching low, I ran to the stairwell.

Entering the flat, Alecos was sitting with his ear glued to the radio. He looked puzzled as he toggled between stations.

"I don't know what's going on," he exclaimed angrily. "I heard what sounded like doors slamming, then CBC English wavelength started with some nonsense about somebody called Toad of Toad Hall and a piglet!"

Despite the anxiety of the situation, I couldn't help laughing. "That's the morning story. It's a children's classic. It must be an extract from Wind in the Willows. But what are they saying on the Greek station?"

"They're playing military music. But what happened to you?" Alecos asked, noticing my bloody knees and my dusty tennis dress.

"Petros and George are on the roof. They tried to get to the Commissioner but were too late to help him. They said that I will be arrested too if I stay in Nicosia. Alec, we must leave. Let's go while we have the chance."

Alecos looked alarmed but hastily collected our documents along with an emergency bundle of money we always kept hidden in the house. Quickly changing from my tennis skirt I threw some clothes into a bag and emptied the contents of the fridge into a shopping basket. Within minutes we had left the flat and were speeding through the deserted side streets back to the checkpoint at the Ledra Palace Hotel.

From the Presidential palace in the opposite direction we could hear the guns booming as it was being bombarded by the tanks.

At the Turkish checkpoint, Alecos showed his pass, which allowed us to use the thirty-mile road through the Turkish enclave. Greek Cypriots generally had to join the UN convoy that left for Kyrenia in the morning and back in the afternoon during the week, otherwise they had to drive past the airport and the sixty mile route round the perimeter of the Turkish enclave to Kyrenia.

We employed a Turkish salesman who visited customers in the Turkish quarters of the island. It was one of these customers who had arranged the pass for Alecos.

The Turkish guards at the checkpoint were eager to know what was happening and were not surprised to hear that the army was on the move. They knew that Athens was behind the present troubles and they were happy to be safe within their guarded enclaves while the Greek Cypriots fought it out between themselves.

As we left the city confines and sped through the almost uninhabited countryside of the Turkish zone, the martial music on the radio was interrupted by the first announcement of the coup.

"Hellenism lives in Cyprus," the announcer proclaimed. "The National Guard intervened today to prevent bloodshed and civil war in Cyprus." The voice continued curtly: "There will be an immediate 24 hour curfew throughout the country."

"We got out just in time," Alecos said with relief.

"Won't we be stopped when we leave the Turkish area on the Kyrenia side?" I asked anxiously.

"No, I don't think so. I'm sure the fighting has been confined to Nicosia so far. Once Nicosia is in their hands there won't be much resistance elsewhere on the island. In fact, that news broadcast was probably the first indication for the rest of the island that there has been a coup, so before any road blocks are set up we should be able to make it through Kyrenia and home."

13

Kyrenia, later that day

As we arrived in Kyrenia pockets of bewildered people stood around in doorways and on corners, but we passed through without being stopped. We drove the three miles east to our home without trouble. As Alecos has predicted no road blocks had yet been set up.

The house, set back from the cliffs, looked out across the sea to the mountains of Anatolia, thirty miles away on the Turkish mainland, and clearly visible on the horizon.

Alecos switched on the radio as soon as we entered the house. He fiddled with the knobs, but the only sound was a distorted babble and crackle from most of the broadcasting stations and only monotonous martial music from CBC. He snapped the radio off impatiently.

"Relax, Alec. Just be glad for the moment that we got here safely," I said, putting away the tins and packets I'd thrown into the basket on leaving Nicosia. "Why don't you make us a coffee while I sort out my provisions?"

Mumbling irritably he filled the kettle.

"It was lucky I grabbed this frozen leg of New Zealand lamb as we left. That should do us for a few days while this curfew lasts."

"For goodness sake, Sally, the country's in chaos and all you can think about is food," he snapped.

"Don't you get angry with me," I said indignantly. "There's nothing we can do now except wait for news of what's happening. I know it's a nerve-racking situation but it doesn't help either of us if you lose your temper."

"You're right. I'm sorry, Sally mou," he apologised. 'I'll take my coffee onto the veranda and keep my bad temper to myself."

"Good idea," I replied thankfully. "Why not take the portable radio onto the roof terrace instead. The Kyrenia Mountains always interfere with the reception here but perhaps it'll be better on the roof. See if you can get BBC World Service or British Forces Broadcasting. Leave the other radio on in the kitchen so I'll know if anything happens."

"Good thinking! Practical as ever! That's one of the reasons I married you!" he laughed, his good temper returning.

With his coffee in one hand and the radio in the other, he went upstairs. I heard the shutters of the bedroom squeak open and the scrape of a chair on the tiled floor of the terrace as he pulled it close to our small wrought iron Sunday morning breakfast table.

We hadn't been to the house for several weeks and I realised that the shelves were almost empty.

"I wonder how long before the curfew is lifted and I can get to the market to stock up?" I mumbled to myself, darting round the kitchen, opening cupboard doors and drawers, checking what was there so I could feed us. It helped to take my mind off the fighting in Nicosia.

My parents had bought the house several years earlier. They'd come across a derelict barn and donkey stable whilst visiting Kyrenia. It was set back off the road overlooking the sea. They realized that, with a little imagination, it would make a comfortable family holiday home with an outstanding view.

They converted the stable and barn into a family sized kitchen and spacious living room at the front facing the mountains. Then added a small entrance hall with cloakroom on the side, turning the ground floor into a practical and roomy area. Overlooking the sea view to the north at the back they added a sun lounge off the living room. The original ceiling beams of the barn were retained and a large stone wood burning fireplace added, as the winter evenings could get chilly once the sun went down. The main bedroom and guest rooms with bathrooms en-suite were built on top. The house was decorated in rustic style. It's white washed walls, brick tiled floors and wooden shutters reflected the simple charm of a typical Cypriot village house. Pine furniture and soft furnishings in terracotta and sunshine yellows completed the atmosphere.

I always felt safe and secure in this house as it held many happy family memories.

The cool, vine covered, north-facing terrace was our favorite spot for reading and eating in the heat of the summer and overlooked the sea. In winter, we watched television or listened to music in the sun lounge which had been warmed by the sun during the day or sat by the fire in the living room where I worked on my needlepoint and Alecos read the newspapers.

But my favorite room was the kitchen.

The window sills and shelves of the old pine dresser were filled with brightly painted Cyprus pottery. Large copper pots, spilling with greenery and flowers, glowed golden in the sunlight. Terracotta dishes and plates were stacked in the open cupboards. Here, I spent many happy hours contentedly pottering away preparing and cooking up the colourful tasty vegetables and fruit that we grew in the garden.

Suddenly I was jolted out of my reverie. The martial music droning monotonously from the radio came to an abrupt end and a voice sounding like doom, announced...

The National Guard intervened today to stop internal strife between warring factions of the Greek Cypriots. It is now in control of the situation and the President is dead. Anyone putting up resistance will be executed at once.

Gasping in horror, I stared numbly at the radio as Alecos came hurtling down the stairs, his face ashen "Did you hear that?" he spluttered. "Makarios is dead!"

I nodded silently.

He dropped onto a chair and buried his face in his hands.

Alecos' Uncle David had been a close friend of the President and Alecos, as a teenager, had accompanied his uncle many times to the Palace. The two men would drink coffee and talk over old times. Alecos admired the President's calm handling of the volatile political situation that had reigned over the island during the last few years. From this earlier association, Alecos knew him to be a warm and likable man with a fine sense of humour.

"What will happen now?" I asked, almost in a whisper.

He shrugged: "It depends on who they elect as the

new president, but you can be sure whoever it is, will be under the thumb of Athens, so it won't be good."

"What will happen to the business?" I asked, with a sinking heart.

"Oh, Sally mou, I hate to think," he groaned in despair. "You remember the Commissioner warned us that people we knew might well be secret supporters of the new regime. I can think of a couple of competitors who are jealous of our success. They would love to get their hands on our agencies. Now could be their chance to use their allegiance with the new power to make things difficult for us."

A prickle of fear ran down my spine. Putting my arm around his shoulder, I said, trying to reassure him: "We'll manage somehow. We'll just have to work hard and keep out of trouble."

"I hope it will be as easy as that. Perhaps Spiros got to the office before eight o'clock this morning. He might be able to tell us what is happening in Nicosia." Jumping up, he hurried into the hall to make a call.

"Damn! The lines are dead," he exclaimed, slamming the phone down angrily.

Back in the sitting room he couldn't settle, one moment staring out of the window, then crossing the room to pull a book from the shelf, only to drop it onto the coffee table and return to grab another one. "This waiting around not knowing what's happening, is driving me mad," he exploded. "I don't know what to do with myself. I'd better go upstairs again. Maybe there will be something more on the radio," he muttered, stomping out of the room.

I was also restless, so went outside to look at the garden. The heat had proved too much for my hardy fuchsia, which now drooped sadly. Running some water into the ancient stone donkey trough, I stood the pot in the water to revive it. Wandering around listlessly, I collected a few tomatoes and cucumbers. The herbs had shriveled up in the heat but I picked some anyway. By now, the fuchsia had perked up after its good drink so I stood the pot to drain, in the shade by the kitchen.

With the bits and pieces from the garden I started to make a salad for lunch adding some Feta cheese, black olives and mixing the limp herbs into the dressing. Fortunately, on the way to my tennis lesson, earlier in the day, I'd picked up a warm crusty village loaf, so I cut some thick slices to mop up the dressing.

Calling Alecos who was still upstairs, I set the table for our meager meal.

Filling his glass generously with wine, I hoped he'd have a good sleep after lunch. But he woke after only an hour and immediately started fiddling with the radio again.

Just before three came a shattering announcement.

The new President was to be Nicos Sampson.

We were appalled. He was the worst possible choice the new regime could have made.

It was common knowledge that Nicos Sampson, an ultra right wing journalist was a convicted killer. His murderous atrocities went back over many years. In 1955 when the Greek Cypriots started a guerilla War of Liberation against British rule in Cyprus, the British governor of the island was obliged to employ the Turkish Cypriots to police the country against the insurgents. This, naturally provoked secular hatred where before, Greek and Turkish Cypriots lived side by side.

Sampson, one of the leaders of the liberation army,

destroyed and massacred the population of three small Turkish Cypriott villages near Famagusta. Again in 1963, he and his gang of terrorists burned to the ground the Turkish suburb of Omophita in Nicosia.

He had been called, 'the Killer of Murder Mile' by the British, when, dressed as a woman, he'd pushed a pram full of guns down the main street of Nicosia and opened fire killing several British soldiers on patrol. He'd been imprisoned in England for the murder of so many soldiers but was released under an amnesty agreement when Cyprus finally gained its independence from British rule.

His appointment as President of Cyprus would be greeted with as much apprehension by Britain as it would be received in Ankara. Sampson's name alone was enough to send panic through the Turkish Cypriot population. Ankara would be obliged to take some sort of action to protect them.

It was evident from the proclamation on the radio that the new regime was trying desperately to reassure world opinion that the coup was strictly an internal affair between Greek Cypriots, therefore. No external intervention by Greece, Turkey or Britain, the three guarantors of Cypriot Independence and Sovereignty, was warranted.

"Why would they choose Sampson of all people?" I asked, in disbelief. "They must have plenty of other credible individuals among their supporters that they could have chosen as an acceptable President."

"I would have thought so too," Alecos agreed. "But I imagine this coup was a last minute desperation attempt before the final batch of Greek Officers was due to leave today. Their serious candidates would have been taken by surprise and distanced themselves. So the organisers had to scrape the bottom of the barrel and Sampson was the only rotten apple left."

He shook his fist and growled in disgust.

We sat for ages in the dimmed bedroom, numbed by the horror of the latest news and the outrageous propaganda trying to justify it. Eventually Alecos could take no more and changed stations to find out what the rest of the world was making of the situation.

On most stations, all he could hear was static, but suddenly there was a weak signal from an Israeli station. A faint voice was saying: "The President of Cyprus had escaped from Nicosia". Looking at each other in disbelief, Alecos fiddled some more.

Suddenly, through the crackle, we picked up another faint signal coming from a station calling itself Radio Free Paphos. To our amazement we recognised the blurred but distinct voice of President Makarios. "I am not dead," the President said. "The unlawful Coup of the Junta in Athens to take over Cyprus has failed. Together we can carry on the resistance and win freedom. The only thing they managed to take over was the radio Station!"

The interviewer then described how Makarios had escaped from the Presidential Palace among a group of school children who had just arrived for a visit. He was then driven to a monastery in the mountains, then on to Paphos where the broadcast was coming from a secret radio station.

We listened in disbelief. The takeover had been achieved so quickly and the bombardment of the Presidential Palace had been so heavy, that it seemed impossible the President had not been killed. But here he was, risen from the dead, speaking to the people

117

of Cyprus and giving us back our hope.

From utter despair, our mood changed to elation. Alecos gave a whoop of delight and jumping off the bed danced round the room like a naked banshee. Suddenly the whole situation had changed. With Makarios still alive, world opinion would support him against the illegal regime and before long he would be back in power.

If we could just go quietly about our business for the next few weeks, everything would eventually return to normal. Our relief was indescribable.

"There's a bottle of champagne in the fridge. Instead of your infernal English afternoon tea, we'll open it right away and get drunk," Alecos shouted happily.

We celebrated well into the night. Our ears were glued to every radio station we could distinguish through the poor reception.

The next morning we woke late despite the sun streaming into the room. The filmy net curtains at the open windows hung motionless.

"It's going to be a scorcher today," I said, getting out of bed and closing the shutters to keep out the heat. "We'll have to go for a swim later to cool off."

Alecos sat up and stretched. "No, we can't, we're still under curfew. Come back to bed, there is nothing else we can do!"

Around lunchtime, a news flash from BBC World Service reported that the President had been rescued from Paphos by helicopter and flown to RAF Akrotiri, part of the ninety square mile military area belonging to the British. From there he was flown to Malta, before flying on to London.

"That's fantastic news," I said happily. "But, as

the champagne's finished, let's cool ourselves off in sea water this time."

Alecos shook his head. "No, that's not a good idea."

"Oh come on, we can't stay cooped up all day. It's too hot!"

"But someone will see us if we drive to the beach."

"No, I don't mean the proper beach, I meant the inlet just below our headland here. I know it's nothing special but there's a small sandy shelf and at least we'll be able to have a swim and cool off. Nobody goes there."

"Oh yes, I'd forgotten about that place."

"Well, shall we go?"

Alecos hesitated, then he nodded: "Yes, it really is very hot! Let's do it. We should be safe."

14

Tuesday 16th July

As we got to the main road at the end of our drive, we looked both ways to make sure no one was about, then quickly slipped down the dirt track next to our boundary that led to the beach.

Parking the car in the sandy clearing behind the olive grove that hid us from the road, we slithered down the steep slope to the welcome coolness of the shady narrow cove below.

The air smelt salty from the dried seaweed covered rocks, but the waves whispered gently as they receded over the fine shingle.

I screamed with shock as my hot sticky body hit the icy water but quickly became aware of the wonderful invigoration of its salty coolness. Floating on my back I gazed at the cloudless blue sky. For a few moments, my mind was empty of everything save the physical perfection of the moment.

Lulled by the movement of the sea, I let myself be wafted gently towards the shore by the swell. My hands touched shingle, the next swell deposited me on the land like a beached whale. After the coolness of the deep water the incoming water, that now lapped over my body felt warm.

Soon Alecos followed. I got to my feet to walk the few steps to the outcrop of rocks where we'd left our clothes. Wrapping a beach towel around me, it too felt warm against the cool wetness of my shoulders

"That was marvellous," I said, vigorously towel-drying my long hair.

"Yes, I must admit it was a good idea," Alecos said. "But now we should be getting back. We don't want to push our luck."

I nodded, quickly pushing my feet into my flip flops before starting up the steep track. At the top, pausing for breath, I looked back at the sea, framed between the cliffs of the cove. Over the narrow inlet of sand the water was aquamarine but further out, where the shelf fell away, it turned a deep indigo, ending in a hazy lavender blue at the horizon.

For a few moments I forgot the troubles we were living through and breathed in the beauty of the surroundings.

As Alecos reversed in the narrow parking space, the wheels of his heavy Mercedes car spun on the loose surface and the back sunk into soft sand.

"Damn," he swore. "Now we're in trouble!"

As he gently pressed down on the accelerator, the tires screamed and churned deeper into the soft ground throwing dust and sand all around.

"You'll have to get out and give it a push," he told me. But though I leaned all my weight on the back of the car, it had little effect.

"You take the wheel and I'll push," he said in exasperation, as he got out. But even his strength didn't help, the car just settled deeper into the sand.

By now Alecos was getting anxious. "I'll go to the farm and see if they can help," he said, hurrying away. Before long he was back with the farmer's fat wife followed by her eleven year old twin grandsons. They didn't look much like a rescue party, though any help was better than none. But even with the extra weight the wheels spun ineffectively.

"What about folding the towels and putting them under the wheels. It might give them a bit of a grip," I suggested.

After a couple of tries, the car jumped forward as the towels were catapulted out behind, showing us all with sand and grit that settled in our hair and stuck to our bodies. "Hooray," we all shouted. "We did it!" Though covered in sand everyone smiled as the wheels settled on firmer ground.

After dirty handshakes and profuse thanks for their help the lady and her grandsons left us. We parked the car safely further up the track and ran down once more to the cove to rinse our dusty bodies off in the sea.

Coming out of the water, we heard the crunch of gravel above us. Looking up to the cliff top, we saw the silhouette of three soldiers against the sky line. They emerged in slow motion as they moved closer to the cliff edge. It could have been a scene from a Spaghetti Western where the Indians appear over the ridge!

They each held a rifle at hip level pointing down at us. It was so bizarre, I wanted to laugh, but that feeling quickly evaporated.

"Stay where you are," the Greek National Guard officer leading the group shouted, as he and the two Cypriot corporals, their guns still pointing at us, made their way gingerly down the steep slope, sliding on the loose surface in their leather soled boots.

On reaching the beach the officer indicated with his rifle that we should put our hands up, though as we were in our wet swimming costumes it must have been obvious we weren't carrying any weapons.

The officer, a big man with a narrow black moustache, that echoed the line of his thin mean mouth, blatantly looked me over in my tiny bikini, his dark eyes lusting. I shivered.

He spoke roughly to us as though we were peasants, saying disdainfully that we were part of a group that had been spotted from the military camp on the headland further along the coast.

Apparently they'd already apprehended the farmer's wife and her grandsons but after a harsh warning they had let them go. We were not going to be so lucky.

"Don't you know there is a curfew? Or don't you ignorant people know what that means?" he asked, sarcastically.

Alecos took a deep breath to control his anger. "I know we shouldn't be out," he said, trying to reason with the officer. "But we live on the cliff top and only came down to the beach for a quick swim as it was so hot."

"You Cypriots think you can do what you like," he sneered, contemptuously. "We're in charge here now."

Alecos flinched. I hoped he wasn't going to answer back.

"Excuse me, Sir," said one of the corporals, whom I recognized as his mother had worked in our bottling plant some time ago. "I know these people and I'm sure they were not intending to make trouble."

The officer glowered at him and shrugged dismissively. "All you Cypriots are trouble makers. Now get your clothes on," he ordered Alecos, harshly.

"You're under arrest."

"What for?"

"You're breaking the curfew and organising a gathering. It's against the law and if you try to resist arrest you could be executed." he taunted.

"But they were only trying to get the car out of the sand," the corporal pointed out .

"We cannot be sure of that, can we?" the officer sneered.

The corporal standing behind the officer looked at Alecos and shrugged his shoulders. "He's a swine at the best of times. I'm sorry," he murmured, in English

"Never mind," Alecos replied. "You did your best."

The officer who obviously didn't understand English, spun round angrily. "If I hear another word from you, you'll be in trouble too," he snarled at the corporal. "Now get going all of you," he said, jabbing his rifle at us to indicate we should all move off in front of him.

After collecting his shirt and shorts from the car Alecos was bundled into the jeep and without another word they drove off.

I drove the car home in a daze. The day seemed to have rushed by at a bewildering speed. I wanted to rewind it and start again. The silence of the house pressed down on me like a physical presence, just the slow ticking of the clock relieved the tension.

Although Alecos was gone, he seemed to have left an energy behind him, a sense that when he was around things happened, as they usually did, though neither of us could have anticipated this present horrific situation.

And, to make it worse, it was all my fault. If only I hadn't insisted on going for a swim. Alecos hadn't been keen on the idea but, laughing off his fears in my usual carefree manner, it had got us in to real trouble. What would happen to him?

Naturally, he would be questioned and they could charge him with causing a disturbance, but then what?

Normally, Alecos temper was slow to rise but it could be very explosive if it boiled over. I prayed he would make an effort to stay calm and not let himself be provoked by that sadistic Greek officer who would obviously delight in goading and bullying him.

As I went into the kitchen, I automatically switched on the kettle.

Why did the English always make tea when their wits were frazzled? What had they done in a crisis before tea? But nevertheless, the familiar ritual helped to settle my thought into a more logical rhythm.

I had to get hold of someone influential. The Commissioner was my first thought, but as he'd been arrested even before the coup had started that was useless.

Who else was there? Maybe Ann would know someone!

I grabbed the phone. Breathlessly, I explained to her what had happened.

"Don't worry," she told me calmly. "That bloody Greek is just throwing his weight about. They can't keep Alecos at the military camp. He's a civilian. They will have to release him sooner or later. But I'll phone around to see if anyone I know can pull strings. I'll call you back as soon as I've got anything."

Her reasoning made sense, but I still felt uneasy.

Trying to put my fears out of my mind, I wandered listlessly around the house. In the bedroom

I noticed that several of Alecos shirts had fallen off their hangers. Absently rearranging them next to his jackets, I touched the cloth and caught the scent of his aftershave and his indefinable male odor. After all that had happened it was this smell that finally unlocked the emotion of the day. I leaned against the wardrobe and cried silent tears of bewilderment, pain and rage. But before my emotions could really take a hold, I quickly padded into the bathroom and splashed cold water onto my tear stained face.

One thing I knew for sure, I must hold on with great determination to all my positive qualities, in order to get me through this new trouble. Dabbing more cold water onto my puffy eyes and briskly drying my face, I brushed my hair and walked out onto the veranda to look at the garden. The magenta coloured bougainvillea seemed more abundant than usual and the oleanders were thick with pink blooms. The grass was yellow in patches, Alecos had intended to water it this evening but I told myself sternly not to think about it now as I watched the sun, swiftly dropping behind the mountains, turning them to a misty purple. How could such terrible things be happening in this beautiful island? It looked so peaceful and lovely. "Don't get maudlin, again. Think positive," I said aloud.

Suddenly, I thought of David in Paphos. Surely he would be able to suggest something constructive? Once again I resorted to the phone but after several attempts to get through, I gave up. Probably all the lines in Paphos were still down as Makarios had fled there from Nicosia before he was rescued and flown to the Akrotiri airforce base.

By seven o'clock I was chewing my nails. Disinclined as I was to phone Spiros because he was always so hostile towards me, surely, as Alecos stepbrother, he would be concerned and anxious to help him? So with some misgivings I phoned him.

He listened without interruption as I explained what had happened. Sounding strangely elated, he said he'd see what he could arrange.

Shortly afterwards, Ann called back with the news that none of the people she'd approached could help as they were loath to bring themselves to the notice of the new regime. I could quite understand their reluctance. It was the same decision we ourselves had come too before my foolish whim to go swimming had landed us in trouble.

15

Late evening

The quiet of the house made the evening seem endless. Switching on the television, I soon switched off after a burst of senseless voices from the screen. The silence pressed in on me again. It was only just after nine; I couldn't go to bed so early as I'd never fall asleep.

Doing my embroidery normally made the time fly by as I got involved in the intricate stitching, but tonight I couldn't concentrate. I threw it down in exasperation and the coloured silks, canvas and scissors scattered over the floor. I stared at them listlessly

Eventually, bending forward to pick them up, the blunt tipped embroidery needle jabbed under my fingernail. I gave a cry of pain and watched a drop of blood swell into a bead and trickle down my finger in a miniature scarlet river. As though in sympathy, my eyes welled in tears and overflowed, running in a silent stream down my cheeks. Then, tired and confused and utterly wretched, despite my earlier resolve, I sat on the floor and wallowed in sobs of self pity.

The sound of the phone brought me back to earth. Dashing away the tears and recovering my composure, I answered it.

"Mrs Lytras?"

I recognised the voice of the young corporal who had tried to intervene for Alecos on the beach. He sounded very guarded. "Your husband has been taken to the prison in Morphou."

"Why didn't they just release him?"

"They were about to but then a call came through from Nicosia and he was taken away."

"But what has Nicosia to do with it?" I asked in surprise.

"I don't know. But I can't speak more, someone is coming," he said, hurriedly hanging up.

Puzzling over this new twist to the day's events, I wondered why they would have taken him to Morphou? It was a small town, far away on the north-west coast!

Now, there was a mystery to add to my fears and frustration. I was no nearer reaching a sensible answer when eventually I dragged myself off to bed.

Waking with a start in the early hours, I could hear the murmur of the waves breaking at the base of the cliffs and the hum of the cicadas as the warm wind gently blew through the mimosa trees by the road. The almost full moon shed a silvery light into the room. I felt uneasy. Something had woken me. It sounded like a car moving on the road, but as there was a curfew, nothing could be about, so it couldn't have been!

Had I locked up before I went to bed? I couldn't remember. Perhaps that lecherous Greek officer had decided to come to the house. He'd undressed me with his eyes on the beach yesterday afternoon. Suppose now he'd come back to finish the job!

A shiver of fear ran through me. Groping for my wrap and crossing the room, I pulled back the curtain a fraction to peep out. The moon illuminated the garden but, apart from the oleanders along the drive moving gently in the wind, nothing stirred.

I thought maybe the noise was a loose shutter banging in the breeze downstairs, trying to reassure myself that my fear was groundless. I'd better go and fix it otherwise it would keep me awake for the rest of the night.

Still feeling wary, I crept cautiously down the stairs to the hall.

The house keys were still in the lock on the inside of the front door where I always left them. I gently pressed on the door to make sure it was closed and touched the keys to stop them jangling. Peering through the arched opening into the moonlit living room and through into the sun room, I could see the coloured silks still scattered on the floor but nothing else seemed to be out of place. The shutters at the French windows were open and secured and the ones in the kitchen were fixed too, so it hadn't been the shutters that had woken me. But something definitely had.

Suddenly, there was a loud crash outside the kitchen. I gasped and my skin crawled with fear. I realised it was the fuchsia pot I'd left to drain on the step. Something or someone had just knocked it over!

I spun round as the kitchen door opened. A heavy figure stood silhouetted against the moonlight. I screamed, and almost stopped breathing, as the figure stepped towards me.

My hand groped for the light switch. Snapping it on I gulped for air and grabbed the back of a kitchen chair to stop myself falling.

"Oh, Spiros," I gasped. "Thank goodness, it's only you! You gave me such a fright."

"Sorry, Sally, I break pot with flower."

"To hell with the pot," I laughed in hysterical relief. "You really scared me. I need a drink to steady my nerves."

Snatching the bottle of red wine I'd left on the table earlier, I filled a glass and took a deep gulp.

"Ahh! That's better. Would you like some too?" I asked, holding out the bottle.

"I like whisky," he replied, in a thick voice, helping himself from the bottle on the shelf. His hand shook as he held the glass.

I looked at him sharply. "Are you all right? You'd better sit down."

"I OK." he replied. "I try phone you but no answer so I come from Nicosia to tell about Alecos."

"What have you found out?" I asked eagerly as I sat down with him at the table.

His eyes narrowed and he hesitated before he answered. "I speak to friend in Police in Nicosia - he say Alecos in prison in Morphou."

About to say that I already knew that, a disturbing thought stopped me.

The young corporal said that Alecos had been taken away after a call had come from Nicosia. Could that order have come from Spiro's friend?

"Did your friend call the camp?"

"Yes, he do me a favour."

My throat became dry and a chill ran down my spine. Taking another sip of wine, a dark puddle spilled on the pine table as I shakily put down the glass.

While I stared at it mesmerised, Spiros, in one gulp, finished his whisky and picked up the bottle to pour himself more.

"How were you able to drive from Nicosia?" I

asked, as another horrifying thought struck me. "There is still a curfew!" I blurted out.

Gulping back his second whisky, he glanced up with the thin cold look he gave to people he didn't like. I'd seen that look many times, it would freeze water!

Then he laughed harshly, the sound like gravel running down a metal shoot.

"Ah, Sally," he breathed, triumphantly. "I waited long time for this day. Makarios, he cheats us. We fight British and when they go he change his mind and he not make union with Greece. So now he go and my good friend Nicos Samson, he President now and he give me good job in new government." He preened, raising his shoulders proudly. His lips curled as he sneered: "Alecos, he think he more clever than me. I only good to work machines! He never make me partner in company. But now I make sure he stay in prison for long time," he gloated.

His flinty eyes mirrored the grudges of a lifetime. I was shocked at the malice and loathing that he'd harboured for so long. Danger warnings started ringing loudly in my ears as I realised he'd already been drinking heavily before he arrived.

Sniggering drunkenly he grinned, baring his nicotine stained teeth.

"So now I take Alecos business, but first I take Alecos wife!"

With that he reached across the table, his stubby fingers curling round my arm.

Pushing his hand roughly from me, I sprang up and edged away.

His chair crashed back as he stood up unsteadily. He stared at me, his eyes glittering with menace. As he lunged toward me, I screamed and jumped back but his hand caught the edge of my wrap pulling it apart to reveal my naked breast.

His hand dropped as his breath came out in a loud orgasmic gasp, his tongue flicked wetly across his thick lips as his pupils dilated.

Whirling round I managed to side step and run into the living room. He snarled, his aggressive instincts fully aroused. Despite his drunkenness he was fast and grabbing my arm, spun me round, his big callused hand flying towards my breast. I tried to pry his fingers off my arm but he threw his other arm round me and spread his legs hauling me hard up against him, his gloating face and foul smelling breath, only inches from mine.

I wedged an arm between us trying to push him away. "Let me go," I cried, my rising panic seeming to add to his ardour. He laughed triumphantly. As the struggle intensified, so did my fear. I tried to knee him but, the bulk of the sofa behind me, blocked my movements.

He grabbed my hair and yanked my head back. The pain was excruciating. His wet mouth contacted mine as he thrust his tongue against my locked lips. His breath, reeking of whisky, garlic and nicotine nearly made me retch. I turned my head away from his foul smell but his hips pinned me to the sofa and I could feel the ever increasing hardness of his bulging groin pushing into me.

I kept pushing at his chest, pushing, pushing, till he let go of my hair and caught at the pushing arm. With his other hand he fumbled to open the zip of his trousers.

Instantly, as the pressure of his body momentarily slackened, I lowered my head and sank my teeth deep into the flesh at the base of the thumb of the hand holding my arm, my mouth filling with the acrid taste of metal and engine oil. Letting out an agonised yell, he released the grip on my arm. I punched my fist hard into his nose hearing the muscle splat. The force of the blow made my knuckles scream, but his pain was more. He bellowed in agony, raising both his hands to cover his broken nose.

In that split second I rushed for the door of the sunroom. But as I fumbled frantically to undo the lock, the key fell to the floor. In the reflection of the window, I saw his stocky body charging across the room behind me like a huge angry bull, blood streaming from his smashed nose.

I jumped quickly to the right and his outstretched hands hit hard against the doorframe. My hasty movement brought a pot of ferns toppling off the windowsill. As I tried to rush away a shard of terracotta pot pierced through the thin sole of my slipper, the sharp pain made me stumble and fall sideways to my knees.

With a howl of triumph, Spiros heavy body crashed down, pinning me to the ground. His hands tugged roughly at my wrap, smearing it with blood. I kicked and struggled, my body writhing and twisting in a frenzy to escape. My fingers tore at his hair but it made no impression as he dragged the wrap open to get to my naked body. I felt the burning flesh of his erection on my thigh as I fought in frantic terror.

I had to get away before he raped me. But he was too strong and heavy and I could feel myself weakening. Suddenly my flaying hands tangle in the embroidery silks. In the middle of the pile I felt the thin cold steel of the scissors. I snatched them up and with all the strength I had left, plunged them into Spiros back. Roaring in pain, his body stiffened and in that instant I dragged myself out from under him.

This time I raced for the front door. The key turned easily in the lock and I threw it wide open as I raced across the moonlight lawn. Crashing my way into the shrubbery, impervious to the sharp branches tearing at my bare legs and arms, I kept to the shadowy darkness of the trees, trying to stifle the sound of my heaving gasps. I crouched in the undergrowth like a wounded animal, gasping for breath and shivering violently from terror and shock.

At some time during the night, a car started up in the distance. My numbed brain registered that it had to be Spiros, no one else would be about during the curfew.

But I was too terrified to leave the darkness of the trees until the first welcome light of dawn broke over the headland to the east. Still shaken , frightened and now cold as well, I crept back to the house, keeping to the cover of the trees. The front door was wide open. The keys, hidden against the wall behind, still hanging in the lock. I thanked my lucky star that Spiros hadn't seen them. I would have been too scared to stay alone in the house if the keys had been missing. I couldn't go through that horrifying experience again. Even to think about it made my flesh creep.

I grabbed an old shirt of Alecos to cover my scratched naked body, then rushing round the house, I locked and bolted every outside door and closed all the shutters. The house became a dark fortress but at least it felt secure. Switching on the lights, I took stock of the surroundings. There was blood everywhere; on the back of the sofa where Spiros had griped it with his bloody hands; more on the floor where the blood had spurted from his nose. The white paint of the sunroom door was marked with bloody hand prints and on the rug too where the embroidery silks still lay in a tangled heap. Nearby, lay the blood encrusted scissors.

Being squeamish, this blood bath was all too much for me. Feeling the bile rising in my throat, shuddering and gagging, I dashed into the kitchen and threw up in the sink.

After recovering, I took stock of the mess. All the chairs had been overturned.

Shards of glass from the bottles and glasses that Spiros, in his drunken fury, had swept off the table, glittered on the floor. Sweeping up carefully, I then filled a bowl with cold water and still gagging, I frantically sponged at the blood stains tying to remove the memory of that terrible ordeal. Finally, picking up my torn soiled wrap, I stuffed it into a plastic bag and threw it in the dustbin, never wanting to see it again.

When everything was cleaned up, I ran a bath, pouring a generous measure of Badedas into the running water. The bubbles quickly rose up into a pure white cloud. I eased myself into the scalding bubbly water. My whole body felt dirty and befouled. Scrubbing till my skin felt sore I tried to rub away the filthy feeling of Spiros bloody, grease ingrained hands on my skin, and the foul smell of his breath from my hair. Sometimes tears spilled over but I dashed them away angrily unwilling to be humiliated by anyone as low and despicable as Spiros.

The perfumed water soothed my tortured mind and aching body. I lay there till the water was almost cold. Then, in a last desperate attempt to remove the feeling of violation and disgust, I rubbed my entire body vigorously with a rough bath towel, liberally applying antiseptic cream to the scratches and bruises on my arms and legs.

Now, to put everything else out of my mind, I concentrated all my energy into working out how I was going to get Alecos released from prison. At that moment, I really had no idea how it could be done. Obviously, Spiros would do anything to ruin Alecos and he'd want his revenge on me too for wounding him. I shuddered, realising that the situation had now got even worse and more dangerous than before.

Somehow the day passed. I couldn't bring myself to tell Ann about Spiros's attack when she phoned to see if I'd had any news of Alecos. The nightmare was too horrible to relive. When eventually I went to bed, leaving on every light in the house, I hardly slept. My ears strained for any sound of traffic on the road and my heart jumped with every creak and groan of the house as it settled.

16

Thursday 18th July

Next morning, the eight o'clock news reported that the curfew would be lifted from two till six o'clock. in the afternoon.

"Four hours! Just enough time to get to Morphou and see Alecos. Somehow or other I'll get him out!" I told the radio announcer firmly.

Minutes before the curfew lifted I was in the car and on my way at full speed west to the market town of Morphou. Road blocks had by now been set up at all main junctions. My hand bag, stuffed with money to bribe my way through fortunately wasn't needed. Calling out cheerfully in English to the soldiers at the barriers, they let me pass without trouble.

At the police station, I told the constable at the desk that I'd come to see my husband. He was surprised to see a British passport and went into the back office. I heard him talking urgently to someone inside.

"There's nothing I can do. Tell her to leave," an angry voice replied. Then another murmur from the constable.

After a moment, a bald aggressive little man stalked out of the office, obviously ready to do battle.

But I'd anticipated trouble. Most Cypriot men were very macho so, in order to appear as vulnerable and helpless as possible, I'd chosen a blouse with a froth of soft pink frills cascading down the front and a long sleeved matching summer jacket to cover the scratches on my arms. I reckoned this outfit would appeal to the protective instincts of most men! In this case, it worked. His angry eyes softened on seeing me and his aggressive expression melted like butter.

"I hope you can help me, sir," I said, in a meek little voice.

"Come into my office and tell me what I can do for you," he gushed, ushering me inside in an almost fatherly fashion. From the corner of my eye I noticed the constable smirking at the change in the inspector's manner.

"Now what's this all about?" he asked, after offering me coffee.

Opening my eyes wide, I simpered as innocently as possible: "I'd like you to release my husband."

He chuckled indulgently, as though I was a child asking for sweets. "Now why should I do that, my dear?"

"Because I think there's been a mistake, sir."

"Really? You'd better tell me about it."

"Well, sir," I replied breathlessly. "It was so hot last Tuesday, we thought we'd just go quickly down to the tiny beach by our house. Our car got stuck in the sand and a neighbour and her eleven year old grandsons helped us push it out. A Greek officer from the camp came along and arrested my husband.

Lowering my eyes meekly I said: "I know we were breaking the curfew but we weren't causing any trouble!"

"I see," he said, seeming surprised. "I was told your

husband was trying to organise a demonstration."

"Oh no, sir, nothing like that. It was only my husband, me, the farmer's wife and her two grand-children. We were just trying to push the car out of the sand. There was nothing political going on," I repeated again. "The Greek officer was very rude and arrogant to us when we tried to explain. He said all Cypriots were stupid peasants."

I saw the inspectors eyes narrow at the insulting words of the Greek officer.

"Uhm, I know the type," he said angrily, nodding his head.

"Surely that's not a reason for my husband to be locked up?" I pleaded, looking up at him, my eyes misting with unshed tears. I had the feeling he wanted to reach out and pat me reassuringly on the head.

"Don't worry, my dear. From what you tell me there has obviously been a mistake. We'll sort it out."

I gulped, tearfully. "Oh, thank you, sir. Our good friend, Phillip Christofides, said you were a kind man and would help me. He and his wife live in Nicosia but he comes from Morphou originally. Perhaps you know him?"

We hadn't seen Phillip in months but I didn't think a little lie would hurt and it turned out to be in my favour.

"Ah, Phillip," he beamed delightedly. "Yes, he's a relative of mine. My sister is married to Phillip's uncle. They live in that big house you pass as you enter Morphou. You must have noticed it as you drove through?" he said, lifting his shoulders proudly. "Costa and I were at school together. He followed me everywhere but now he's a very rich man with his acres of orange groves. And, I'm just a poorly paid employee of the government," he shrugged resignedly.

I detected a touch of envy in his tone. Maybe his comment was just an innocent statement or perhaps he was suggesting that he could be 'persuaded' to help me.

I wasn't sure, but anything was worth a try.

Pretending to fiddle nervously with the clasp of my handbag resting on my lap, it suddenly opened revealing the bundle of bank notes. His eyebrows rose slightly as he saw them and his tongue flicked to the corner of his mouth. As we continued to speak about Phillip his eyes darted several times to the open bag on my lap.

As he finished telling me the family history, I lifted the bag for a fraction of a second before closing it. "If you can help us I know my husband would be very grateful."

He cleared his throat, his eyes resting on the hand-bag. "Yes my dear, I could certainly arrange his release. Unfortunately, we will have to keep him here while the paperwork is sorted out but don't worry, he'll be quite comfortable and we'll feed him well!" He chuckled again, patting his own protruding belly "Come back on Saturday morning and you can take him home."

"Oh thank you, sir," I gushed. "I knew as soon as I saw you, you'd understand. You look like a kind man. Everything's so upside down at the moment. Nobody knows what's happening, so that's probably how the confusion occurred."

He nodded understandingly. My impression was that he too was unhappy with the new political events.

"I'm very grateful to you and my husband will be too," I said again to enforce the point.

Grasping my handbag prominently in front of me I stood up. He nodded his head imperceptibly as he eyed the bag. Then, leaning across the desk, I planted a grateful kiss on his forehead. He looked startled, and then beamed with embarrassed pleasure.

"Could I ask just one more small favour, sir?" I asked, sweetly.

"Of course, little lady. What is it?"

"Would it be possible to see my husband just for a moment."

"Of course. No problem, my constable will take you to him."

Alecos threw his arms round me and beamed in delight. "Sally mou! How did you get here?"

"The curfew was lifted for four hours so I dashed over to see if I could get you out."

"What's going on?" he exclaimed, looking me over in amazement. "I've never seen you dressed up like a baby doll before!"

"Shh, never mind that, it served its purpose," I replied laughing self-consciously. "But, what about you? Are you alright?"

"Yes I'm OK and it's comfortable enough in the circumstances but I don't understand why they brought me here."

"I found out Spiros is behind it. He's mixed up with Sampson's lot. He wants to keep you locked up so he can take the business. He really hates you, you know." said Alecos, eyes opened wide in disbelief. "But how..," he continued.

I interrupted quickly, giving him no time to question me too closely. "I managed to charm the inspector. Fortunately, he's partial to the baby-doll look even if you're not," I said, flicking playfully at the frills of the blouse. Anyway, I indicated discreetly that you'd show your appreciation when he releases you." I opened the bag and he nodded in understanding.

'But, Sally mou, how did you find out about Spiros and how did you get that bruise on your neck?" he asked, pushing aside the pink frills.

"Don't worry; I'll explain everything when I pick you up. The inspector says he will have to do some paperwork before he can release you but it will be ready by Saturday so I can come for you then. I've brought you a change of clothes and a pair of shoes in case you needed them. Now I must hurry or I won't get home before that damn curfew starts again. If I'm out on the road, I'll be the next one to be arrested and we're in enough trouble without that too!"

The next morning it was announced that the curfew would no longer be in force during the day I made a quick dash into Kyrenia early in the morning to the market to collect some necessary provisions. But after that, I stayed close to the house. I was terrified that Spiros might turn up while I was out and surprise me.

During the afternoon, hearing a car turn into the drive as I was watering the pots outside the kitchen, I had a nasty moment. Dashing into the house and banging the door behind me, I soon realised my mistake.

By a strange coincidence our friends Phillip Christofides, and Joanna his English wife, arrived with their new baby. They had a village house in the old town of Kyrenia and had decided to pop in as they were passing when they saw the car outside. Having lied to the inspector in Morphou that Phillip had given me a personal recommendation, I felt his arrival at my door at that moment in time was a good omen and my spirits lifted.

I told them what had happened and Phillip promised to phone his uncle to make sure that everything would be done to get Alecos released the next day.

We all settled down to the inevitable cup of tea and Joanna placed the baby in my arms whilst she drank hers. His huge dark eyes stared up at me and his little mouth seemed to smile. I felt a stab of longing as I rocked him before gently placing him in his carry cot where he gurgled contentedly and kicked his fat little legs.

The conversation naturally turned to the upheaval taking place on the island and the possible consequences.

The BBC that morning had announced that the Turkish fleet were mobilising on the Anatolian coast, just thirty miles north of where we were sitting. Phillip laughed at the idea of an invasion. "No," he said firmly. "It won't happen. Don't you remember when the Turkish president threatened to invade Cyprus some years ago? President Johnson told him that if he sent his forces to the island, the US wouldn't guarantee Turkey's protection against any Soviet response. The Turks had to climb down in humiliation. And again in 1967 they made threatening noises but nothing happened."

"But that happened years ago," I said. "Nixon and Kissinger are running the show now and they detest Makarios."

"Yes. But they have achieved their aim of getting rid of Makarios now. The US is behind the Greek colonels anyway and Kissinger has given his blessing to Sampson, so there's no need for more interference.

Their envoy Mr Sisco is running between Athens and Ankara trying to stop any aggression between those two Nato countries. They've almost forgotten about what's happening in Cyprus."

"Perhaps you're right," I replied. "And now Makarios is out of the way, Nixon can concentrate on trying to wriggle out of the Watergate scandal!"

Changing the subject I indicated the wooden planks on the roof of Phillips car in the drive.

"Oh yes," he replied. "We decided to come to Kyrenia and do some work in the house. Nicosia feels uncomfortable now and we'll be out of the way here."

Joanna nodded. "We'll feel safer here in Kyrenia. There is such an atmosphere of violence and brutality in the city now with Sampson and his armed bully boys throwing their weight around. Ordinary people feel intimidated and frightened to move about," she said, peeping into the carry cot to tuck the baby more comfortably into his bed.

"Yes, I can imagine," I said, nodding in agreement. I thought of Spiros on the rampage, taking out his grudges on all the people he felt had slighted him in the past. I shuddered at the thought.

Later that evening I had a call from my parents who had been frantically trying to get through since the coup took place. It appeared that the Turkish government was asking Britain to intervene. The Greek backed coup in Nicosia, as far as the Turks were concerned, was the final move towards enosis which they could not tolerate. They would have to retaliate.

My parents were worried enough, especially as they too had heard that the Turkish forces were mobilising for an invasion. I told them that we were safe, though of course I didn't mention that Alec had been arrested.

"Don't worry," I assured them as confidently as Phillip had assured me earlier. "Nothing will happen."

But not far away over the dark sea, the Turkish forces were ready to go.

17

Invasion, Saturday 20th July

By Friday evening I felt much happier. Tomorrow I would go to Morphou and bring Alecos home. Going to bed early I had no trouble falling asleep but was woken with a start, at dawn, by a strange noise outside on the road.

Imagining that Spiros had returned again, my heart hammered. The house was well battened down so he'd find it almost impossible to get in, unless he had an axe or a battering ram! Nevertheless, I lay rigid trying to identify the sound.

My hearing picked up on the low purr of motor engines moving slowly nearer, but in addition to the engine sound was an unrecognisable rhythmic creaking.

Mystified, I crept out of bed. Squinting through the shutters, I made out a slowly moving procession of covered lorries. Through the open back flaps I could see they were full of National Guard soldiers, faces blackened and fully kitted out with helmets, back packs and rifles. Then came several jeeps painted in khaki and olive, towing behind them creaking gun carriages, covered in camouflage netting.

The convoy turned off the road onto a dirt track, opposite the house, leading into a densely planted orange grove.

It was just before six and already quite light as I crept upstairs to the roof terrace to get a better look. I watched until the last of the convoy disappeared into the trees, then turning to go back down I let out a startled cry. Moored just off the coast were the menacing shapes of three enormous grey battleships, each flying the red and white crescent moon flag of Turkey. Clinging to the huge bodied ships, like puppies at their mothers teats, were several flat rafts. As they broke away from the mother ship, I saw they were landing craft crammed with soldiers, coming fast to the shore.

Despite the radio announcements the previous day about the mobilization of the Turkish Army on the Anatolian coast, nobody had really believed they would come. But here they were, just a short distance from where I was standing.

It was such an astonishing sight, I had to blink hard to make sure I was really seeing it.

As the realization sunk in, I flew into the bedroom throwing on the nearest clothes that came to hand. Rushing downstairs, I grabbed the phone in the hallway and dialled Ann's number. A sleepy voice answered.

"Ann, wake up! There are battleships just off shore. Turkey is invading Cyprus." My voice rose. "Get dressed quickly."

"I can't believe it, I thought they stopped it after all that diplomatic shuffling between Greece and Turkey," she gasped, now fully awake.

"What is happening in Nicosia?" I asked urgently

"I don't know I've just woken up, but hang on, I can hear a lot of aircraft noise and shooting coming from the airport."

"Don't hang around," I shouted urgently. "Pack some things into a bag and don't forget your passport. Get over to my place, you've still got a key. You're too close to the airport. It's the first place the Turks will try to knock out. I'm going to make a dash for it before all hell breaks loose here. Hopefully I'll be there in about half an hour. See you soon!" I said, slamming down the phone.

Grabbing a basket as I dashed into the kitchen, I threw in the bits and pieces from the fridge and cupboard and flew out of the house, but stopped short, hearing the sound of a fighter aircraft coming very fast and low. The Turkish crescent was clearly visible on the fuselage. I pulled back into the safety of the hallway banging the front door behind me. As the jet swooped low over the area, anti-aircraft guns opened fire from the orange grove.

There was not a moment to lose. I had to get away before the plane returned to destroy the guns hidden in the orchard. If I stayed here I would be a sitting duck, directly in the line of fire from either side.

Adrenaline pumped as I banged the door shut and dashed to the car. I shot off with a screaming spurt of gravel, down the deserted road like a formula one driver, first off the grid at Le Man. I drove with my foot hard down on the accelerator to cover the few miles east to get to the recently completed mountain pass to Nicosia avoiding the Turkish enclave.

In my rear view mirror, I could see the fighter plane, just a dot in the distance, banking round to come in again over the orange grove. It was trying to wipe out any resistance and protect the troops landing from the warships.

At tremendous speed it bore down behind me, I

could almost see the pilot's eyes as he opened fire just before the orange grove. Wrenching the car off the road to shelter in the protection of a thick canopy of trees, the plane whooshed deafeningly overhead. Shards of tarmac showered the car, as stray bullets strafed the road. Instantly I was off again making for the opening between the mountains where the pass began. The fighter plane banked steeply left out to sea to come in for its next sortie.

I was only moments from the turn but this time there were no trees to protect me, just a wide new road with no cover. I had to make it into the pass before the plane got there. With my heart hammering so loud I could feel it thumping in my ears. I was sure I was staring death in the face. The plane hurtled along behind me again at an unbelievable rate of knots discharging it's ammunition into the orange grove. Racing at breakneck speed into the right hand bend of the pass, there was an ear piercing crack as a bullet hit my back bumper. The car rocked violently skidding across the road almost crashing into the rocky cliff face on the other side. My breath came in heaving gasps and my eyes stung as the sweat poured off my forehead. Once within the safety of the steep sides of the pass, I slowed down to catch my breath, the bumper clattering loudly behind me as it hung precariously only inches from the road surface. In seconds, with my heart pounding, this time in relief at my narrow escape, my foot was on the accelerator again and I was off, desperate to get to the safety of home.

As the steep sides of the pass levelled out onto the plain, I gasped in wonder at the sight that met my eyes.

To the right of me, over the sixteen miles of

Turkish enclave between Nicosia and the Kyrenia mountains, the sky began to fill with the mushroom shape of parachutes opening up as they streamed out like ribbons from low flying fat bodied transport planes. The scene before me had all the grace and beauty of a ballet. Despite the danger, I slowed right down to watch this once in a lifetime spectacle.

Wave after wave of parachutes filled the sky. The early morning sun, shimmering on their silk canopies, turned them into huge pearls as they billowed and swayed gently dropping to earth carrying their lethal load of armed troops who, from this distance, looked as harmless as toy soldiers.

I watched in fascination, but as the first of the paratroopers hit the ground, rapidly gathering in the billowing parachutes behind them, my awe and fascination evaporated as I became abruptly aware that this was not a beautiful theatrical scene but an ugly real life war.

Behind the first wave of troops six huge Hercules cargo planes lumbered into view, their engines droning like angry wasps. But by then I was clattering off down the deserted road again.

Suddenly a huge shadow appeared on the road in front. Looking up, I saw an enormous crate suspended from a parachute. It was dropping completely off course and would land on the Greek side of the enclave. But more to the point, it looked as if it was going to drop directly onto the road in front of me.

Oh no! This can't be happening to me, my brain screamed. If I go on, the crate could land on top of me and crush me into the ground. But if I stop, it will crash down and block the whole road and I will be trapped on this side with Turkish soldiers all around me.

What should I do? My foot hesitated over the brake peddle. No, I daren't stop, I'll have to keep going and pray that my luck holds. I've escaped being shot dead by a jet fighter, so there's no way I am going to let myself be squashed to death by a crate!

So, again, with my foot pushing down even harder on the accelerator, I kept going.

I was mesmerised by the parachute and its lethal load swinging ever nearer.

Pulling as far over as I dared, the tyres juddered on the uneven, gravel strewn surface alongside a storm ditch at the left sides of the road. Either I was on a collision course with the crate, or, if, by luck, it passed over me, there was every possibility that I could be smothered by an octopus of silk and webbing from the parachute. Neither situation was worth thinking about.

The huge parachute was almost above me. The crate, hanging nearly in front of my eyes, was going to land. I was only feet away from its point of impact. It was going to hit me.

Gripping the steering wheel, my knuckles were white. I pushed myself back against the seat to brace my body for the collision. My eyes screwed tightly shut in terrified anticipation of the bone breaking crash. This was finally it!

It didn't happen.

Instead, the car was jolted to the left, the near side wheels spinning into the ditch. With a shattering noise, the bullet- riddled bumper was wrenched off, clipped by the corner of the crate as it smashed on the ground, spilling its load of heavy boxes on the road.

I fought with the steering to get the car back onto the tarmac just as the parachute slowly settled, like a gigantic deflated balloon over the jumble of boxes, completely blocking the road behind me.

I'd made it.

Tears running down my cheeks, the whole of my body trembling violently with shock and my stomach churning in spasms, I sat in a daze, stunned and disorientated. Eventually all these sensations turned into a great feeling of relief at my miraculous escape. This time tears of happiness poured down my cheeks in a cascade as I instinctively drove the battered Mercedes slowly, towards Nicosia, completely unaware of anything around me. I woke from my semi- trance when I eventually arrived at the flat.

18

Back in Nicosia

Driving through the eastern suburbs of Nicosia before six thirty in the morning, I had only vaguely been aware of the people standing in their doorways mystified by the distant sounds of explosions and gun fire. But as I arrived home the Cyprus Broadcasting network on the car radio brought me back to reality with a jolt.

It was a call for all Greek Cypriots men to take up arms to resist the invaders.

This broadcast would be the first indication to the population of Cyprus that the island had been invaded.

Ann was already there waiting anxiously, but before telling her about my horrendous journey, I said urgently: "We'd better start taping up the windows. They always do that in war films to stop flying glass imploding into the buildings. Any minute now the shooting and bombing will start in earnest."

"Okay, let's get cracking," Ann replied. "Where's the tape?"

"I've only got parcel tape. I'm sure it's not what they really use but it will have to do."

We busied ourselves taping large Union Jack type crosses to the French windows, stopping constantly to gape at the ballet of hundreds of paratroopers landing in the Turkish area.

"It's so beautiful to watch," Ann said. "It doesn't seem possible they're the enemy and they're here to kill us."

As if to prove the point, the quiet of the moment was shattered by the boom of tank fire and the sharp rattle of machine guns coming from the Venetian walls of Nicosia that divided the Greek from the Turkish area.

The fire was returned by Greek Cypriot fighters who appeared to be gathered in the football stadium a short distance from us. Bullets began ricocheting off the walls of our building as we both made a frantic dive for the safety of the apartments' central hallway, shutting all the doors leading off it.

We huddled there for some time cowering from the uproar of the battle erupting around us.

Suddenly I gave a yelp of dismay. Ann looked at me in alarm.

"I've completely forgotten about Alecos," I wailed. "I was supposed to get him out of jail today. but so much has happened to me this morning, I haven't even thought about him till this moment and now I can't get to him. He'll be frantic with worry wondering if I've been captured."

"Yes, you're right. He'll know by now that the Turks have landed but he won't know that you've already left Kyrenia. I wonder if the phone is still working. You could try to phone the prison," she said. "Give it a go."

I opened the door into the entrance hall and slithered across the floor to get to the phone.

I hadn't a clue what the phone number of the prison in Morphou was but I could look it up once I knew if I could get through. I lifted the receiver but there was silence. I tapped out Ann's home number, just to make sure, but the line was dead.

"It's no good," I called to Ann. "We're cut off. What do I do now?' I asked desperately, slithering back into our hideaway."

"Calm down and let us think. Alecos will be safe in Morphou for the moment," Ann said, thoughtfully. "He'll know by now that the Turkish landings were to the West of Kyrenia so, there would be no way you could get to Morphou from Kyrenia."

"Yes that's true," I nodded. "He'll know that I wouldn't hang around when the fighting started and the only logical place I would go to would be Nicosia, through the new pass on the east side of Kyrenia, so he'll have a pretty good idea that I'll be safe. He'll probably think I'm at your place."

And then I paused. "But," I wailed. "I still can't get to him from here because the airport road is being bombarded."

I slumped against the wall banging my head against it in frustration.

"Uhm! The situation is pretty awful but at least you can both assume that the other is safe for the time being, thank goodness," Ann replied, pragmatically.

Then, to take our minds off our personal situation, she said: "We should get the portable radio? At least we'd have some idea of what's going on out there. And it would be something else to listen too instead of the racket outside."

So we settled down to hear what was going on. The reporter said that Cyprus navy boats had set out from Kyrenia to engage the approaching Turkish flotilla but had been sunk by a combined navel and Turkish air attack and Greek Cypriot forces had failed to halt the Turkish landing force as their tanks and armoured vehicles had been destroyed.

"That's awful," I wept. "What chance have our tiny army got?"

The report continued...

The United Nation Security council is demanding immediate withdrawal of all foreign military personnel. They made it clear that they disapproved of the Greek coup that had precipitated the crisis, as well as the Turks for taking military action.

"What good is slapping them on the wrist going to do? It's too late to stop them now," I said scornfully.

Right on cue, the booming explosion of a mortar shook the building. "My god," Ann said in a shaky voice. "That was too close for comfort. It must have landed in the eucalyptus trees behind the building. We're pretty vulnerable in this building you know."

"Yes, I realise that now," I said. "I thought your building would be too dangerous to stay in, but I think there wasn't much to choose between them. I'll close the rolling shutters. Then we can open these doors and get some air. It must be almost 40 degrees in this enclosed space. It's stifling!" I said, flapping my hands around my face to move the air.

"While you're doing that, I'll get some wet towels to wrap ourselves in. That should keep us a bit cooler too," Ann suggested.

Keeping my head down, I crawled over to the French windows in the living room. There was nothing moving on the streets but I could see a thick haze of gun smoke over the football stadium nearby, where the deafening shooting was coming from.

Hoping to get a slight breeze into the room, I didn't close the light vents in the shutters but slid open the full length glass doors. The longed for fresh air, turned out to be thick with the metallic smell of cordite which caught at the back of my throat and made me gag.

Going into the bedroom to close up there too, old Mrs Panayiotis was sitting at her usual position at the window. I doubted if she even knew that anything unusual was happening as she wasn't able to see the stadium from the position of her window and she was probably too deaf to hear much noise.

Ann had already dampened down some towels, which we thankfully draped around our necks. It helped a bit, but we were sweating again before long, so I filled a bucket with water then we could wet the towels whenever we needed too. I'd grabbed a few books while I was in the living room and now tried to read but my thoughts kept turning to Alecos, worring about what might be happening to him.

So the hours passed. Sitting on the tiled floor with our backs against the wall, we managed to keep as cool as our uncomfortable and dangerous circumstances allowed.

By mid morning with no let up in the fighting and nothing to do, we were restless and bored. We felt alone and abandoned as the battle continued around us.

"Shall I get us something to eat?" I asked.

"Good idea, I'm starving. I rushed out of the house this morning without eating anything," Ann said, as her stomach gave a loud gurgle.

"Oh no," I cried. "I can't believe what I've done."

"What now?" Ann raised her eyebrows impatiently.

"I left all the food behind in Kyrenia. I must have put the basket down when I rushed back into the house as the plane flew over. Goodness knows what I've got here. I took most of it with me to Kyrenia when the coup started."

Forgetting the danger, I rushed into the kitchen. A bullet shot through the window, it lodged in the lintel above the door, splattering me with fragments of plaster. I dropped to the floor like a stone, staring aghast at a perfectly round hole between the strips of tape stuck to the now crackled glazing of the window.

"Are you all right?" Ann called, hurrying through the door.

"Stay down," I shouted. "It's dangerous in here. This room doesn't have shutters."

I crawled across the floor to the fridge hoping I'd left something there. Apart from a jar of pickle, a half empty bottle of tomato sauce, some walnuts in syrup plus a rather shrivelled lemon the fridge was empty. The good thing was, there were a couple of bottles of water and also some bottles of white wine.

I had better luck with the cupboard though. There, I found a packet of tea, a packet of crackers and a couple of tins of butter beans.

"If I was Jesus Christ, I could almost feed the five thousand, with what I've got here," I joked. "But as I'm not, we'll have to go easy. So for now, we'll have water and dry biscuits. I'll make a pot of tea soon with tap water. We can have that cold later with a squeeze of lemon juice, it will save on the bottled water. Who knows how long we'll have to stay here! We might not have much food but if the worst comes to the worst, we can drink ourselves to death. I know there are several bottles of whisky, gin and vodka in the cabinet and there's plenty of red wine in the rack.

At one o'clock we managed through the noise outside and the static of the radios, to switch to the

BBC World Service for the news. From the cultured tones of the BBC announcer we learned more specifically about the fighting and destruction that was taking place all around us on our beautiful island.

At dawn this morning Turkish forces invaded Cyprus. 6000 troops and 40 tanks made air and sea landings on the island a few miles west of the northern port of Kyrenia and dropped forces and arms into the Turkish Cypriot enclave of Nicosia.

Nicosia International airport was attacked with bombs and rockets by high performance jet aircraft. There was fierce fighting in the Famagusta area between Greek and Turkish Cypriots and British families in the Dekalia military base have been told to prepare for evacuation.

British tourist are advised to make their way to the RAF base at Akrotiri in the south of the island where British warships are standing by to evacuate them.

Due to repeated harassment by Turkish jet fighters over the island, RAF planes based at Akrotiri are unable to mount an air evacuation at the moment.

We were heart-broken, but the newsreader sounded unemotional - it was unreal.

His refined voice continued:

The invasion of Cyprus has sent shock waves around the world.

In Brussels the headquarters of the NATO High Command was put on alert in the event of all out war between Greece and Turkey, both members of NATO.

The Soviet Union and her Allies, declared a state of alert while aircraft carriers of the US 6th Fleet based in the eastern Mediterranean moved toward

Cyprus in readiness to evacuate US citizens. The UN Security Council are meeting in emergency session in New York in order to arrange a ceasefire.

"Ugh!" I spluttered indignantly. "A fat chance they'll have. The Turks aren't going to land all that firepower only to agree to a ceasefire before they've even taken Kyrenia and got themselves an outlet to the sea. I wouldn't be surprised if their real intention is to capture a big chunk of the island. All the talking to and fro in the UN isn't going to stop them now that they've finally got their foot in the door."

"I wonder how long we can hold out," Ann pondered. "Cyprus has nothing, only a few thousand soldiers and no air force. It's up against the huge Turkish invading army with the latest modern equipment and jet fighters supplied by NATO. By the time the Greeks get here it will be all over," she snapped. "Our soldiers don't even have any weapons. The arsenal just outside Nicosia burned down during the fighting in the coup. I could see the fire burning for days from my place."

"Well, let's hope the mediators can get them to agree on a cease fire," I said.

Ann shook her head. 'From the news reports this last week, they've been going backwards and forwards between Ankara and Athens like yoyo's specifically to stop a war between Greece and Turkey. so the invasion of Cyprus seems to have become almost irrelevant.

The broadcaster's unemotional voice continued...

And now for the rest of the news. Cricket. The Benson and Hedges Cup one-day match between Surrey and Leicestershire started this morning at

Lords. Surrey was first to bat with Edrich and Skinner the opening batsmen. Skinner who was bowled LBW for nought was followed by Howath. The score now is 12 for one wicket.

I groaned in frustration: "Here we are, trapped in the thick of battle with rockets and guns going off outside while the British public are more concerned with the cricket results! It makes me feel so helpless I could cry. They don't seem to realise that, if two NATO powers go to war, it would cause an international catastrophe. Do they think that Cyprus is some obscure place in Africa or the Far East? It's all happening right on their doorstep in Europe, to one of the world's most beautiful and historic islands."

"You're right," Ann agreed. "Next time I hear of the suffering of ordinary people involved in a war situation I'll have more compassion, now that I'm going through it too. Though it won't make them feel any better!" she added wryly."

For the rest of the day we sat almost in silence. Our only contact with the outside world was through the radio, telling us about the battle for Nicosia airport and Kyrenia town, both of which it appeared were still in Cypriot hands.

"I wonder how long our limited forces can hold out?" I brooded.

"I don't think they can last too long, unless they get reinforcements from Greece," Ann replied. "The only hope is if the mediators, Joseph Sisco from Washington and Mr Callaghan can get them to agree on a ceasefire sooner rather than later. But, there's absolutely nothing we can do about it," she added, in her conciliatory manner. "So let's get the mattresses off the spare beds and we can at least be a bit more comfortable. My bottom is getting quite numb from sitting on this marble floor."

"That's a good idea. Why didn't we think of that before? Then I'll get us something to eat. I think perhaps tonight I'll serve butter beans in a piquant tomato and pickle sauce on Jacob's crackers, accompanied by a full bodied red wine. Followed by Walnuts marinated in heavy syrup with a palatable dessert white wine! How does that sound?"

"Not bad in the circumstances, Jeeves," Ann laughed.

"How about an aperitif now to start? Perhaps madam would like a whisky and water or vodka and shrivelled lemon?"

"I think I'd like a double whisky. You can go easy on the water, we might need it tomorrow!" she said. "But seriously though, Sally, we're pretty close to the fighting. We're safe for the moment but let's hope no stray mortar lodges itself in the building during the night."

"Don't even think about it," I insisted. "If it happens, it happens. I'm so used to the noise now, I almost don't notice those rockets going off anymore. Never the less, I'm going to have a good few drinks tonight to knock me out so I won't know what's happening out there."

19

Sunday

Probably due to our meagre supper and our very generous alcohol intake, we both slept reasonably well. We woke at first light worrying what the new day would bring.

By now we were hot, sticky and hungry, having been shut up in the small airless hallway all night. After taking a quick shower, I made a pot of tea and we gobbled the last of the dry biscuits smeared with the remains of the jam. I was concerned that our food supply was very low but I put that thought out of my mind. We would have to cross that bridge when we came to it.

As we settled back into our safe, hot little hallway, we tuned in once again to the BBC World Service News. During the night there had been frantic negotiations by Mr Sisco the American envoy, trying to agree a ceasefire in Cyprus but without success. The right wing government in Athens had fallen after the humiliating debacle of the invasion. Nicos Sampson had been replaced in Cyprus and the rightful government had now been restored with a call for the return of Makarios as soon as possible.

"That's at least one bit of good news," I said in delight. "Those corrupt colonels in Athens have been disgraced and that gangster Sampson and his violent mob in Cyprus are finished. Now I'm almost satisfied. So even though we are still incarcerated and under fire, wider events seemed to be moving in the right direction."

We switched to The Cyprus Forces network for the local news, which gave us new cause to celebrate.

A ceasefire had been agreed to evacuate foreign nationals trapped on the island. Anyone holding a British or foreign passport, other than the Republic of Cyprus, should pack one bag only we were told and proceed to a designated assembly point. From there they will be escorted by UN armoured carriers to the British base area of Dekalia and airlifted to RAF Akrotiri outside Limassol for onward flights to their home countries.

Those residing in the Nicosia district should assemble at the Nicosia Hilton Hotel for departure at 14.00hrs.

Residents of Famagusta and Larnaca will be escorted to the Dekalia Base and residents of Kyrenia will be evacuated by sea on British Navy Frigates.

"Hooray, that's great news too," I shouted happily. "Thank goodness Britain is doing something constructive at last and using the bases for the evacuation. They were supposed to be a guarantor of the islands independence and sovereignty but it hasn't seemed like it so far. Now, you'll be able to get to England to be with your family," I said, patting Ann on the back.

"What do you mean? I'll be able to go to England?" Ann frowned. "What about you?"

"Well, I can't leave. I have to stay and somehow

or other get to Alecos."

"And how do you think you can do that?"

"I don't know yet, but as they are all trying to arrange a cease-fire, they should come to an agreement sooner or later and then I'll see."

Stubbornly, Ann shook her head. "No, I'm not going, I can't leave you here on your own."

"Don't be silly. Much as I want your company there's no reason for you to stay. Go while you've got the chance."

"No, I'm staying," she said obstinately."

"But there's nothing to keep you here. Your family are all in London. You'll be safe there."

She shook her head: "No, this is my home. I can't go back to England and live with my parents again. Who knows how long this situation is going to last? If I have to be in England for more than a couple of weeks, I'll go mad!"

"But you can't stay in Nicosia. Your flat is much too close to the airport. It looks likely that your flat and our lovely new office could well be destroyed. They are bombing the airport right now by the sound of it."

She looked startled at the prospect of losing her home, but she shook her head with a determined look in her eye that I had never seen before.

I backed off and tried a new tactic.

"Ok, then. What about this as a solution? We'll both make for the Hilton. It's the only safe way out of Nicosia while there is a ceasefire. Then just before we get to the Hilton, I'll peel off and you carry on as though you are going to Dekalia. But before you get there, turn-off to the right towards Dhali. From there, cut across to the Limassol road, and keep going till you get there. I know you have an Aunt or cousin you can stay with once you arrive. Then you can easily get to Akrotiri if you decide to go back to England after all. You can phone your parents from there to let them know you are safe."

She thought for some moments then nodded. "Yes, I do have a cousin there I don't know her too well, but I'm sure in the circumstances she'll take me in. But what about your parents? They need to know you're OK too."

"Well, you can phone them too. Just tell them we got out of Nicosia on the convoy and went up to the mountains as Alecos can't be evacuated because he doesn't have a British passport. You don't need to say anything else about Alecos. When I get to the mountains I'll get through to them somehow and explain everything. I imagine it's only in Nicosia and Kyrenia that the telephones are down.'

"Well, OK, that part sounds feasible she agreed. But where will you go?"

"Humm! I hadn't thought that far ahead yet."

I pondered for a while then came up with a solution.

"Ahh! I know. You remember that time when we were marshalling in the Cyprus Rally and they stuck us in the forest on one of the special stages?"

"Yes, I remember that night. I never understood why they'd put us two girls in such a remote place. The night was pitch black and the only sound was the hooting of owls. It was really spooky. Maybe they thought as we were English we were too tough to be frightened!"

"Goodness knows why they did it. But anyway, when we finished, we stayed the night in that new little hotel run by a rather colonial English couple. I could stay there again?"

"Yes, I remember it. I think it was calle Pinewood Valley Hotel. It was near Spilia village, wasn't it?"

I nodded. "That's the one."

"Yes, that's a good idea. It won't be full. The Cypriots will go to the hotels in Platres or Prodromos if they don't have relatives living in the mountains."

"Well then, that's another problem solved. So, we'll leave together for the Hilton. Then I'll turn off and take the back roads through the fields behind Strovolos and make my way up to the hotel. Once I'm there I'll try to get hold of David. He'll know what to do next. So does that plan sound alright to you?"

"Yes, that sounds good and I won't have to worry about you."

"Right then! Now you have nothing more to argue about," I smiled in relief.

"But we'd better get ready. The fighting seems to have quietened down for the moment. Let's see what's happening outside."

Crouching low, I peered out of the bullet hole in the kitchen window. A few cars were already heading in the direction of the Hilton. One pulled into the forecourt of the garage below. A National Guard officer got out to put petrol in his tank.

Ann's Greek was naturally fluent so I called: "Quick, Ann, go down and talk to that soldier in the garage. He should be able to give us an idea of what's happening."

A few moments later, with a great deal of nodding and shaking of heads, she was talking earnestly to the officer.

"Ok," she said breathlessly on her return. "He confirmed that both sides have agreed to a cease-fire but he said it's not safe to stay here in the flat. The Turks still haven't managed to take the airport but there's heavy fighting in the area. So, if a stray mortar hits the petrol tanks in the garage downstairs, the whole lot will explode and probably take the flats with it. The Turks might even decide to take out the government offices across the road, and then this building would certainly get hit."

"Wow! It's a good thing we didn't think of those things before. We thought we were safe here but it seems we've been sitting on a time bomb."

"And, according to him," she added. "They still haven't managed to take Kyrenia either so there is still plenty of fighting going on despite the cease fire for the convoy. He also said that the convoy from the Hilton will be leaving at eleven thirty local time, not two."

"Well, in that case we'd better get a move on. We don't want to get left behind. While I'm packing, you can dig out some Union Jack stickers in the desk drawer to put on the car windows and you'll find some paper flags in the cupboard which we had for a fancy dress party once. They would be useful to wave if either of us are stopped at roadblocks."

As we left the flat there was now a steady stream of traffic on the main road.

At each turning more cars filtered into the queue. We pulled into the stream and inched our way slowly along. At the junction of Diganis and Makarios Avenue, the road up the hill to the Hilton Hotel was jammed with cars, nose- to- tail, in both lanes. There must have been hundreds of them. Many cars were packed with Cypriot families, presumably with British passports, hoping to join the evacuation. Tanks and armoured cars lined the roadside and UN troops, with side arms, directed the traffic converging from every direction, all creeping along desperate to get out of Nicosia.

It was slow going. Even to travel 200 yards to the end of the road took 15 minutes. I reckoned it would take about an hour and a half at this rate to cover the normal 8 minutes drive to the Hilton. But never mind, we were at least moving and felt safe and well protected by the United Nations and British troops lining the road.

Half way up the hill, with a beep of my horn and a frantic wave to Ann in her little red VW Beetle, beside me in the queue, I took the right turn into Drama Street and made my way painfully slowly against the oncoming traffic.

We were all very used to seeing British troops and UN Forces on the island. The British had been in Cyprus since 1878 when the prime minister, Lord Palmerston, had leased it from the Turkish Ottoman Empire. When Turkey entered the First World War on the side of Germany, Cyprus was formally annexed by Great Britain and in 1925 given the status of a Crown Colony. But following years of riots and upheaval between the Greek Cypriots and the British, the Cypriots gained their independence in 1960. But the British still kept 99 square miles as sovereign military base areas, which, thankfully today, were being used in evacuating some 4500 civilian refugees.

The military protection steadily evaporated the further away I got from the convoy. After what seemed like hours, I eventually came to the end of Drama Street. Now I was on my own, with just my wits to get me through to safety and from there to rescue Alecos.

Soon I came to a roadblock. A simple pole barrier set up by the side of the road and manned by what looked like teenagers in National guard uniform, brandishing first world war Lee Enfield rifles.

The red white and blue stickers were prominently placed on the windscreen of my car and as I got near I waved my little Union Jack flag out of the window. One of the young soldiers approached the car pointing his rifle menacingly at me. With a big smile, I wished him 'kalimera sas' - good morning to you - even though by that time it was already well after one o'clock. His aggressive attitude changed and he asked politely where I was going. Concerned that I was making my way alone up to the mountains, he warned me there was heavy fighting around the airport and I should keep well away from the area.

He suggested I go south, skirting the bombed compound of the Presidential Palace till I got to Panayia Christalousa church, then keep going south west on the small road to Pano Dheftera village and get directions from there. Thanking him with a big smile, I was off with another wave of my flag.

By now I was driving through the southernmost outskirts of the city.

Nicosia had been the capital of Cyprus since the first Arab invasions in the seventh century.

The island had been inhabited since 7000 BC. And been fought over and occupied by almost every major power throughout the ages, due to its strategic position in the Eastern Mediterranean. But after gaining independence from the British, it grew steadily with the advent of tourism.

It soon became a base for multinational oil field personnel, businessmen and journalists working in the Middle East. Cyprus became a Mecca for all that was missing in the Arab world. Nicosia, the small but modern city, set in the centre of the island, had an

171

international airport just a short taxi ride from the city centre. It was an ideal location for 'rest and recreation' leave for anyone working in the Arab States, with good roads to all seaside and mountain destinations and the obvious accessibility of fine wines and unlimited booze. The heart of the historic city was enclosed by 16th century Venetian walls containing museums, ancient churches and medieval buildings. It retained the nostalgic atmosphere of the past with its narrow winding streets lined with traditional houses, little artisan shops, galleries and taverns, echoing a bygone age.

The modern city had grown outside the old walls, its wide tree-lined avenues, now home to banks, embassies, restaurants, cafes, new shops and apartment blocks.

The city also boasted a racecourse, a football stadium, botanic gardens, a new eighteen-storey office block. The latest prestigious arrivals were the luxury Hilton Hotel and a Woolworth department store, giving a modern cosmopolitan status to the capital of this small island at the edge of the Middle East.

Now, at the end of the outer suburbs of the modern city with its ancient heart, I was in no man's land. I had never been here before. According to the map, the road I was to take to the mountains was much longer and more tortuous than the more direct road we normally used that passed the airport. But this was now the only option, so I followed the long rough road in a wide south west loop to the Troodos mountains.

The heat stamped down on the flat open plain stretching away endlessly to the shimmering horizon. On either side of the road, the vista consisted of scrub and dust with only a few gnarled olive trees and an occasional clusters of broken down farm buildings to relieve the monotony.

The car windows were closed, as the thick clouds of dust rising from the pot-holed road would have completely enveloped me but the sweat poured off me instead. At last I passed through the twin villages of Kato and Pano Deftero situated at the beginning of the foothills to the mountains. It was hard to believe that the arid area I'd just driven through produced an abundant variety of vegetables that supplied the markets of Nicosia. Today, in the scorching summer heat, everything looked dusty, dry and limp.

Now, at last, the road started to climb out of the plain. The road surface improved, the vegetation became greener and the temperature dropped. I opened the car windows and breathed in the fresh air.

Soon I passed a signpost for the Mitsero Mines giving me a vague idea of where I was but then came the endless climb, up and up, one tortuous bend after another. The constant turning made me feel sick. I was also hungry, tired and gritty, but still only half way there.

Beginning to think I had taken on more than I could manage, my mind churned endlessly. I was worrying how I was to get to Alecos as I seemed to be driving further and further away from him.

Suddenly a huge dark cloud appeared from behind the top of the mountains, blocking out the sun. Then just as suddenly, big fat raindrops smashed noisily on the windscreen.

This torrential downpour in August was a summer phenomenon that only ever occurred in the mountains, but even then, so rarely, that I'd never experienced it.

Now it felt like a gift from the gods.

Stopping the car and jumping out into the middle of the road, I threw back my head and opening my mouth wide, swallowing huge gulps of clean clear mountain rain, refreshing my parched throat. As the rain pour down, sticking my hair in wet strands to my face, I spread my arms wide and whirled around like a dervish, laughing in delight as I experienced the most wonderful feeling of elation and joy.

The rain stopped as quickly as it had started and the sun shone again in a tall cloudless blue sky. The trees and shrubs sparkle with jewelled raindrops and the condensation, rising from the surface of the road, became a golden mist in the sun's rays. Every outcrop of rock, leafy shrub and blade of grass became a glittering silhouette outlined sharply in the radiant light.

After the rain, the smell was unbelievable. Sharp spicy eucalyptus and pine. Earthy damp dust. The lemony smell of cistus and the aromatic herbs of rosemary, sweet thyme and lavender, all combined to make the unique aroma of the mountains. If it could have been bottled, it would be more exotic than the most expensive French perfume.

Each one of my senses felt alive and bursting with joy. It was such a magical experience that I really believed that the mythical 'Gods of Mount Olympus' and especially Aphrodite, Goddess of Love and Beauty, my favourite deity, was looking down and would help me find Alecos.

Getting back into the car I felt so exhilarated, I covered the rest of the journey in a dream without noticing the hardship.

Just outside the village of Spilia, I found the little hotel. Mr and Mrs Fletcher, the couple we'd met before, were still there. They greeted me warmly, and showed me to a comfortable room overlooking the pretty garden and the mountains beyond.

After jumping in the shower, getting rid of the dust and grit which seemed to have settled into every fold and surface of my body during the long drive, I sat on my small balcony drying my hair in the last rays of the evening sun which slanted down through the valley.

I felt safe and relaxed and ready to tackle all the problems I knew were ahead of me.

But first I had to phone my parents who would be frantic to know what had happened to me.

I booked a reverse charge call for nine o'clock Cyprus time, but seven o'clock for them in England. Even if there were the usual conection delays there would still be plenty of catch up time before they went to bed.

Having eaten hardly anything all day, the simple dinner that Mrs Fletcher served felt like a banquet. To top it off I added a couple of extra glasses of white wine, to relax my stiff body and help me sleep. Now, I was clean and fed and ready for the long wait for the call to England.

But Aphrodite was still looking after me and produced another miracle.

The phone rang almost on the dot of nine and the voices of my parents were loud and clear. Ann had already managed to get through to them from Limassol so they were not as panicky as I'd expected.

They were also better informed about the invasion than me, as the Sunday Times had devoted several pages to the invasion.

"You know the invasion began yesterday at 5.45am," my mother said.

"Yes, I know about that, I saw them landing," I told her. "I just managed to escape before the heavy fighting started. I heard her gasp in horror clearly down the phone."

"So where are you now?" my father asked, grabbing the phone.

"Up near Troodos, in a little hotel. It's safe here, so don't worry."

I didn't tell them that Alecos had been arrested. There was nothing they could do except worry even more, so I decided to wait till I had something more positive to report.

After I'd heard all their news, we arranged to phone at the same time tomorrow. "But don't worry if you can't get through, the lines are down all over," I explained. "I'll keep trying from this end too so sooner or later we'll make contact."

"Good night, Sally darling, keep safe and out of trouble," Dad said, fortunately not realising what trouble I was already in.

"Good night Dad. Don't worry about me, I'll manage."

Now the first part of my plan had been completed successfully. I'd arrived at the hotel without mishap. Ann was safe in Limassol and I'd got through to my parents. And, as an added bonus, I felt sure that Aphrodite was looking after me too.

But I knew that tomorrow's plan, to track down David to ask for his help, might not be as easy to achieve.

20

Monday

After the tensions of the previous day, I slept like a log and woke with the sun shinning through the slats in the shutters. Throwing them open, the early morning rays turned the leaves of the trees to glittering golden pennies as they rustled in the light breeze.

Dressing quickly, I went downstairs to the flower-decked garden that overlooked the village. Like the fields across the valley, the garden of the hotel was terraced, the steps down to each level, edged with earthenware pots cascading with flowers. The acacia trees waved their greenish grey fronds in swooping arcs, shading the wide terrace outside the dining room, where round white wrought iron tables and chairs with yellow-striped cushions were set for breakfast. The setting was idyllic and I smiled with pleasure.

The hotel was set on the sloping hillside just out-side the village. The pitched terracotta-tiled roofs of the small houses tumbled down to the river valley. Washing lines on the occasional flat roof, hung with sheets and towels, flapped and billowed in the breeze like the sails of tall ships. It was picture perfect and everything smelt green and fresh.

Then, to add to my delight, a beautiful tabby cat

177

with a tiny bell on its red collar came strolling across the terrace. Draping itself around my legs, it purred like a well oiled Mercedes engine. I loved cats and this one knew it. Looking up at me with its blue oriental shaped eyes, our love affair started at that moment.

Cats in Cyprus have a touch of Egyptian in their high legs, slanted eyes and graceful necks. The country folk keep them purely as rat catchers. They hang around the barns or fishing boats, in scruffy gangs and there are always cats roaming around coffee shops in the villages but rarely ever are they allowed in the house as pets.

But the Fletchers' tabby, called 'Princess' was a real 'aristocat'. She certainly lived up to her name. Sleek, well fed and obviously quite used to luxury living, she vacated her own soft cushioned chair in a shady corner of the terrace, to jump onto my lap purring contentedly as soon as I sat down for breakfast.

This delicious feast consisted of freshly baked village bread, melon with lounza, the special cured ham of Cyprus, Halumi cheese with honey and real percolated coffee. I'd got so used to the small thick Turkish coffee served in Cyprus, that I'd forgotten how good filter coffee tasted.

One thing was for sure, if I had to stay here for long, I'd certainly put on weight. Everything was so perfect. It felt like being on holiday rather than escaping from a war zone, on a rescue mission to save my imprisoned husband.

While I savoured my coffee, with Princess purring on my lap, a retired English couple arrived for break-fast. We smiled and said good morning and before long we were chatting.

They introduced themselves as Frances and Bob Rix. They had arrived just before the coup for a walking holiday in the mountains. They knew that there had been a coup in Nicosia, but to them, it was far away and had never dreamed that it would disrupt their holiday. Their days had been spent walking and bird watching but now, to their horror, they'd heard the island had been invaded in the north by the Turkish Army and there was heavy fighting around the airport. With no flights out of Cyprus, they were stuck with no idea what to do.

Finishing my coffee and seeing they were upset and out of their depth I moved over to their table to try to reassure them.

Explaining the situation as simply as possible, they became more anxious when they realised that the only way of leaving the island would be to join the evacuation of refugees from the RAF base at Acrotiri.

They were in a state of near panic so I assured them that as they were tourists with British passports, and documents from their travel company, there should be no difficulty. But they seemed unable to take it all in.

I suggested we should meet again in the afternoon, over tea, and I would try to answer any questions they might have after they'd discussed the situation quietly together during the day. They still looked anxious but agreed to meet later.

In the meantime, I had to get hold of David. Realising I was probably in for a long day sitting by the phone, I wasn't too daunted as the surroundings were so relaxing and I'd noticed there was a wonderful selection of English language books in the hotel bookcase.

My first job was to phone around to find the

whereabouts of David. I knew it would be tricky as he was bound to be involved with the evacuation so he could be anywhere, other than the front lines. The UN mandate stated that as a Peace Keeping force, they were not allow to fight but only to observe and be involved as a non-combatant force.

So making the most of my enforced circumstances and hoping that sooner or later, my patience would be rewarded, I settled down by the phone in the reception.

It was no surprise when there was no answer on his private number. Eventually, I got through to the British UN Command Station in Paphos and asked to speak to Major David Hamilton. The operator told me he was not available at the moment.

I was more or less expecting him to be out, but still my heart sank.

"Please can you tell me when he would be available?"

"Sorry, madam. I can't do that."

"Please help me, I need to speak to him urgently."

He was still reluctant to say anything, so I pleaded with him. "Look, I know you are not supposed to give out information, but I'm a very old friend of the major. He promised to help me any time he could and I desperately need his help now."

Eventually, the operator took pity on me. "Major Hamilton will be back in camp on Wednesday, madam."

Thanking him profusely, I gave my name and the number of the hotel. "But please, please, pass it on to Major Hamilton as soon as he arrives back in camp," I begged. "It really is urgent."

Assuring me he would, he hung up.

I was left holding the phone with the hopeless

feeling that I'd got to the winning post but now had to wait forty-eight hours before I knew if I'd won.

Patience is not one of my virtues. While I'm busy trying to achieve what I want done, my adrenaline fires on all cylinders, but waiting around without being able to get thing moving was a nightmare for me. I felt nauseous and drained, my happy holiday feelings evaporating fast.

Frances and Bob had already left the hotel for their walk and I'd seen the Fletchers go off to town for supplies so I would have to wait untill the afternoon before I had anyone to talk me out of my mood. Though I tried pouring my sorrows out to Princess, it didn't help much, she was far too aloof to show any concern!

At four o'clock I sat down for afternoon tea Bob and Frances joined me almost immediately eager to discuss with me what to do next. That alone made me feel better. Even though there was nothing I could do to help myself, at least I should be able to help them!

Mrs Fletcher brought us a pot of English tea and generous slices of home made Victoria sponge cake. I hadn't had such a proper tea for ages and just the sight of it cheered me up. Frances got busy pouring the tea and after our first mouthful of cake, we got down to business.

They were worried how they could get to Acrotiri.

"Our transfer to the mountains and back was included in our holiday package," Bob told me. "So what should we do now?"

"Well, the first thing is to phone your travel representative here in Cyprus. If he's based in Limassol you'll be OK but if it's Nicosia, you'll be out of luck. There is still heavy fighting there and almost everyone will have left the city on the convoy yesterday as I did."

Bob pushed his cup to one side to shuffle through their travel papers.

"Oh dear! The forwarding agent is in Nicosia. So now what do we do?"

Taking the last mouthful of the fluffy sponge cake, I asked: "How many more days have you left of your holiday?"

"We were due to leave next Saturday," Frances said.

"Well, in that case, I think you should get a local taxi from here to take you to Akrotiri. Even though you'll be a bit out of pocket, I'm sure the taxi fare won't cost too much. You can take it up with your travel insurance company when you get back to England. Though you probably won't get much joy out of them."

Despite his worries, Bob chuckled: "Oh, we wont worry about a few extra pounds. It won't break the bank!"

"Well, as you've already booked and paid for the hotel, you might as well stay till the weekend. Unless of course, you are really scared and feel it's not safe to be in Cyprus?"

"No, we love it here and are sorry we have to leave," Francis said wistfully.

"In that case, arriving at Akrotiri on Saturday will be soon enough and still be within the terms of your holiday package. You'll get a process form from the British authorities in Akrotiri which will prove you were evacuated."

"Yes, that makes sense," agreed Bob.

"Good. We'll still have time to go up to Troodos on the bus to see if we can spot the Short Toed Tree Creeper again," Francis said, excitedly. "I might be able to get some better photos this time."

She looked at me enquiringly. "You do know, of course, that the Short Toed Tree Creeper is not only endemic to Cyprus but is only found in the Troodos mountains too. So it's very rare and very special!"

"No, I didn't know that," I said, with a wry smile.

What a bizarre situation! I thought to myself, Here I am, stuck up a mountain, not knowing what is happening to my husband. The country has been invaded by enemy forces: my house in Kyrenia is now in enemy territory: my home in Nicosia probably damaged or in ruins: the whole population of the island in the middle of a major chaotic upheaval that will change their lives forever: and here are two tourists on a bird watching holiday in Cyprus. And now, her only thought is to get a better photo of a short-toed bird, completely unaware about the devastation happening around them! I shook my head in amazement and gulped the tea down in disbelief.

Fances was still chattering on about her birds but suddenly she snapped back to practical realities.

"Where do they put everyone when they arrive at Acrotiri?" she asked.

"I think they'll convert the school and use the classrooms and the hall and whatever other space, as dormitories to sleep as many as possible."

"I don't like the sound of that, it will be very uncomfortable," Francis complained.

"You'll be one of the lucky ones," I answered impatiently. "It won't be comfortable but at least you'll be safe and know that sooner or later you'll get back home. The Turkish Cypriots from Limassol went to the base because they were scared they'd be harmed by Greek Cypriots who have already attacked several Turkish villages. They have all had to sleep together on the beach and will stay there as they have nowhere safe to go to. All the national airlines are sending flights to evacuate their own citizens to their home countries. Apart from foreign tourists, there will be the military families and International company employees and their families too. There were at least 4000 people just on the convoy from Nicosia alone. They all have to be processed before they leave. But at least they have homes somewhere to go to," I said in exasperation, trying to convey the magnitude of the situation.

"What about the Greek Cypriots who can't leave? They've lost their homes and everything. They have nowhere to go either," I added angrily.

I think she got the message as she shut up, looking rather sheepish.

"That's why I think you should hang on here till you have to leave," I said, trying to calm down. "Some of the chaos should have been sorted out by then."

Bob, wanting to keep the peace, nodded his head in agreement. "Yes that really sounds like the best option."

I was still angry at her thoughtlessness so I continued to drive home the more unpleasant aspects of the situation.

"Once you get to the airbase, you'll have to wait till there is room on a flight back to the UK. But it should be less hectic than it is at the moment, so you might not have to wait more than a few days!"

"My goodness," Francis exclaimed. "This will certainly have turned into an unusual holiday!"

I laughed ironically. "It will give you lots of stories to tell your friends when you get home. You'll be celebrities!" I pointed out, sarcastically.

"Thank you very much, Sally, for your advice," Bob said gently, still trying to calm me down. "I think you've given us a pretty fair picture of what to expect. Now we'll just have to enjoy the next few peaceful days left to us here, before we go and face the maddening crowds," he finished wryly, sipping his tea and settling thoughtfully back in his chair.

"Oh, just one more thing," he said. "Do you know where we land when we arrive in England?"

"I heard on the British Forces news that people living in the south of England will go to RAF Brize Norton, near Oxford."

Bob gave a grateful sigh. "Well, that's the best news yet. At least we'll be almost home then. We live in Bicester. It's not too far from Brize Norton."

"Do you really?" I said in amazement. "My parents live near Woodstock, in Lower Heyford. Alan and Jill Cooper, perhaps you know them?"

"No, but we know Ruth and Peter Darvill from Heyford.

"Good gracious! They are the nearest neighbours; they live on the other side of the canal bridge from my parents."

"Well isn't that a small world!" exclaimed Francis. "Ruth is an artist and I go to her classes in the village hall."

Naturally, after such a coincidence, the tension evaporated and we chattered away about people and places we knew. I softened towards Frances and had to assume her thoughtlessness had been from fear of the unknown, because now she was relaxed, she turned out to be quite a comedian. Bob was an ex police inspector and had a lot of stories to tell. The evening flew by and suddenly it was late and we were ready to say goodnight.

I had been dreading going to bed as I knew in my agitated state, my mind would be churning over all the problems of getting to Alecos and I would be tossing and turning with worry. But, after such an unexpectedly jolly evening, I felt cheerful and relaxed and confident that somehow or other everything would work out satisfactorily.

21

Tuesday 23rd July

When I woke the next morning, I lay in bed planning what I could do to make the day pass pleasantly and keep my mind busy to stop myself worrying about Alecos.

My first task was to get up to date with the invasion situation. Fortunately, I'd hastily thrown my little portable radio into the suitcase before we joined the convoy. Generally, there was too much static for it to receive much, But up here in the mountains, the British Forces Broadcasting Service came through loud and clear as their antenna was on Mount Olympus nearby, at the very the top of the mountain range.

Most of the news was about the evacuation...

Since mid afternoon yesterday, 36,000 people of all nationalities, including one from Puerto Rico, have been airlifted out in 61 flights.

Receiving centres had been set up in RAF Lyneham in Wiltshire and Brize Norton in Oxfordshire where food and clothing is being provided for those who have arrived with nothing.

Conditions are basic as refugees continued to crowd into the Sovereign Base Areas. At Akrotiri alone, the number of civilian refugees has been put at eight thousand.

In response to the food shortage and other essentials, two Britannia flights brought in 22 tons of cargo and 6000 lbs of powdered milk.

This statistic made me laugh out loud. My imagination pictured rows and rows of tiny refugee babies lined up screaming for their powdered milk ration! Even in the worst of times, there was always something to bring a smile to the situation.

It was staggering to think of the logistical problems such an evacuation must entail. The co-ordination of the operation was immense but thankfully, between the Brits and the UN everything seemed to be running as smoothly as possible in the chaotic circumstances.

Yesterday while telling Bob and Frances about the situation, I'd tried to play down the hardships they would encounter, but after our entertaining evening together, I realised I needn't have worried. Though Frances would probably grumble when she heard the latest update, they were both much tougher than I'd given them credit for, so they'd get through the ordeal with humour.

As I'd expected, they took the news stoically, realising it was just something they would have to manage. Now, all that was left was to enjoy their last few days in the mountains till they got the taxi on Saturday to Acrotiri. Once there, they would start the unexpected and dramatic climax to their otherwise peaceful two weeks holiday in the mountains. After her initial reservations and fears, Frances now seemed to be quite looking forward to the adventure to come.

"As you have a few days left, what are you going

to do?" I asked.

"We'll definitely go up to Troodos again to see the birds," she said eagerly.

"We thought we'd go tomorrow," Bob said. "As we are already too late to catch the bus today."

"I was going to suggest that I drive you up there but I have to be here tomorrow to wait for my UN friend to phone. But I could take you today or perhaps I could drive you around the area. There are some beautiful villages round about. Have you been to the village of Kakopetria yet?" I asked.

"Oh, that would be lovely. If you don't mind taking us," Frances enthused.

"No, it's my pleasure. It's one of our favourite places in the mountains. We could take a drive up the valley and have a coffee and a stroll in one of the other villages, then back to Kakopetria for lunch. The restaurant there cooks fresh trout like a dream They get it from the trout farm nearby. It's so delicious; it makes me salivate just to think about it.

"That sounds perfect," agreed Bob, rubbing his tummy at the thought of lunch. "What time shall we leave?"

"Let's meet in the lounge after we've collected our things. Then we can leave just after the BBC World Service news. I want to know if the National Guard is still holding the line outside Kyrenia. They put up a fierce fight in the area to keep the Turks back when they landed at Zefiros. That was three miles west of Kyrenia. My house is three miles to the east, so hopefully, it's still safe."

"Yes," Bob agreed. "I'd like to know what's happening too. We seem to be living in a fools paradise up here in the mountains with no newspapers or television we can understand. Up to now, that was part of the pleasure of being here. But now we are in the middle of a war zone, it's rather unnerving not knowing what's going on in the real world outside."

"Oh no, I don't feel like that at all," Frances replied. "It's so lovely up here. I don't want to get back to the real world. I could stay here forever," she said wistfully.

Just then the news began...

Early today in Cyprus, Turkish landing ships reach the beachhead and unloaded battle tanks and supporting equipment. Greek Cypriot forces in the area were unable to contain the new landing force and retreat towards Kyrenia town but after heavy fighting, the last defence at Kyrenia collapsed. Greek Cypriots trapped in the castle managed to escape from the city. Turkish forces have now successfully created a bridgehead between Kyrenia and Nicosia, forcing Greek forces to retreat south.

"Oh no!" I groaned. "That's my home gone. I loved that house. I had so many happy years there with the family and with Alecos since we've been married. It holds so many memories.' I said, near to tears."

"It's very sad, but you are safe and no one can take your memories away," Frances sympathised.

The broadcast continued...

On the political front it appeared the Greeks and Turkish governments have agreed to discuss a cease-fire. Mr Callahan, the British Foreign Secretary, announced that the Turkish government have accepted the British initiative to hold talks in Geneva on Wednesday afternoon. It is now up to the Greek government to agree to Wednesday, rather than Friday as they had initially requested.

"God, those bloody Greeks! It's their fault this all started. Now they are quibbling over a couple of days!" I exclaimed angrily. "Both Athens and Ankara are stalling in order to gain substantial military advantage before officially agreeing to a ceasefire. I can't believe they care so little about people's lives. Now the fighting will continue till Wednesday. Then, if we're lucky, they'll sit down for tea in Geneva!"

I banged the table angrily. "That's such awful news. We are helpless, just waiting around in limbo with no idea of our fate. Goodness knows how long they will drag it out."

I was so furious, this time that tears of rage started to well up. I brushed them away angrily.

The Rixs looked at me in concern. Then Bob said: "Look, Sally, if you don't feel like going out, we can do it another day. Frances and I can go for a walk."

"No, I'm sorry. I just feel so helpless. I wake up every morning feeling sick with worry and afraid of what might be happening to my husband. The longer this stand-off continues the more frightened I get and I can't do anything about it, except wait. And the waiting is driving me mad," My voice rose to nearly a scream.

"We wish there was something we could do to help," Frances said, putting her arms round me in a sympathetic hug.

"Sorry," I said again. "I seem to be getting more depressed and hysterical all the time. Without your company I'd be a complete wreck. You certainly help to cheer me up. I'll really miss you when you leave on Saturday," I said, brushing away more tears.

"But now come on, let's go out. The drive will take my mind off things and I can show you more of our lovely mountains."

The next morning, waking even earlier, my stomach tight with cramp, I was on tenterhooks, hoping that David had got my message and would phone so I could at last get moving to find Alecos.

Yesterday, after my depression of the morning, the company of Bob and Frances on our drive through the mountains had relaxed me and we'd had a wonderful day together. They were delighted to explore the picturesque villages, the cottage walls purple with bougainvillea or shaded by vines heavy with grapes and their little vegetable patches lined with tomatoes and beans neatly strung up across bamboo poles, clumps of potatoes, yellow flowered courgettes and, fronds of carrot tops in orderly rows. Their humour and enthusiasm for the beauty of the area made me feel proud to be able to show them that Cyprus was a really lovely place. Its reputation as one of the most beautiful islands in the Mediterranean was no exaggeration. Seeing it through their eyes, confirmed it to me, and I forgot all my troubles.

But this morning, the realization that this most lovely of islands was being decimated by war, made me cry. Beautiful buildings, ancient churches and antiquities were now in ruins. Forests and fields were burnt. People were displaced from villages they'd lived in for generations and so many killed in the fighting.

The pleasure of yesterday evaporated and I felt worse than I had ever before. With an effort, I pulled myself together and got ready for the long day.

Breakfast was a lonely meal today. I only had Princess to keep me company.

Bob and Frances had caught the early bus to Troodos to get one last glimpse of their cross-eyed bird, or whatever it was called!

I missed their lively company, and was grateful they were still around for a couple more days as it was going to be hard living without them. Being dependent on forces outside my control, before anything could improve, gave me such a dreadful feeling of impotence and helplessness.

After breakfast I sat outside on the veranda reading, waiting for the phone to ring.

I couldn't concentrate and stared into space not even aware of the beauty around me.

Suddenly the telephone rang in the reception. Sitting forward on the edge of my chair, I waited expectantly for Mrs Fletcher to call me. But she didn't.

Tears of disappointment welled up again. It was unlike me to feel so down but I was in such an emotional state, I felt completely out of control.

A few minutes later my heart leapt as the phone rang again. This time, it was for me. Mrs Fletcher discreetly disappeared into the kitchen as I took the receiver.

"Sally, what's the matter? I came off duty late last night and phoned as soon as I could," said David, sounding worried.

"Oh, David," I whispered in relief. "I was so scared that they wouldn't give you my message."

"Are you alright? Has anything happened to you?" he repeated.

"No, David, nothing's happened to me. It's Alecos. I know you must be frantically busy with all that's happening, but you're the only one I can turn to for help."

"Don't worry about my duties; you know I will always help you if I can. So tell me, what's happened to Alecos?"

I explained about him being arrested during the coup and ending up in Morphou prison.

"When they lifted the curfew on Wednesday afternoon, I managed to get to him and arrange for his release at the weekend. But then the Turks invaded and I had to escape from Kyrenia back to Nicosia and couldn't go back for him."

"But you're phoning from a Troodos area number?"

"Yes, I'm in Spilia. Ann and I got out of Nicosia on the UN convoy. I had nowhere else to go so I made my way up here. Ann went to a relative in Limassol. Now, I need to know what's happening in Morphou and if it's safe to go there."

"Look, Sally, I'm due back on duty this evening but in the meantime I'll contact our Morphou people to discover what the situation is there. I'm on a 36 hour pass next week, so I'll have a better idea then. We could meet and discuss how I can best help you."

"Oh, that's marvellous," I said. 'I knew I could rely on you to come up with something. Should I meet you somewhere or can you come up to Spilia?"

"Yes, I think that's the best idea. I can borrow a car and come up to you. If I stay around here, they are bound to find something urgent for me to do and I'll never get a break and I'm exhausted. But, Sally, don't be tempted to go rushing around on your own. It's not safe."

"OK, if you come up here I'll ask Mrs Fletcher to arrange a room and prepare us a meal. She's a great cook."

"Good idea," David agreed. "I'll come up next Wednesday

"That's great," I said. "There are only a couple of visitors left here and they're leaving for Akrotiri at the weekend, so it will be private and quiet. There are no Cypriots here. You know how they would gossip if they saw me having a quiet dinner with a UN officer while my husband is away.

"You know, of course, Sally, that the diplomats are gathering in Geneva today to discuss a ceasefire, so maybe something will be resolved. But from what I hear on the grapevine the Turkish army has got its feet firmly on the ground now in Cyprus and they are not going to let anything go. They want to make it worth their while and get as much territory as they can, even though they claimed that they only wanted a beach head between Kyrenia and Nicosia, so they could protect their people."

"That's what I was worried about and now you've confirmed it. The fighting could go on for months and that would be disastrous for both communities," I said, in alarm.

"Yes, Sally, you're right," he agreed. "Anyway you're safe up there in the mountains for now. Hopefully, when I see you next week, I'll have some good news."

"Thanks, David, you're an angel. I've been waking up each morning in a state of panic but now, with your help, thing will get moving and I won't feel so useless and out of my depth. Thank you again and I'm looking forward to seeing you soon."

"Bye, Sally, I'm so glad you called me to help," he said wistfully. "Look after yourself and see you on Wednesday."

The phone went dead but I felt almost light headed after talking to David. He really was such a capable and reassuring person. It was such a relief to know that something would be done to find out what had happened to Alecos.

I had no plans for the rest of the day but felt so elated that I needed to do something.

I packed a few bits into a bag and strode out to the village taking deep breaths of the air reputed to be the purest in Cyprus, due to the fact that the village of Spila was about six thousand feet above sea level. What a difference now from my miserable mood earlier. It felt like I'd been drinking champagne! My spirits lifted and I felt elated. My body still felt stiff after cowering on the floor of the flat as bullets flew around. Then sitting for hours in the car, first on the convoy then the long drive up the mountains to escape. Apart from the amble through Kakopetria for lunch yesterday I'd had no exercise. I needed a good walk to get my body working properly again and now I felt raring to go.

I made for the modern church whose belfry dominated the skyline above the trees of the village. Apparently this large church with a red tiled roof had been built recently, after the roof of their small ancient stone church at the far end of the village became unstable and the old church was no longer safe to use. The new church had been built entirely by the highly religious folk of the village. But so as not to lose everything from the place where they had worshipped for generations, they removed the large church bell. They suspended it in a majestic pine tree which shaded the new church. Now the old bell rings out across the valley every day, pulled by the bell rope hanging from the tree.

The uphill climb was good exercise and I hummed happily to myself as I strode along. Leaving the church the track dropped gently down into the valley. The sun filtered through the leaves of the plane trees, warming my bare arms. It glittered on the trickle of water that gurgled over the rocks in the almost dry riverbed. Even the birds seemed happy. They chirped and chattered in the trees and in the distance could be heard the tinkle of bells from a herd of goats. The heady pungent perfume of wild thyme and sage, that grew abundantly in the dry climate of the mountains, filled the warm air.

From the church I wandered through the village. The old people and children left behind to care for the animals and crops, while their men folk had gone off to fight for their country, stared at me suspiciously as I passed but I greeted them with a smile and a hello and they began to smile back.

As I passed the village shop, the yeasty aroma of freshly baked bread enveloped me. Unable to resist it, I entered the dark interior and bought a small crusty loaf, then added a chunk of salty Halumi cheese, a big juicy tomato, some grapes and a few plump black figs to my shopping list. This would be my lunch and now I would find a good spot to enjoy it in.

As I walked along the riverbank the scraping of my walking shoes on the smooth rocks startled the basking salamanders. The scuttling of their bodies in the grass was the only sound in the stillness of the afternoon siesta, apart from the buzzing of the bees, collecting pollen from the tiny flowers of the sweet smelling thyme.

Finding a sun dappled spot by the river's edge, I collapsed on the soft grass and dangling my tired feet in the cool sparkling water. I tucked into my alfresco lunch then settled back in the sunshine to read.

I never went anywhere without a book but it was difficult to find foreign language books in Cyprus. My spoken Greek was good enough for general conversation, but I couldn't decipher the Greek characters quickly enough to read a book properly. I could only manage advertisements and newspaper headlines. But now, to my delight, English books were readily available in the recently opened Woolworths store in Nicosia. Unfortunately I'd only thrown a couple of novels into my bag when we'd left Nicosia, so the last thing I expected to find in the mountains was a huge collection of English books, left behind by Mrs Fletcher's tourist guests. There were novels, biographies, classics and reference books. So, during my enforced stay in the mountains, I intended to make the most of this wonderful windfall and lose myself in this unexpected variety of subjects.

For one afternoon at least, I could relax and enjoy sitting quietly in the warm sun by a cool river, reading a good book, safe and away from the horrors of reality.

22

The following week

After my peaceful afternoon by the river, the previous day, I enjoyed the time I had left with Bob and Frances. We'd made the most of their last few days knowing they would face a chaotic time at the camp before they eventually returned to their home in Oxfordshire. We had a lot of fun together, going for long walks, Frances pointing out the different birds, then, picnicking by the river or in the forest.

Frances was especially sorry to leave. "I really love it here in Cyprus," she enthused. "It is the best place we've ever been too. I can't understand why we never thought to come here before. I admit we haven't seen much of the island but I'm sure I'd love it all."

"You should come in March and stay by the sea in Larnaca," I told her. "The weather is mild at that time of year on the coast, much the same temperature as it is up here now. There are lots of lovely coastal walks and ancient sites to explore. In the winter, the sea seeps into the nearby lake forming a salt marsh and hordes of migrating birds make a stop off there on their way north or south."

"Yes, I'd love to go there. I've read about it in my bird books," Frances said. "Is that the place with Flamingos?"

"Yes, that's right. Great flocks of beautiful pink birds stalk the shallows of the salt lake, feeding on the tiny brine shrimp that breed there. There is a beautiful minaret shrine built in 1816 when Cyprus was part of the Ottoman Empire. It's dedicated to the foster mother of the Prophet Mohammed and one of the principle places of pilgrimage in the Moslem world. It's a lovely peaceful spot and the cypress and palm trees surrounding it are reflected in the lake..."

Breaking off abruptly I felt the blood drain from my face as I realised that from now on, nothing would be the same.

"What's the matter?" Frances asked, with a worried frown.

"I can't believe it. Here I am chattering about the lovely places to visit in Cyprus yet now it's all being destroyed. The Turks seem determined to get as much of the island as possible. Larnaca is far from the fighting but who knows how far the Turks intend to go especially as they have a religious shrine in the area. There is nothing to stop them. Our soldiers have very few weapons; they must be running out of arms and ammunition. During the coup, the armoury, just outside Nicosia, was destroyed so that Makarios supporters couldn't get hold of weapons. The Sampson regime expected to get their necessary supplies from Greece. But since the Colonels were toppled after the Turkish invasion, nothing has been replaced so they have nothing left to fight with," I despaired, as the consequences of the war overwhelmed me.

The happy mood of the afternoon dissolved and though I tried my best to put these dreadful events out of my mind, I could no longer chatter light-heartedly, even though both Bob and Frances tried their best to cheer me up.

Saturday morning arrived. Their taxi came to pick them up at seven-thirty as it was a two hour drive to Akrotiri and there was no knowing how long they would have to wait around in the queue before they were processed.

I'd written a long letter to my parents telling them what had really happened to Alecos. On the infrequent occasions we'd managed to get through on the phone, I'd never mentioned Alecos, only the course of the fighting. They always had more knowledge about the war than I did as they listened avidly to the news reports on the BBC and watched TV. I knew they were worried enough, without the added knowledge that I was alone and didn't know where Alecos was.

As she left, I handed Frances the letter and asked her: "Please will you deliver this to my parents when you get back. I've told them what happened to Alecos and you can fill in the gaps when you meet them. Maybe by the time they receive it, Alecos will be back," I added hopefully.

Frances tucked the letter into her bag and hugging me said: "Of course I will, Sally dear. It will be the first thing we do when we eventually get home. I'm looking forward to meeting your parents and I'm sure we will all become good friends. After all, we now share a daughter!"

I was so touched by her comment, I hugged them both, and once again, the tears fell, almost blinding me.

They have become very special to me. They'd pulled me through a very difficult time with their fun, laughter and concern and I knew I would be distraught without their company.

I kissed them both and, still weeping, said: "I'll

miss you so much, I really don't know how I would have managed without you here."

As they got into the taxi, I said: "Have a safe journey. I look forward to seeing you again soon. You can be sure that when I'm in England you'll find me on your doorstep, and you'll meet Alecos too."

Tears rolling down my cheeks, I watched till the taxi was out of sight.

As I returned to the hotel, Mrs Fletcher came out of the kitchen and handed me a mug of tea. "Drink this, Sally. It will make you feel better, you look done in. It's still early, why not go back to bed for an hour or so? A sleep would do you good."

I felt drained and had no energy to argue so took the tea without protest. I think she must have put something in it as, unexpectedly, I fell into a deep sleep and didn't wake till midday.

I sat around for the rest of the day in a daze. 'Mrs F', as I had now named her, bustled around, making sure I ate and drank whatever she put in front of me.

In the evening she suggested that I joined them for a light supper. I pointed out that I wouldn't be much company but she insisted. They didn't seem to mind that I hardly joined in the conversation. But their quiet presence helped get me through the first evening of being completely alone since I'd arrived a week ago.

The next morning still feeling nauseous and helpless and despite getting up later to make the day seem shorter, it stretched in front of me as though it would never end.

I missed Francis and Bob and their jolly company and now all I could do was count the hours till David arrived to help me get to Alecos.

The reports on the radio didn't help me feel better

either. Each day events just seemed to get worse and worse. Turkish forces has used a clear and hold strategy when they landed. By the time the UN cease fire convoys were agreed, the Turkish forces had only secured a narrow corridor between Kyrenia and Nicosia, but since that time, three thousand Greek Cypriots in the north had already fled their homes in fear. Then there was no stopping the Turkish army. With their superior man power and NATO supplied weapons and tanks, they steadily encroached east and west of the agreed corridor. So the fighting continued with the Turks advancing even further.

The Cyprus National Guard to their credit, were managing to put up a heroic defence, But with the fall of the Greek Colonels after the Turkish invasion, there would no longer be a supply of arms and ammunition arriving from the mainland, so they were steadily forced to withdraw south.

The whole situation was demoralising and frightening.

In Geneva, the talks between the foreign ministers of the three guarantor powers which had begun on 25th July, continued. But all they could agree on was to hold another set of talks at a later date!

I'd lost track of the days but now I realised that today was Sunday. I had an urge to visit the church even though I wasn't religious,

When I arrived, the old ladies of the village, in their black Sunday clothes, were just leaving. By now they recognised me and greeted me warmly as I waited outside while they gossiped before slowly dispersing to their homes. Then I entered the cool enclosure of the church.

In Greek orthodox churches everyone stands, but inside this church were a couple of benches as the congregation now only consisted of old ladies. I sat down and gazed at the frescos and icons of the saints on the beautiful gold painted iconostasis, the partition dividing the congregation from the priests and altar behind it. The peace and calm of the atmosphere seemed to sooth me. I closed my eyed and my mind became blank and my tension fell away. Maybe I fell asleep but on leaving the church, I felt recharged and refreshed and ready to face the world again.

During the week, I'd got into the habit of borrowing a book from the Fletcher collection. Then in the shade of the vine-covered terrace with Princess curled up on my lap, I would lose myself in the pages.

This time, without thinking, I'd picked up *Bitter Lemons* by Laurence Durrell.

I'd read it before and enjoyed it but today it was a bad choice.

The story was set, in the beautifully romantic village of Bellapais where the author Laurence Durrell had a home, quite near to our own house just outside Kyrenia.

The village nestled in orchards perched high on the hillside. It was crowned by the loveliest ruined abbey, the gardens filled with roses and geraniums, with views of the sea through the ruined arches of the cloister, through which swallows darted and soared.

In the centre of the cloister, delicate tracery still clung to some of the arches and, four old cypress trees rose like green fingers pointing to the sky.

Built around 1270, the white monks of Bellapais had enjoyed royal patronage and wealth but over time they had become corrupt.

They feasted and drank to excess and took wives, some as many as three and only accepted their own children as novices. This immorality continued for almost one hundred years.

It was easy to see how the monks had become decadent. In the balmy air and luxuriant countryside, the whole area has a sensual, seductive feel. But it came to an end when the Genoese army lay siege to Kyrenia and looted the Abbey.

Today I read the story with deep sorrow; I knew by now, that this time it was the invading Turkish army who had captured and sacked Bellapais. It was too sad to contemplate.

Putting the book down and wiping away the tears, I pulled myself together and set off to walk through the village.

Over the previous week the villagers had got used to seeing me and greeted me with smiles and gossip. With their gappy teeth and heavy mountain accents, it was sometimes hard to understand what they were saying, but I smiled back and nodded and they seemed quite happy with my limited response.

Once I'd been to the local coffee shop. When I'd entered, the place fell silent and the old men raised their eyebrows. Custom had it that the *Kafeneon* coffee shop was basically the reserve of men so women were rarely seen in such a place.

But as they'd got used to seeing me about in the village the fact that I was invading their sanctuary was more or less accepted. After all, what could a foreigner know about the rules and manners of the village! They greeted me politely and then ignored me.

The only woman there was the old lady who owned it. Her face was shrunken and seamed with wrinkles, like a peach stone, but her moist brown eyes were alert and friendly.

I ordered a coffee, and with a toothy smile she

presented me with her house *glyco*, a whole green walnut embalmed in heavy spiced syrup.

Even though I didn't have a sweet tooth, this sticky, spiced walnut was absolutely the most perfect accompaniment to a strong bitter black coffee that I had ever tasted.

Apart from the fact that it was so delicious, it would have been an insult to her hospitality to refuse anything that was offered

The ladies of the villages made sweetmeats from whatever fruit was in season. They were offered to every guest who visited the house and served with a tiny two-pronged silver fork on small glass saucers. Even melon and orange peel were steeped in heavy syrup. During the years of living in Cyprus I'd tasted them all but the walnuts were my favourite.

As the young men had left the village to fight, only the old men were left in the kafeneon. They spent their days there drinking coffee and brandy and arguing about politics. They wore long leather mountain boots supposedly protection from the vipers in the fields. As the same last was used for both right and left feet the boots made them look bandy legged while their baggy black trousers 'vrakas' were worn like large babies nappies. It was a style that had been worn for generations. Rolling their worry beads between gnarled fingers, they gazed out at the passing world, though nothing much was passing these days. But these old men kept up the traditions of a lifetime, often dozing on their cane-covered chairs, their empty coffee cups balanced on another chair in front of them.

Some played cards, slapping down their trumps with histrionic fierceness.

The others, playing Backgammon *Tavli*, throwing

the dice on the table with a clatter, shouting loudly as they slapped their counters on the wooden *Tavli* board, all the time arguing or gossiping about their neighbours. It was amazing that these wizened old men could make such a deafening noise. They pressed pale brandies on one another with insane generosity and covered the floor with cigarette stubs, before finaly, heaving themselves unsteadily away to their families for lunch, leaving one or two still sleeping on their chairs in the untidy bar.

After their siesta, they returned to take up their positions again on their chair and continue with their drinking, smoking, card playing and noisy politics till it was time to return home once again for supper and bed. Life was simple and predictable for these old mountain men, most of whom lived to a great age.

So the day passed. When I got back to the hotel Mrs F came out to greet me to make sure I was OK. She certainly was taking a maternal interest in my wellbeing and I was grateful as it made me feel less alone. Again she invited me to eat with them.

This evening I was on better form after my miserable contribution the previous night. The talk flowed and we got to know each other on friendly terms rather than as hotelier and guest. Colin Fletcher had been an RAF flight commander posted to exotic countries during his working life but, they had chosen Cyprus with all its simple charms, to retire to and had several very happy years there already.

Clare Fletcher had worked in the city as PA to some important banker before she met Colin but had settled without trouble to the military life of an officer's wife with its constant entertaining and moving to new and exciting places.

She knew I was depressed and worried about

Alecos so she asked if I would like to join them the next day when they went off to Limassol for their weekly shop.

I was pleased to accept, as it would keep me busy and distract me from moping about.

Mrs F was thoughtful and caring and I felt that she, like Frances, was treating me like a surrogate daughter. I hadn't realised how much I missed my mother but now, I had suddenly discovered two new ones. It gave me a warm feeling. I no longer felt so completely alone.

So off we went the next morning. It was stimulating to be in the hustle and bustle of a town. Going to the busy market with Mrs F (I hadn't got used to calling her Clare yet) comparing prices of the fish and vegetables or window shopping for the latest dresses and shoes, felt as though life was normal again. But it also made me aware of just how cut off and lonely I was in the mountains. I had no idea how long I would have to stay there. And more to the point, would I find my home intact if and when I was finally able to return to Nicosia?

23

Wednesday 1st August

The day spent in Limassol made me feel much better and the good feeling spilt over into Tuesday, which I spent in the sun on the terrace contentedly reading.

Then it was Wednesday. The day I'd been waiting for had finally arrived. David would be here today.

After breakfast, I took up my regular spot on the terrace with my latest book and the cat. I was spending so much time reading I was getting through almost a book a day.

Mrs F came out to clear away the breakfast things. She had taken to calling me the Sphinx as I sat so long in that particular chair. She definitely sounded like my mother who use to make me go out to play when I was a child instead of sitting all day reading.

"What time are you expecting your friend, David?" she asked.

"He won't be earlier than eleven. He has to drive from Paphos, and it's a difficult journey across the winding mountain roads."

She nodded. "I'll bring you a coffee a bit later but now I'll leave you to your book as I know you won't move from that chair."

As it got to mid-morning I began to get anxious, perhaps he couldn't make it after all. Maybe he'd had an accident or got lost! My stomach began to churn again with worry. I couldn't sit any longer. I threw my book down and stood up. Princess, who had been sleeping soundly on my lap, slid to the floor with an indignant 'meow'.

I wandered out to the front entrance to wait. Within minutes David pulled up and jumped out of his car.

"Sally!" he exclaimed in pleasure as his strong arms enfolded me tightly. The sensation of being crushed against him was exhilarating. It was so long since I'd had any physical contact with anyone and I yearned for it. His hands moved affectionately over the curve of my shoulders to just above my elbows.

"You were always there waiting for me when we were together' he whispered, stroking a lock of hair from my face as he gently kissed my cheek before reluctantly releasing me. Then taking me firmly by the elbow, he steered me in the direction of the reception desk."

Mrs F was there waiting. She smiled conspiratorially at me and raised an eyebrow in appreciation. He was a very good-looking man!

The formalities over, we strolled out to the terrace. Mrs Fletcher was there in a moment, placing a bottle of wine on the table.

"On the house," she smiled mischievously, then disappeared back into the kitchen.

"She seems a very nice lady," David exclaimed. "You must be very well looked after here."

"Oh yes, I am," I nodded vigorously. "I'm the only one here now so she seems to have taken me over. The other guests went to Akrotiri to get away on the airlift. They were a very nice couple who were here on a bird watching holiday. They were good company and I gave them a letter to deliver to my parents as they live quite near each other in Oxford-shire. I hope they are back safely by now, they left five days ago and I really miss them," I said wistfully.

"Oh yes, I'm sure they'll be home now," David said stretching his long legs out under the table and settling back into the deep cushions of the sun chair. "It was chaos when the first huge wave of civilians descended on the base. But the RAF is doing a fantastic logistics job bringing in planes from all over to get everyone safely through the system to their various destinations."

"Yes. I heard on the news they even had someone from Puerto Rico!" I laughed. "But I'm sure they didn't send a special plane to fly him back there!"

He smiled too, making deep creases in his sunburned cheeks. "Anyway, enough talk about refugees and airlifts," he said. "Let's relax and enjoy the day and start with a glass of wine to help us along."

He opened the bottle and poured the wine. It was golden and cold and in the warm sun, the glasses frosted at once. We lifted them and briefly touching the rims together, I looked into his familiar deep blue eyes.

"Sally," he sighed. "I'm so glad to be here with you again. You look marvellous. I was so looking forward to your company and your mischievous sense of humour. What more could a fellow want?"

I laughed happily. "You still have a way with words, don't you?"

David's flirtatious chat and powerful presence was so magnetic, that I allowed myself to enjoy it for the moment.

He stood the bottle in a patch of shade on the table and took off his jacket. His open necked shirt was almost as blue as his eyes. I remembered how I'd always teased him about being vain and wearing blue shirts to emphasise their colour. We'd had such good times together, I thought nostalgically.

Enough! I warned myself. Alecos should be first and foremost in your mind. You're very vulnerable at this moment so don't let yourself be seduced by past feelings and old memories. It's too dangerous.

I shook my head to clear my mind and took a deep breath.

"What news did you get from Morphou?" I asked, to put us back on a neutral course.

His eyes flashed with disappointment and running his hand through his thick blond hair, he stared intently at me for a moment, but then, he too seemed to realised we should keep our conversation neutral.

"So far things are more or less normal there. The Turkish army seems to be concentrating on the area to the east of Kyrenia, steadily expanding up the Karpas peninsula. It's very sparsely populated, just tiny villages with old people, their few animals and small farms so there is hardly any resistance. To the west they've captured St Ermoloas but that is still far from Morphou so everything is still quiet in that area."

He stared off into space for a moment as though he was reluctant to say something that would upset me. Then he continued quietly: "Alecos could still be in the prison, where at least he would be safe, but according to my information, it's more likely that when the Turks landed, the prisoners were released. Every able-bodied man was needed to fight."

"Oh, that's terrible. He was never a soldier. He doesn't know how to fight. I must get to Morphou somehow," I said anxiously.

"No, Sally. I don't think it would be a good idea.

There are roadblocks everywhere and pockets of fighters roaming the countryside. You could be caught in cross fire on the empty roads or stopped by renegade soldiers and goodness knows what could happen to a woman alone. No, you can't do that. It's much too dangerous!"

"But I have to do something; I can't just sit here not knowing if he's alive or dead," I moaned in anguish, realising this was the first time I'd allowed myself to acknowledge the fact that Alecos might have been killed. A cold shiver ran up my spine and I pushed the thought from my mind immediately.

He drummed his fingers absentmindedly on the table, his brow furrowed trying to come up with a solution. Finally, almost resignedly he apologised. "I don't know what else to suggest, other than for me to take you there."

"Oh David, would you?"

"Of course I will but the trouble is I don't have leave again for another fourteen days."

"That's such a long time to wait. I think I'll have a nervous breakdown before then." Tears rose uncontrollably into my eyes.

"I hate to see you cry, Sally," he said reaching for my hand. "But I don't know what to do to solve this problem."

"No, don't worry. I know it's very difficult for you now. It's not your fault I can't stop crying. I'm just so emotional and frightened these days," I sniffed. "I really am grateful that you are willing to take me, so I'll just have to be patient and sit it out."

"Good girl, you were always tough," he said, patting my hand encouragingly. "The time will pass and we can go together. But I certainly wouldn't suggest you to go by yourself. It would be madness.

If anything happened to you I'd never forgive myself."

"Yes, I'm sure you're right. Thank you," I said tearfully.

At that moment Mrs F appeared with lunch. "It's not much but it will see you through for a while and I have made dinner for you tonight. I hope you like trout?" she said eyes twinkling as she looked at David. He really could make women's heart's flutter.

We enjoyed our 'not much' lunch, which was more than enough, while we chatted about old times, without getting involved with the romantic side of our relationship. Then, we strolled around the garden and down to the river. We didn't go into the village as the villagers would have been scandalised to see me with a man in uniform.

The day passed in a warm haze. I felt so comfortable and relaxed with him. Everything about David was so familiar but that was no surprise as we'd been really close before Alecos came into my life.

I had to keep reminding myself that now he could only be a good friend and not a lover. But in this romantic setting it was very hard to hold myself back. He was a perfect gentleman but I could feel it was a struggle for him too. What we'd had together was over and now my life with Alecos was my priority but I felt guilty that I still found David so attractive and was enjoying his company, while Alecos was somewhere out there suffering.

Mrs F popped in and out, fussing that we had everything we wanted, her eyes lighting up as David smiled and flirted with her. She had definitely fallen under his spell.

She was a good looking woman and must have been used to plenty of flattering attention during the busy exciting social life she'd have enjoyed in the exotic places she'd lived as a senior officers wife. Although she and Colin were obviously happy together, it must have been lonely for her, sometimes, in this small mountain village.

"What time would you like dinner this evening?" she asked David.

I knew tonight's dinner would be special as she wanted to impress him.

"Not too late if you don't mind," he told her. "I have to be back on duty by nine thirty tomorrow morning, so I must leave by six- thirty at the latest. It's a long drive."

"Right," she said. "I'll have a good breakfast ready for you by six. We can't send you off on an empty stomach. So will eight o'clock be OK for dinner then?"

"Yes that will be perfect," David beamed.

I smiled to myself. This time she was fussing over him, like a mother hen!

Eventually the sun set over the valley, the heat went out of the day and I went upstairs to get changed.

I'd hardly been out of my well-worn teeshirts and shorts since I'd arrived in Spilia.

I needed time to make the transformation from scruffy to glamorous for this evening. David had always loved it when I'd dressed up for his regimental dinners or officers' parties. Although he was good looking he never minded sharing the limelight with other attractive people around him.

After I'd showered and washed my hair. I slipped into my one and only strappy cotton sundress, which I'd thrown into my bag in a hurry when we left from Nicosia.

Then, just to make myself feel feminine after so long, I sprayed myself with a light flowery perfume.

David was waiting for me in the reception talking to Mr Fletcher. Breaking off their earnest conversation about cricket, they looked up as I came down the stairs.

"Wow! You look fabulous, that turquoise colour looks amazing against your suntanned skin," David exclaimed in admiration.

Mrs F looked amazed. She'd never seen me really dressed up. She nodded her approval.

"And you are ready on time too!" David remarked.

"Of course I am. Have you forgotten? Punctuality was one of my hang ups."

"Yes, I remember. It's not a bad fault. You know how bad-tempered I get if I have to stand around waiting," he grinned mischievously.

Just as he had when he arrived, he reached out and touched my hair but this time he wound a lock of it around his finger. "Your hair always looks so sleek and shiny. As though you'd polished it. It's so much nicer than the backcombed birds-nest styles that seem to be the fashion nowadays."

I acknowledged his compliment with a happy smile. My hair, thick and dark, was my best feature and I was proud of it.

The night was warm and balmy as we strolled out to the terrace. From below, in the garden, came the guttural croaking of frogs and the monotone burr of the cicadas harmonising with the melodious cords of the nightingale.

Mrs F had already placed a bottle of cooled white wine on the table. We sipped it quietly while we nibbled on the juicy black olives and crispy toasted almonds, which accompanied it.

By now it was dark. Moths circled, round the lanterns on the terrace, casting romantic flittering shadows around us. But, with moths came the mosquitoes spoiling the romance. Picking up a coaster from the table, I batted them away as they hovered over me ready to pounce.

David chuckled, his smile making deep grooves in the tanned skin between his high cheekbones and strong angular jaw. "Still the same gorgeous Sally, even the mosquitoes can't keep away."

I gave a resigned shrug.

I'd inherited my dark Mediterranean skin from my grandmother, but even that didn't protect me from every biting insect that saw me as a delicious target. Mrs F had obligingly placed smoking mosquito coils under the tables to keep them away. But it was a losing battle.

"I'm really looking forward to dinner," David said. "The food in camp is good but sometimes we are so busy we hardly get time to sit down and enjoy it."

"I'm sure you'll love it tonight. She's a really good cook, but I've been feeling so awful lately I can hardly eat without feeling sick. I'll do my best this evening though as I'm sure she's gone to a lot of trouble."

"Yes, Sally. Just relax and enjoy it. I'm sure you'll be fine. You always had a healthy appetite, as I remember," he said, with a twinkle in his eye.

At eight Mrs Fletcher announced dinner was ready. On the table the candles made the crystal glasses gleam like iridescent prisms casting rainbow patterns on the soft white lace tablecloth and napkins. The silver cutlery glowed beside the beautiful porcelain dishes.

"The table looks absolutely beautiful!" I exclaimed in delight.

Mrs F smiled proudly. "Yes, it's a long time since I felt like doing anything special. The clients who come here are mostly walkers and bird watchers and they like things rustic. They don't want 'five star' elegance. I enjoyed decorating the table tonight because I felt it would be appreciated by such a beautiful couple."

"Thank you. We really feel grateful for what you are doing for us," I said, genuinely touched by her kindness.

Then she brought the food.

First she served us a delicious platter of baked vegetables with a thick creamy yogurt dressing with fresh herbs. At the end, we mopped the succulent juices up with hunks of freshly baked village bread. It wasn't exactly, 'five star' behaviour on our part, but it was so delicious and I didn't even think about feeling sick!

"That was absolutely wonderful!" David beamed, as Mrs F removed the plates, smiling proudly at his reaction.

Next, came the special main course, two big rainbow trout, fresh from the fish farm up the mountain. These beauties had been baked in lemon juice, oil and garlic, garnish with fennel fronds and served with small, waxy potatoes.

Both of us had always loved our food so we relished the exquisite flavours and textures and hardly spoke a word until everything was completely gone.

David was in raptures. He shook his head in astonishment. "That was without a doubt, one of the best meals I've ever had," he told Mrs F when she came out of the kitchen, this time blushing from so much praise.

"Yes," I said. "It really was delicious. The flavour of the fennel with the fish was a taste inspiration. I loved it. The trout at Kakopetria is famous but you've outshone them."

She almost burst with pride at our genuine pleasure.

"I'm glad you enjoyed it. Now I'll let you rest for a while before I bring you some mixed fruit and nuts with the cheese to finish," Mrs F said, as she bustled off with the empty dishes.

David gave a contented sigh and sat back in his chair stretching out his long legs, pleasure written all over his face.

"Here I am with you again, Sally, in this beautiful, peaceful, relaxing place, eating the most wonderful food. All that war and fighting feels like it's happening on another planet. I wish this could go on forever. I feel like I've gone to heaven. I've never felt like this before," he said in amazement. "It almost makes me question the choice of my life as a soldier, rather than a life of a hedonist!"

For the rest of the meal he remained thoughtful until we took our coffee and brandies down to the garden so Mrs F could clear the table and finish in the kitchen.

The moon was nearly full casting a silvery glow on the shrubs and trees as we settled on the hammock with our drinks. After our delicious dinner I felt relaxed and satisfied and in the romantic glow of the moonlight I slowly allowed the atmosphere to take over my caution. David must have felt it too, as he moved closer to me.

"Now it's time to finish off this wonderful evening

by kissing you," he said firmly, taking me in his arms. Locked in his powerful embrace he pushed me gently back against the cushions. I closed my eyes in expectation. I could feel the strong beat of his heart along with the rapid pulse of my own. But caution returned almost immediately when I felt him slipping the thin straps of my dress off my shoulders.

"No, David. Stop," I pleaded, opening my eyes and pushing his hand from my arm as he kissed my neck.

He stopped and looked at me with a puzzled expression.

"Why not?" he asked. "I can feel you want it as much as I do."

"Of course I do, but I can't do this. It wouldn't be right." I said desperately, my mind warring with my body that wanted him to continue making love to me.

"Please, David, let me go. I can't think clearly with you as close as this."

"Don't think, feel. Feel my heart beating like yours," he murmured still holding me, refusing to let me go.

"No, David. Stop! My voice made it clear that I was serious. "Of course I want you but I can't let it happen. How could I ever look Alecos in the face again if we made love while he was in prison or wandering wounded round a battlefield? I'd never forgive myself! I'd feel guilty for the rest of my life."

He pulled away and stood up. "I'm sorry too, Sally," he apologised, looking guiltily down at me. "I should never have put you in this position. But being with you here has been so wonderful - like it used to be. I just forgot that our lives have changed and things that were so natural to us before don't apply anymore," he sighed unhappily. "I've never really got over you, you know!"

"Oh, David, I'm so sorry. It's my fault, I took advantage of your kindness and offer of help," I said near to tears. "I love being with you but we're just opening up old wounds."

He sat down again, next to me but not touching and we lapsed into a thoughtful silence. Then taking my hand we walked slowly back through the garden and into the hotel.

At my bedroom door, David drew me to him. We kissed gently, before saying a sorrowful goodnight and he walked dejectedly to his room down the hall. I wanted desperately to run after him but held myself back. I knew that just to take one step towards him would be my downfall. However hard it was for both of us, we realised that now a line had been drawn in our relationship. The romantic ties had been broken but in their place we still had a special lasting friendship.

24

Ann's visit

My alarm clock woke me from another nightmare.
I'd set it early to make sure I didn't miss breakfast
with David before he left. I felt lousy, but David was
pleased that I'd made the effort, as he knew from old,
that early mornings were not part of my normal day.
His mood was subdued but never the less, he was still
insistent that he take me to Morphou on his next
leave.

After breakfast, we studied the map and arranged
a meeting point on the northern side of the Troodos
Mountains overlooking the plains of Morphou.

David's route from Paphos was long and tortuous,
but it didn't seem to bother him, and he was adamant
that he'd be there to meet me.

I was grateful that despite everything, he still
cared enough to want to be there to support me if the
situation turned out to be bad. The meeting was set
for ten thirty in the morning on Tuesday, August 14th.

He thanked Mrs F for her fantastic hospitality and
asked her to keep an eye on me. Then with a cheeky
grin, he gave her a hug and planted a kiss on her
cheek, waving her goodbye as we left the hotel.

At the car, he drew me to him and burying his face
in my hair, held me tightly. Then he pulled away and

without a word, got into the car and drove off. I watched till the car disappeared from view. I missed him already and my spirits fell.

Now the long wait had begun.

Seeing the weeks stretching before me, I couldn't imagine how I was going to live through the endless days. Generally, I was, quite active but there just wasn't enough to do up here alone in a small village tucked away in the mountains. I was reluctant to go off exploring in the car as it was necessary to save my petrol for the long journey to Morphou. The nearest petrol station from here was about twenty miles away.

When I'd taken the Rixs out for the day, I'd gone via the garage and topped up as much as was allowed. Due to the war, petrol was scarce, so there was no way of filling the tank once it was empty.

Mrs F was clearing the breakfast dishes away when I went back into the hotel.

I'd already told them over supper the other night what had happened to Alecos during the coup. And I'd also briefly mentioned my previous connection with David. I now told her that David had insisted on taking me to Morphou to look for Alecos, but it would be almost two weeks before his next leave. In the meantime, he'd forbidden me to go off alone, insisting it was much too dangerous.

"Yes, I agree with him. There are roadblocks everywhere and gangs of trigger-happy youngsters in uniform roaming all over. You can't go wandering off on your own in the present circumstances. Actually, I was surprised to find David such a caring type of man, especially for one so good looking," Mrs F commented. "That type is usually pretty arrogant. We came across quite a few in our time. They thought because of their good looks, they deserved more from life than anyone else! But David was different, very charming and considerate and he certainly thought the world of you."

"Yes, he's a good man. As I told you, I've known him for a few years. He wanted to get engaged, but by then I was in love with Alecos so our relationship ended unhappily."

She raised her eyebrow, waiting expectantly for me to explain. So instead of clearing away the dishes, we sat down together on the terrace and the whole story poured out.

Finally, I concluded: "I'm sure David would have been a very good husband but even if Alecos hadn't been in the picture, I couldn't have married him because I couldn't see myself as a good army wife!'

Then, shaking my head, I continued: "The rules and regulations of military life frightened me. I would probably have been a disadvantage to him before long. I know wives are vetted when there is a promotion due. I'm sure they would have noticed that I'm a bit of a rebel. David thought it was an amusing trait. But he was besotted and couldn't see that it would cause trouble between us and his career sooner or later."

"Yes, I was a bit nervous marrying into the military myself at first," Mrs F agreed. "But fortunately, it worked out fine."

"But in your case, Colin was already a commanding officer when you married, so the dynamics were quite different for you than they would have been for me, starting as a wife of a junior officer."

She nodded. "Yes, knowing what I do now, wives attitudes could certainly be a problem, so you were probably right in your decision."

As our earnest conversation continued, we found we had a lot in common and the morning slipped by. Suddenly Colin put his head round the door to see what had happened to his wife.

"Ah, there you are, my good woman. I've made myself a sandwich and coffee as nothing seemed to be forthcoming. I thought you must have eloped with David," he chuckled. "He really impressed her you know," he said, winking at me.

"Sorry, darling. Sally was rather down after David left so we've been having a girls heart-to-heart," she said, smiling innocently. "We've also made plans about occupying herself while she's here."

Mrs F had confessed that she too was worried what she was going to do with herself now. She had unexpected time on her hands as there were no longer any summer guests to look after due to the war. Colin was always there in the background. He too, had no hotel duties, but it allowed him the guilt free pleasure to spend his time undisturbed in his office, working on his autobiography.

Mrs F didn't have enough to satisfy her active mind so, apart from seeing to Colin's simple needs, her days were empty too.

After our long talk, she and I became friends. We laughed a lot and her lively company helped to keep away my depressions. A couple of times we went off to spend the day together in Limassol. We window-shopped and had long lazy lunches by the beach. It did us both good to have female company and a change of scene.

Sometimes, as she knew I loved to cook, she let me make lunch for the three of us, which gave her a whole day's break to potter in the garden.

In the evening after supper we played cards,

listened to music or Colin would read an extract from his manuscript to see our reaction. He had a highly developed dry sense of humour and our hilarity confirmed his writing was on the right track.

Being occupied helped me sleep better, though I still had horrible nightmares and woke up each time in a sweat, feeling sick with fear.

On the political front there was no cause for laughter though.

According to the Cyprus Broadcasting news, the Turks had started building an airstrip on the plain to land propeller cargo planes. They had moved further west to Lapithos and had captured 30 Greek villages and towns to form a rectangular enclave from Kyrenia to Nicosia. Turkish forces, ignoring the limits agreed at the original ceasefire, had now secured a bridgehead five miles west of Kyrenia and had advanced five miles east so my home was now in enemy hands. Every time I thought about it, I felt like weeping.

In the local newspaper, the General leading the formidable Turkish Commandos, based in the Kyrenian Mountains, was quoted as saying...

We went to Geneva with a plan. We want a division between the Turkish and Greek Cypriot communities to enjoy autonomy in the separate sections. The Cypriots can agree either by diplomatic talks in Geneva or fighting us on the ground. But in the end we'll get what we want, so it's up to them!

The newspaper also reported that, the second round of peace talks in Geneva would be held on Thursday 9th August. But both the Athens and Ankara sides were already threatening to boycott the talks for various reasons so the advance would proceed unhampered and the Generals confident arrogance seemed horrendously feasible.

David had explained to me that this 'threatening to boycott' manoeuvring was part of the normal technique of political pressure. But for us, the population of Cyprus, it was a tragedy.

We waited like helpless bystanders as they played games with our lives.

It was also reported that at the UN headquarters near Nicosia airport, talks had resumed between Turkish, Cypriot and British officers, in an attempt to reach agreement on the ceasefire lines to establish a UN buffer zone between the two sides in Nicosia. But, just like the stalemate in Geneva, hours of talking got nowhere so the Turkish attacks around the airport kept going!

Despite this depressing situation, there was a heartening note that the atmosphere seemed to be less tense in the capital. Some shops were reopening and people were slowly returning to work. I felt my spirits rise as this tiny chink of light appeared.

So the days passed. Then one morning, sitting in my usual place on the terrace with Princess purring contentedly on my lap while I read yet another book from the Fletchers rapidly diminishing stock, my concentration was disturbed by a very distinct chug-chugging noise coming up the hill to the hotel. It sounded exactly like Ann's little red Volkswagen Beetle, as it trundled along.

Jumping up and spilling a very indignant Princess onto the floor, I rushed out to the front entrance, just as the car came to a shuddering halt at the door.

"Ann," I called excitedly. "What are you doing here? I thought you would be in England by now!"

Uncurling herself from the little car, she grinned from ear to ear.

"I fancied a trip to the mountains. I thought you might like some company," she explained, hugging me warmly.

"I'm so happy to see you. I've missed you. Come in. Do you want to stay over? The place is empty so there's plenty of room,' I babbled in excitement."

"Slow down," she ordered. "I'm gasping for a coffee and a cigarette. Let's sit down and when I get my breath back, we can decide. Then we can catch up on the news."

Hearing the excited chatter, Mrs F popped her head round the kitchen door.

"Mrs Fletcher, this is my best friend Ann," I introduced them.

"I'm delighted to meet you, Ann. Sally has told us all about your adventures. I'll bring you some coffee," she bustled off, delighted to have another guest.

"My goodness," Ann exclaimed. "You're well looked after here. I hope the food is as good as the service."

"Yes, without a doubt. Mrs F is great. She fusses over me all the time. I'm the only one here now so we both appreciate the company. We've become good friends. Anyway, you will stay over won't you? We've so much to catch up on. You look absolutely great, by the way. Something must be going very right in your life. I've never seen you looking so good."

"Yes," she nodded excitedly. "I've got lots to tell you, but please let me finish my cigarette first," she insisted.

I was on tenterhooks while she slowly sipped her

coffee and puffed on her cigarette.

"Hurry up," I urged. "You're dragging it out on purpose. I haven't spoken to you for weeks and now you're teasing me with your smelly fag."

She laughed and stubbed the butt into the ashtray. I knew that before long it would be overflowing, as she was almost a chain smoker.

"Now, let's have the news. You look like the cat that's had the cream."

She settled back comfortably in her chair and, in her deep rich voice, she began.

"Do you remember Karl, the Austrian UN doctor I was going out with when you were with David?"

"Of course I do. You were really smitten with him."

"Yes, that's him. I suppose you could say he was the love of my life. I was absolutely devastated when he was transferred," she sighed, remembering her loss.

I nodded. "Yes, I know. You moped around hardly saying a word for weeks."

"Well, now he's back again," she laughed, her eyes sparkling with pleasure.

"That's fantastic! I'm really happy for you. But how did you meet him again?"

"It was fate! I went to stay with my cousin, as you'd suggested. But that really didn't work out, so I decided I would be better off staying in England with my parents after all.

"I went to Akrotiri and had to hang around for a couple of days before my turn came to get on a plane. It was chaos. There were thousands of people to be sent off. Planes kept arriving and taking off almost immediately crammed full of people.

"Anyway, one night, on the way to dinner in the

canteen, I fell into a storm drain. You know how deep they are! It was dark and I was chatting with some people and didn't notice it. I disappeared down the hole and everybody laughed till they pulled me out and saw the nasty graze on my leg which had hit the concrete side of the drain as I fell in. It was a horrible mess, so they took me to the base hospital to be bandaged up, and, who do you think was the Doctor on duty that evening? Karl!"

"Wow!" I exclaimed. "That was a lucky coincidence."

"Yes, amazing. Apparently, he'd volunteered to help during the crisis, as they needed doctors immediately. He'd hardly had time to settle in before he was on duty. So now he's in Cyprus again and all the old feelings are still there?"

She nodded happily.

"But, he's married!" I said hesitantly.

"Oh, No! Not anymore, he isn't," she exclaimed triumphantly. "While he was away in Cyprus all those years ago, his wife met someone else, so eventually they divorced."

"I'm so glad for you, I was worried that you'd get your heart broken again when he went back to Austria."

She shook her head. "No, not this time. Apart from being needed here, he wanted to find me again, to see if we could pick up where we'd left off. So, this is it!"

"That wonderful news, but why are you here then? Why aren't you with him?" I queried.

"He's on a 48 hour shift. He lives off base and as I had nowhere else to go, I moved in with him." She grinned mischievously. "So, I thought I'd use the free time to come up and see how you are doing! Aren't you pleased to see me?"

"Of course I am, Ann. I'm delighted. I'm so happy for you, you've waited long enough to find your Mr Right, so I hope it all works out for you both. You deserve it."

"Life is wonderful for me now and I'm so happy. But," she sighed. "I feel a bit nervous and guilty, though."

"Why?" I asked, puzzled.

"So many people are really suffering because of the war, yet that same war has changed my life for the better and I'm walking on air."

"Oh for goodness sake, don't start feeling guilty about your good luck. Enjoy it while you can. Nobody knows what this war is going to throw at us, so we just have to enjoy anything good that comes along and you have Karl now."

'Yes, you're right as usual, you haven't changed. But here's me gabbling on about my life and I haven't even asked you what news you have of Alecos?"

I sighed. "There's no news. I managed to get hold of David and he's going to take me to Morphou, when he has leave in a few days. He says it's too dangerous for me to go there alone even though the fighting isn't in that area. Hopefully then I can find out what has happened to Alecos. At the moment things are so upside down even the UN are in the dark," I said unhappily. "I don't allow myself to think the worst. But you're happy and I'm happy for you. So let's enjoy our time together and you can tell me all the ordinary day-to-day gossip now that we've had the 'highlights'."

We chattered and laughed for the rest of the day, pleased to be together again.

Smoking like a chimney, she naturally talked

mostly about Karl.

I enjoyed the unusual experience of seeing her so uninhibited with happiness.

The time flew. The ashtray was emptied and replaced several times by Mrs F.

She made Ann very welcome and fussed over her as she did me. She popped in and out with lunch, then tea, then some drinks.

"I didn't realise I would miss having guests to entertain," she admitted as we raised our glasses to her in a vote of thanks. "I thought I'd enjoy my new found peace and quiet instead of rushing around, but I find I really like making sure everyone is happy." And now I have two daughters," she said with a happy grin. "So what would my new daughter like for dinner?"

We carried on talking way after our delicious food, until we were exhausted and ready for bed.

It had been a lovely day. Just like old times!

25

Next day

The next day, Ann didn't have to leave till the afternoon. But she wanted to be back in good time to have dinner ready for Karl.

"My cooking is improving. Karl is a typical Austrian. He likes rich sauces and cream cakes. I'll probably be much fatter the next time you see me. When this is all over you'll have to come to dinner." she said, her eyes twinkling happily.

I chuckled. "I'm looking forward to it. You'll be a specialist in rich creamy Austrian food and I'm an oily Mediterranean cook. Maybe we'll set up a restaurant!"

She laughed, and then became serious. "If things go on like they are, we might have to make it a Turkish one!"

We both fell silent, contemplating what could happen.

Pushing these disagreeable thoughts aside, I changed the subject. "Well, instead of sitting around being miserable till it's time for you to leave; we should go out and enjoy the beauty of the mountains."

She nodded. "Good idea, let's do that."

"Have you ever seen any of the Byzantine painted churches?" I asked her. "There are several around here tucked away in the forest."

"I've seen a couple near Nicosia but never got round to visiting any in the mountains."

"I found a book in Mrs F's library called *The Painted Churches of Cyprus*. It explained the history and the symbolism of the paintings. There are several nearby. I've visited a couple already. They were very old and some of the frescos were still so well preserved."

"But why are there so many up here?" Ann asked.

"Well, during the 7th century, the Arab pirates regularly sacked the coastal towns of Cyprus. To escape the constant raids and destruction, the population steadily moved away from the coast and came up here to the mountains. Consequently they built themselves homes and of course, churches too."

"It would be good to know more about the country before it's lost," said Ann. "It sounds like a good idea."

"There's a church quite near here with a funny name," I explained. "'Pagnagia tou Araca - Our Lady of the Pea'."

"That's a peculiar name for a saint. I've never heard of her!" Ann exclaimed.

"It's one of the lesser-known churches, off the beaten track. But it's full of magnificent frescos, according to my book."

"Right, let's go there."

'We have to drive through the pine forest to get there. We could have a morning of culture and a leisurely picnic before you have to leave," I suggested. "I'll ask Mrs F if she could make some sandwiches for us."

"Sounds good, let's do it."

We drove eastwards from Spilia, on a rough road through the forest, and arrived at the small run-down village of Lagoudera. As usual, there were a couple of old men sitting outside the local *kafeneon* fiddling with their worry beads, waiting for something to happen to enliven their day! The place didn't look promising, but my book said some of the finest frescos in the mountains were in the church.

Just outside the village, we came across the church of 'Our Lady of the Pea', almost hidden from the road by pine trees.

We parked the car in the shade and walked to the remains of the 12th century church across a small field with the dust from the dried peas billowing around us.

It had once been part of a large monastery, but now only the north wing was still standing and covered by a steeply-pitched, tiled roof to preserve it from the winter snow and rain.

Through this roof protruded a rare, undamaged dome.

The whole interior was covered with frescos, some dating back to 1192 AD.

"Wow!" Ann exclaimed. "These are really something, and the colours are so clear, it looks as though they'd been painted yesterday!"

"The book says it was restored only a few years ago," I told her.

"There are so many frescos I don't know where to look first," she added, turning round in a circle

"A good starting point would be the dome. It's the symbolic heaven," I told her, walking to the centre of the church. "This church has the most complete series of paintings from the main Byzantine period, in the whole island," I said, pointing to the fresco in the dome. "That's Christ Pentocrator."

"Pentocrator! What does that mean?" Ann asked puzzled.

"Christ the Ruler of the World," I explained with authority, having read it all up in the book. "Symbolically, he's looking into space supposedly away from the sins of mankind."

"With so many sinners, no wonder he looks so miserable," Ann remarked.

I pointed out a few more frescos then, moving over to one of the archways, I indicated a figure of a skinny old man. "This is the one I really wanted to see," I said. "The figure was a naked old man with long hair and what looked like a large beard hanging to the ground."

"He's a real beauty!" Ann remarked, laughing.

"Yes. This is old St Onoufrius."

"I've never heard of any of these saints," she chuckled.

"Apparently, he's an Ascetic. They practise self- denial and abstain from worldly comforts. He lived in the wilderness and refused to wear any clothes when his old ones wore out."

"But why does he look like he is wearing a sporran? Was he Scottish?" Ann giggled.

"No," I laughed. "I don't think they had Scottish saints in the Byzantine Empire! That sporran thing is supposed to be a young pine tree hiding his loins."

She raised her eyebrows and smiled. "It's all rather overpowering, all these angels and virgins and funny saints. It's enough to give you a headache," she said, rubbing her eyes.

"Yes, I agree so I'm going to look around outside," I said, leaving the cool interior of the church for the warmth of the sunshine.

Wandering around the back of the church in the shade of the pitched roof, bits of masonry were scattered around. Probably they were the remains of the monks' cells from the original monastery.

The warm air was heavy with the aromatic perfume of the pines. There was hardly a sound, only the whisper of the breeze through the trees. As I approached, tiny lizards slithered off the warm stones where they were basking in the sun and scuttled into the dry grass. It was very peaceful and I felt a calmness settle over me as I stood there absorbing the spirit of the surroundings.

Then, into the sound of silence, I heard a crunch of footsteps on the crackly grass behind me. Turning around, I froze in horror.

I was looking down a double-barrelled shot gun and pointing it straight at me, was Spiros.

His bloodshot eyes bulged with elation and his triumphant yell shattered the silence.

"You bitch," he screamed, froth forming at the corners of his mouth. "Now here I find you, I look everywhere," he spluttered, his eyes turning into narrow slits. "Now I kill you," he hissed, waving his gun in fury.

Frozen to the spot, a gasp of terror escaped my lips. "How did you find me?" I croaked.

"Ha! I see car pass in village and I follow," he sneered, his gravelly voice echoing loudly off the walls of the church, As his dirty stubby fingers fidgeted on the trigger, I heard the oiled mechanical click as the twin barrels were cocked.

I was terrified but knew the longer I kept him talking the more chance I had to calm him down. "Why do you want to kill me, what have I done to you?"

"You wife of Alecos, you think you special. You is English. You think me a peasant and dirty. I hate you!" he growled, the gun swinging in ever widening

237

arcs, as he swayed drunkenly, shouting loudly and furiously with pent up frustration.

Out of the corner of my eye, Ann appeared silently round the front of the church. She crept up behind him carrying a brass candlestick. With both hands she lifted the heavy object and brought it crashing down on top of his head, the blood gushing from the open wound.

Collapsing like a stone, with a heavy thud, he hit the ground and lay completely still.

Horrified we stared at the body. "Oh, my God. I've killed him?" Ann whispered in terror as the candlestick dropped from her trembling hands, clattering noisily onto the stony ground.

Shaking with fright, ghostly pale and near to tears, Ann bent over the body. Her eyes clouded with fear as she looked up at me. "What are we going to do now?" she said.

Numb with horror, I shook my head in bewilderment - the realization that Spiros had intended to kill me, and now we'd probably killed him instead, robbed me of my senses for a moment.

Eventually I whispered: "We can't leave him here. we'd better hide him somewhere."

The land by the church was completely flat and featureless. All the wild peas had dried up and become brown stubble in the summer heat. The only place to hide anything was deep inside the pine forest, but that was impossible. We weren't strong enough to drag his body that far. I was desperate to find a place. Frantically looking around I finally spotted a slight unevenness in the ground under some trees.

"Look," I pointed. "I think there's a ditch over there."

Ann nodded distractedly, still too numb to react. I

ran across to see.

It was a narrow gully left by some tree roots of a fallen pine. It wasn't much, but it was better than just leaving him where he had fallen.

So together we each got hold of one leg. He was very heavy but, panting and straining, we slowly pulled the body over to the trees. The physical effort had taken us through our state of shock and we both began to think normally.

I was terrified that Spiros might just be unconscious and would come round before we'd managed to bury him. We couldn't take the risk. So, searching around, I found a large stone and bashed him hard again on the back of the head.

Ann looked startled. "What are you doing?"

"I'm just making sure that he is really dead."

"But, Sally, we could go to prison for murder."

"No, I don't think so," I said thoughtfully. "In the present circumstances, many people will use the war as a cover to settle old feuds. Once the fighting is over there will be too many other things for the authorities to worry about. Sampson and his henchmen will be considered traitors, so the death of one of his bunch won't be a priority. Lots of things will be swept under the carpet, so Spiros would be considered just another casualty of war. After all, the coup and Sampson were the cause of Turkey invading Cyprus. The Turks realised from recent history that with Sampson in charge, every Turkish Cypriot anywhere on the island would be massacred."

Ann shook her head. "You can't be so sure. We still might be in trouble."

'No, I don't think so I'm not worried. The crack you gave him might just have knocked him out. Thumping him again on the head was my contribution. After what he's done to Alecos and me, I enjoyed doing it. It goes just a little way to getting my own back. He's the cause of all our troubles. He had Alecos locked up in order to take over the business, then he tried to rape me and now he was determined to kill me," I said, shrugging my shoulders.

"Anyway, even if he isn't dead, we couldn't have him coming round till we've finished. It could take a while as we still have to bury him. So it could be just enough to keep him quiet till then."

Ann paused as she thought it over, and then nodded. "Yes, one way and another, I think you were justified."

We now had to dig to make the hole bigger. Using our bare hands and the spoons and forks from our picnic hamper, we scrapped away for ages till finally we made it long and deep enough to get most of him in. Then lining him up parallel to the lip of the ditch, we bent down and pushed the body into the narrow space. It was still half visible, so pushing back the soil from the hole and scrapping up great handfuls of pine needles from the thick carpet around the trees, we covered him as best we could.

It took a long time so I was glad I'd given him a thump so he didn't regain consciousness before we'd finished. We topped off the mound with twigs and dead branches of pine and eventually we were satisfied that the body couldn't be seen.

Ann, by now, was fully functional. She picked up the candlestick and scrubbed the blood off with the hem of her skirt, then scurried back into the church to replace it. Meanwhile, using a broken off pine branch, I swept over the scuffed ground to even out the pine carpet so, that in the unlikely event of anyone coming to the church, no one would realise there had been a disturbance there.

We found Spiros' car tucked away amongst the trees. We let a couple of the tyres down and pocketed the keys that he'd left in the ignition.

Finally, we hid the rifle under the picnic bags in the boot of my car and drove hastily away.

Pulling up, with a squeal of brakes, at the hotel, Mrs F came to the door.

"You're back early. I thought you were going to have a picnic," she called, cheerfully. Then seeing our shocked faces as we almost fell out of the car she gasped in concern. "What happened to you?"

We staggered inside and collapsed on the settee in reception. Mrs F, realising something bad must have happened, flew back into the kitchen and within seconds brought us both a coffee with a dash of brandy. As the hot liquid slowly revived us, we haltingly told her about Spiros appearing in the forest. She was shocked but quickly took control of the situation.

"Firstly, Sally, you'd better put your car into our garage. If he's alive, he knows now you are in the area and will probably come looking for it. You, Ann, should get back to Akrotiri as soon as possible. If he's not dead, it's unlikely he'll be getting around very soon as you've got the car keys, though he might have a spare set, but you wouldn't want to meet him on the road as you are driving alone back down the mountain."

Ann, still looking very shaken, nodded and ran upstairs to collect her things. Even though she'd never liked Spiros, the realisation that the heavy blow she'd given him, might be responsible for his death. It would weigh heavily on her conscience, so I was glad she had Carl to comfort and reassure her when she got back.

As she left, we hugged each other tightly. Kissing her on the cheek, I whispered: "Drive carefully and don't worry. You've got Karl to look after you now. You're the lucky one!"

After she'd gone, the full shock of what had happened suddenly enveloped me in a wave of nausea, making me feel drained and dizzy. I stumbled up to my room. Stretching out on the bed, I closed my eyes till the nausea subsided, but when I tried to get up, it returned again and I was violently sick. I knew it was shock and fear that was pushing my mind to the brink of frenzy.

Making a conscious effort to calm myself, I tried to concentrate on my happy day yesterday. But, it was the image of Spiros drunkenly waving a gun in front of me that kept springing to mind. It was terrifying to know he'd been crazed enough to kill me. It sent icy shivers through my body.

The sickness had obviously been brought on by the constant tension, frustration and fear that had built up over the weeks. I'd been unwilling to acknowledge it, but today, with the horror of the encounter with Spiros, it had come to a head.

I pushed my head back against the tightness of my shoulders. The muscles in my neck creaked and felt like lumps of lead as I tried to knead the stiffness away. I knew I was wearing myself down and my nerves were bar-tight. It was obvious I should be taking some sort of medicine to get me out of this depressed state, but what I needed more than any medicine was the end to this waiting and uncertainty. No longer in control of my life, I was just responding to events orchestrated by others.

I'd been so alone and stressed. Aching for the touch of Alecos beside me, the intimacy and warmth of him holding and soothing me with soft words and kisses.

It was the first time I'd allowed myself to feel this longing and silent tears of yearning ran down my cheeks to soak the pillow.

Eventually I heard a gentle knock on the door.

"Is there anything I can do?" Mrs F asked as she peeped round the door. "I was worried about you. You've been up here for such a long time."

Here sympathy and concern finished me off and I burst into sobbing tears.

She hurried into the room. Sitting down on the edge of the bed, she took my hand in her squeezing it comfortingly.

"Shh! Shh!" she whispered. "Have a good cry and let it all out. You've been through so much, I'm surprised it's taken you so long to break down."

I cried and cried while she sat patiently soothing me with quiet words. Finally I came to a shuddering stop.

"You look exhausted," she said. "You need a good deep sleep. Why don't you let me get you something to help you?"

I nodded. "I haven't really slept properly for ages. I try not to think the worst but in the middle of the night I have terrible nightmares or I wake up so early, full of dread and feeling sick with fear, worrying about what's happening to Alecos."

"Well, a mild sleeping pill will relax your mind and drive the nightmares away.

Tomorrow, after you've had a good sleep, I'll give you a low dose anti-anxiety pill to help you through the day. They won't do you any harm," she assured me. "When we were in Nairobi, during the Mau Mau uprisings, sometimes I got so scared, I popped a pill and the screaming fear inside me dissolved just like melting ice and I felt calm enough to carry on."

And that's exactly what happened. The next day after my first full night of peaceful sleep I woke feeling refreshed, instead of fearful. Then with the help of Mrs F's magic pill, I floated through the next couple of day, preparing myself calmly for Tuesday, August 14th and my meeting with David.

As I knew I would wake early, I intended to leave strait away. I couldn't just sit around waiting once I was up and ready and I wanted to be sure to get to the meeting point in good time.

I told Mrs F I'd help myself to coffee and take a bottle of water and some fruit from the fridge. Then I'd make my way steadily to Scouriotissa and when David arrived, we'd go down together in to Morphou town to find Alecos.

26

Tuesday 14th August

Last night I hadn't taken another of Mrs F's pills, in case I overslept, so again my sleep was full of night-mares. I dreamt that Spiros came back to kill me and soldiers with guns rampaged across the countryside chasing Alecos. Once again I woke sweating and terrified. I'd tossed and turned trying to escape in my dreams and the sheets were wet and crumpled. Most mornings I'd just felt sick, but this morning I was so frightened I really was sick. It was very early but there was no way I was going back to bed, I didn't want to fall asleep and drop back into that same nightmare.

The early morning mountain air was cool so wrap-ping my cotton robe tightly round me, I crept outside so as not to disturb the Fletchers. The sun was just tipping the top of the Plane trees with a golden light. It was silent except for the distant tinkling of bells as the goats grazed peacefully in the pastures around the village.

Princess sidled up and wrapped herself round my bare legs purring contentedly. She walked with me to the bottom of the garden. I concentrated on the movement of my body, not allowing myself to think too much about the day ahead and the frightening truth I might discover when I got to Morphou.

Never having been to Morphou over the mountain roads before, I mentally went over the route I'd visualised from the map that would take me to the meeting point with David. I didn't want to be late or get lost, as signposts on the mountain roads were few and far between.

Eventually hearing a noise in the kitchen as Mrs F got up to start the day, I put my head round the kitchen door.

"Good morning," I said.

"My goodness, you're up early," she exclaimed, surprised.

"Yes, I had a dreadful night so I went for a walk with Princess."

"I must say you don't look so good. I'll make you a coffee and a piece of toast to get you going."

"Thanks, I could do with it, I feel terrible and I have to leave early to meet David."

"I don't envy you. You'll have a lot of driving to do today to get to Morphou."

As it would take me about two hours to get to the meeting place just outside the mining village of Scouritissa, meaning 'Slag Heap'. I gave myself a good margin for error, so I set off just before eight o'clock.

Since 2000BC, Cyprus owed much of its ancient glory and posterity to the extraction and processing of copper. Even the name 'Cyprus' was the ancient Greek name 'Kypros' meaning copper. The mines fell into disuse for many centuries, but were revived by the British at the beginning of the nineteen hundreds when it was decided there was enough copper extract lying around the slag heaps to make it viable, but as the deposits thinned out, most of the mines were abandoned.

The Cyprus Mines Corporation, with its headquarters in the village of Scouriotissa now worked the few that were left.

The roads were almost empty except for a few people stirring as I passed through the villages. I tried to get the morning news on my car radio but it was impossible. The reception was crackly and the signal kept getting lost round the tortuous bends of the mountain roads.

Switching off in frustration I sang to myself instead. Trying to remember the words of the latest songs kept my mind off what I might find ahead of me. I'd heard on the radio, the previous week that Turkish forces were advancing steadily west, day-by-day getting nearer to Morphou. In the week, there had been heavy fighting in Lapithos and Karavas. These villages were a long way west of the original corridor they'd claimed was their desired target when they landed twenty-five days ago. When would they stop? How much more of the island had they planned to capture?

Also during the past week, yet another Geneva conference had been held.

This time, the newly proclaimed president of Cyprus, Glafcos Clerides and Rauf Denktas the leader of the Turkish Cypriots were present. But still nothing constructive was resolved, much to the anguish of the Greek Cypriot population.

Driving steadily north, on an almost direct route, it took ages to cover a few miles as the road twisted and turned. Provided I didn't miss my turn, I felt that I would make the meeting point in plenty of time.

For David, on the other hand, it was going to be a difficult and tiring journey. He had a three-hour cross-country route, constantly doubling back on himself, climbing round the mountains on rough roads. I didn't envy him. It really was a labour of love that he was willing to do it for me.

Eventually I got to the meeting point, just outside the village, at the junction of the single gauge railway which connected the Company headquarters to its main mine a few miles to the west.

I arrived early but it was a dismal spot to pass the time.

The area resembled a scrap yard. Wooden sleepers and scaffolding poles were scattered in untidy piles. Spilling out of torn sacks onto the dirt yard where crystals of pyrites and other minerals glistened in the sunshine. Several wagons and sections of rolling stock sat empty and rusting on the rail track. The place seemed abandoned, as there was no sign of anybody working, though a big dog was chained up by one of the buildings. I assumed that the mines must be closed as all the able bodied men would be away fighting the Turks.

Sitting in the car, I sipped from a bottle of water and nibbled on a ham roll that Mrs F had insisted I take with me.

I knew David would be on time. Punctuality was part of his daily army life. He loved the military, its organised life and the way it looked at the world. He enjoyed the male bonding and camaraderie with his men and was comfortable in his duties and responsibilities as an Officer. He respected the rituals and the deference to seniority, and the good-natured rivalry between regiments. He really was a born soldier.

I think that if I'd married David I could have been happy with him. He was a generous, considerate and loving man. But, even if I'd managed to live with the rules and regulations of military life, there would still have been the loneliness of long absences as he responded to his duties and the constant threat and perils of war. I would have been in fear for his life on a daily basis. I know I didn't have the temperament to cope in those circumstances without cracking up.

The commercial world was more my scene. It could be nerve racking, dirty and cut throat. One could be ruined financially but nobody would be killed!

Glancing down at my watch, I saw it was nearly ten o'clock, David would be here soon.

I waited, ten, fifteen, thirty minutes. Something must have happened, he was never late. The minutes passed slowly. Eleven o'clock, still no David. Something was definitely wrong. What should I do? I could not just sit here!

I decided to drive slowly to Pendya, the next village along the main road and wait there as I couldn't stay in this miserable place any longer.

There was no one to leave a message with so scrabbling in my bag for a piece of paper I wrote that I'd wait at Pendaya till twelve thirty. Then searching round in the wooden piles, keeping well away from the barking guard dog, I found a couple of rusty nails to stake my message securely to an electricity pole by the road. David, with his army-trained awareness, was sure to notice its pristine whiteness standing out against the dusty debris.

Driving slowly to the main road through Scourio-tissa village. I saw that too was deserted. On a normal day it should have been bustling, being the administrative hub of the mining community. The whole area was empty. It felt spooky. Something was very wrong.

The road to Pendaya, unlike the winding mountain roads, was completely straight.

In the distance was the great sweep of Morphou Bay. The sun sparkled on the waves out at sea but there seemed to be a pall of mist hanging over the vast green plain where huge orange plantations and cut flower farms flourished in the fertile soil of the richest farming area in Cyprus.

Far down the straight road something shimmered like a mirage. As I drove nearer it appeared to be straddling the road. Getting closer I realised it was a heavily sand-bagged roadblock defended by several well-armed soldiers, waving their guns frantically and shouting.

I approached cautiously. David had warned me about roadblocks and trigger-happy young soldiers. There was nowhere I could turn around. If the worst came to the worst I would have to put the car in reverse and put my foot down hard.

I crept slowly nearer till I heard what they were shouting.

"You can't pass," they yelled.

"I'm going to Morphou," I shouted back.

"No, no you can't go there."

"Why not?" I asked frantically as I crept close enough to talk.

"The Turks have captured Morphou. They attacked during the night and anyone who didn't escape in time is either a prisoner or dead."

"No," I screamed in agony. "My husband was there, in the prison."

"No, he can't have been! Everyone was let out to defend the town. He could have escaped in the dark but you must go back. The Turks are advancing fast and we will have to withdraw from here soon, before they reach us. Go now quickly. If they catch you they will rape and kill you."

Shocked and distraught, I drove blindly back, my mind a blank, not aware of time, or distance, not anything. The car must have driven itself on autopilot.

Now, the Turks had captured Morphou. I had lost Alecos completely.

I didn't know what to do next. The future was a void.

Eventually I arrived in Spilia, though how I got there without coming off the road I don't know.

Mrs F came rushing out as I pulled up at the hotel.

"Thank God you're here. We thought you'd be back hours ago. Just after you left the radio announced that the Turks had advanced in the night and captured Morphou. We thought you would have heard it on the radio?"

"No, the reception was terrible. There was a lot of crackle and interference and I couldn't make out anything, so I switched off."

"So did you go all the way to Scouriotissa?"

"Yes, I waited there for David but he didn't come. I couldn't understand why he wasn't there."

Mrs F nodded knowingly and explained: "They would have cancelled his leave when the Turks advanced during the night. He'd have been sent out somewhere on observation duty, probably near Morphou. He must have been frantic wondering if you were waiting at Scouriotissa. Hopefully, like us, he would have thought you'd heard the news and turned back."

"Yes, you're probably right. I was so worried. It was so unlike him not to turn up."

"So what did you do then?" she asked, as Colin hurried into reception with a worried look on his face.

"She's ok," Mrs F said to him over her shoulder.

"Well, after waiting for an hour I drove on towards Morphou," I explained. "I was stopped by a road-block. The soldiers told me what had happened and insisted I go back as the Turks were still advancing. They reckoned Alecos had been released as the army advanced, so he might have been captured or escaped from Morphou and joined up with whatever Cypriot forces were fighting in the area," I burst into tears as I finished in a rush.

Mrs F threw her arms round me. "My poor Sally," she said, patting me comfortingly on the back as I sobbed. "I think another of my magic pills is what you need and something to eat. You didn't have any breakfast. You must be starving."

"Colin," she called. "Will you make a sandwich for Sally and a cup of tea? She's shattered."

Slowly, my sobbing quietened and I was able to eat. I washed the pill down with the tea and sat quietly staring in anguish at Mrs F. She could see I was in shock and couldn't think for myself.

Gently, she took my hand and speaking calmly said: "The best thing for you now is to go back to Nicosia tomorrow. Now the Turks have started on the second stage of their obviously pre-planned opera-tion, in complete contravention of the UN ceasefire, and captured Morphou, the only place left is Famagusta. By then they will have captured the entire north coast, in fact almost half of the island. They've got what they wanted and more. And, unless they intend to take the whole island, I think they will settle in the next few days. If Alecos has escaped, he will eventually be able to make his way home and you should be there when he arrives. He'll have been through a terrible ordeal and probably be traumatised. He'll need you there with lots of love and reassurance so he will feel safe again, just as you will. You can mend together in each other's arms!" she smiled, encouragingly.

So the next morning, after another medicated sleep, I collected my things together.

Paying my bill, it seemed suspiciously small.

"This can't be right. I've been here more than two weeks! The bill is so little, I have enough money to pay for everything," I insisted.

"No, Sally. Keep your money, you've been no trouble. In fact, I consider you family now. And who knows what you'll need in the future."

"That's very kind and generous of you. I'll be eternally grateful to you both for all you've done for me and I'll never forget you," I sniffed, almost in tears again.

Not only was she very considerate but, just like my mother, Mrs F had anticipated my needs for the days ahead and set out my programme.

"You'd better take the main road down to Limassol. Colin has topped up your petrol tank so you have enough to get there and fill up at the garage in town. You've been up and down that road a few times these last weeks so you know the way. It will be much safer than the cross-country route you took when you arrived here. Then take the main road into Nicosia, which you obviously know. There probably won't be much traffic on the roads, but I'm sure there will be someone coming along who could help you if you need it."

I was overwhelmed by their kindness. All I could do was tearfully nod my head in thanks.

"And another thing," she said, ticking off the instructions on her fingers. "I've packed you a few staples to take back with you, as I know you've got nothing at home. I remembered the story about the 'feast' you had with Ann the evening the Turks invaded."

Mrs F chuckled at the memory. "So I've packed eggs, tomatoes and cucumbers and water for the journey with some fruit. Colin went to the baker earlier and got you some bread and cheese. That's another reason why you should go via Limassol. You can stop off at a grocery shop and get a few more provisions. Who knows what shops you'll find open in Nicosia after it's been deserted for so long."

She'd thought of everything, realising that my mind was still only functioning on go-slow. She really was a good woman. I was so grateful. They had helped me through some of the worst weeks of my life and I would never forget it.

I promised to phone to let them know I'd arrived safely as soon as I got home.

Then, with lots of tears, hugs and kisses, we said goodbye.

27

Return to Nicosia

The journey back from the mountains had been tiring but uneventful.

Fortunately our building seemed to be undamaged though the apartment smelt musty and neglected but it began to feel more like home once I'd opened the shutters and widows to let in some air and light.

Walking into the bedroom I noticed old Mrs Panayiotis was still sitting by her window across the way. Nothing seemed to have changed. She looked as though she'd been there all the time I'd been away. I gave her a wave and could see her smile as her frail arm waved back.

So much had happened in a few days, it made my head spin. It felt as though I'd been in turmoil forever but in fact, all the real upheaval had started just one month ago, with the beginning of the coup.

In that short space of time the lives of everyone on our wonderful island had been turned upside down. Thousands of people had lost their homes and their livelihoods and many more had lost their lives. Now, the Turkish invaders had captured almost half the island, what new horrors would be inflicted on us?

I'd completely lost contact with Alecos for almost this whole month and now, for the first time, I acknowledged the fact that I might even be a widow!

But the very moment that dreadful possibility entered my head, I pushed it away. I wasn't ready to live with the possibility of that fact yet.

I wish I'd thought to ask for some of Mrs F magic pills before I'd left the mountains. I knew I was going to need them, as I was ready to burst into tears again.

Thinking of the magic pill reminded me to I pick up the phone. Relieved to find it still connected, I let the Fletchers know I'd arrived. Their concern and best wishes helped to boost me up again and after a long encouraging conversation I hung up and vowed to pull myself together to start my life once again in Nicosia.

I went into practical mode. My first job was to make sure the electricity and running water were working. Next, I set about moving the mattresses that were still in the hall. Enough had happened to me one way or another without tripping over them and adding a broken ankle to the list.

It was heavy and awkward work. I felt stiff and dizzy when I finally finished, I had to sit down and rest before I had enough energy to generally tidy up after the long absence.

A couple of newspapers were still on the settee in the lounge where Alecos had dropped them when I'd rushed in from the roof. The thought of him sitting there brought a lump to my throat but I wouldn't let myself cry anymore. In the last few weeks I'd cried, sobbed and howled more than in my whole life. I was amazed that there were any tears left in my system but there always seemed to be more lurking close to the surface.

The food parcel Mrs F had thoughtfully prepared for me plus some bits and pieces I'd picked up on the way through Limassol were a godsend. The larder was practically empty so it would see me through till I could do some shopping if I could find somewhere open.

Looking through the bullet hole in the cracked glass of my kitchen window, I noticed signs of activity in the garage below. First thing next morning I would fill up both the cars. Although I didn't expect to be going anywhere, it would be a sensible idea.

At the same time I'd take a run out to the supermarket. If it was open I'd stock up on whatever was available. Not that I anticipated having guests, but I still had to eat!

By now it was dark and I was exhausted. I prepared the picnic Mrs F had provided and I switched on the radio to listen to the British Forces news.

It was reporting that during the day, the last defence of Famagusta had collapsed. However, as the Cypriot forces had withdrawn, they had managed to destroy two Turkish M47 tanks.

"Hooray!" I threw my arms in the air. Even a tiny success was heartening.

There had also been fighting around Nicosia too. In the encounter, one Turkish tank was destroyed by fire and a number of others were forced to retreat. To date, this had been the only tank-to-tank battle of the conflict. At least the Turks hadn't had it all their own way. Anything was better than nothing!

That night, after my tiring drive back to Nicosia and the relief of being in the safety of my own home, I slept the sleep of angels in the comfort of my own bed.

On waking next morning I made myself a light breakfast in preparation to face the first day of a new life. I still felt nauseous but by now I'd become used to the feeling so it didn't bother me.

In the carport I looked more closely at the damage the Turkish air force had made to Alecos' Mercedes car on my frantic escape from Kyrenia. But despite the battering, it was still usable, so I filled both cars with petrol.

Then on to the supermarket. It was open and I found enough basic rations to last me for a few days. The store itself was almost empty of people. The few that were there huddled together in groups recounting their various experiences in subdued voices. They were still shell shocked at what had happened but determined to put it behind them and carry on with their lives as best they could. Just as I was!

After that, I took a slow careful drive out to our office block. Nobody was about apart from a few soldiers manning a roadblock further up the road towards the airport. Thankfully, our building was still intact, except for some broken windows on the upper floor. So far so good. Part of my life was still intact.

Back in the city, it, too, was almost empty of people but there were walls splattered with bullet holes, smashed windows and piles of rubble from buildings that had been hit.

Arriving back at the flat, I set about putting groceries away and doing mundane jobs, anything to keep myself and my brain occupied.

CBC news was constantly on. The statistics they were reporting were overwhelming. I could hardly believe my ears.

It seems that in the last two days, in an obviously pre-planned and rapid advance, the Turkish forces moved to occupy all of the north of the island. The advance halted almost precisely on the 'Attila' line proposed by Turkey in 1965, but rejected by the United Nations mediator of the day. So now, after a twenty year wait, they had finally achieved their aim and almost a third of Cyprus was under their control.

Over 180,000 Greek Cypriots had been dispossessed and had fled their homes. This Attila line put Famagusta, Kyrenia and Karavas as well as Morphou and the northern half of Nicosia in their possession. The area represented almost one third of the island and contained two thirds of its tourism, two thirds of cultivated land and sixty percent of water resources, industrial plant, mining and quarrying.

The amount of land and resources the Turks now controlled was devastating. How was the south ever going to survive?

They had invaded on the pretext of ensuring the safety of the Turkish Cypriot population and acquiring a land corridor to the sea. It could be argued that they had right on their side, as they were joint guarantors of the independence of Cyprus and Turkish Cypriots had to be protected.

Now it was clear, this argument had been just an excuse to keep the diplomats and NATO powers out of the way while they got a foothold in order to capture the whole of the north coast. Even when they pressed on and captured land on either side of the corridor and then advanced steadily east and west, contrary to their original agreement, the Western Powers stood back and let it happen.

All they had to do now, was to proclaim an Autonomous Turkish State in the northern area of the island and no one would, or could, stop them.

I was reeling from the impact of these facts. How could the Greek Cypriot population pull itself up from such unimaginable losses? It seemed an almost impossible task.

Then, to bring this terrible situation closer to

home, I had to consider what would happen to our business without Alecos at the helm?

I knew nothing about the finances except that we owed a lot of money to the bank for the loan on the machinery of the new production line.

I had no idea who I could go to for help. There was no one around. Most of my friends were foreign women married to Cypriots. They, by now, with their children, would have been evacuated to their home countries. Their husbands would be fighting in some capacity against the Turks. Once the war ended, the men that were left would trickle back to their businesses. But for now there was nobody around.

The only person who came to mind once again, was Commissioner Marcos.

When the Sampson regime was toppled by the Turkish invasion, the supporters of Makarios had formed a new government to carry on his work. The Commissioner would most certainly be back at his post in the new set-up.

As there was no one else I could think of, I decided it would do no harm to phone him.

The Commissioner's private phone rang for a long time. Just as I was giving up in despair, a female voice answered. I assumed it was his secretary.

"I'm sorry to disturb the Commissioner. My name is Mrs Sally Lytras. I'd like to speak to him if he is available?"

"I'm sorry," she said, rather bossily. "He's very busy. Try again later."

My heart sank. She didn't want to put me through. Then I heard her whispering. Some moments later the Commissioner spoke. "Mrs Lytras, where are you?" he asked in surprise.

Explaining as simply and briefly as possible, he

listened as usual without interrupting.

"I don't know what to do or who to turn to. Everyone I know has left and I desperately need help and advice," I said.

There was a long pause. Then he replied: "Of course I'll help you if I can, but everything is piling up today. You know the Turkish Army now controls a third of Cyprus?"

"Yes. I heard it on the news. It doesn't bear thinking about. It makes my troubles sound trivial but I still need help."

"I'll try to come over tomorrow morning early and see what I can do for you."

"Thank you. I know you are frantically busy so it's very kind of you to spare me some time. I hope to see you tomorrow."

As I put the phone down a wave of relief swept over me. But it was short lived. For hours now I'd felt my inner strength ebbing. The effort of holding myself together and trying to be positive about my new situation was proving almost impossible.

In my weakened state, my desperate longing for Alecos and the yearning to be held in the safety and reassurance of his arms was growing to such a pitch that I could feel I was coming ever closer to the brink of panic.

But I mustn't think of Alecos. I had to push all thought of him out of my mind. To imagine him coming back was a dangerous fantasy. It could cloud the brutal and stupefying reality of what was really happening.

Collapsing onto the settee, the tears started to fall again. There was nothing I could do to stop them. I cried and cried. I felt my body was being rung out like a wet dishcloth. Eventually the only sensible thing I could think to do was make myself the proverbial 'cup of tea.'

As I set about making it the thought of it made me feel sick. This had never happened before. A cup of tea had always been the 'cure all' for my troubles, but now I couldn't face it. Perhaps a coffee would be better. I started again but just the smell turned my stomach over.

What was happening to me? My body was rejecting habits established over a lifetime!

Suddenly, stopping dead in my tracks, the cup fell from my hand and smashed into a thousand pieces on the floor. Rushing to the telephone desk in the hall, I snatched up my calendar. When did I have my last period?

I'd gone through one harrowing experience after another and the days had become muddled. I couldn't remember having had a period recently. Maybe some event in the calendar would jog my memory.

Looking back at my engagements on the pad, I remembered my period finished just before Alecos left for Germany on 15th June. He'd been away just short of two weeks. We'd gone straight to Paphos for the weekend when he returned.

After that we were working flat out making the new hair colours.

My periods were always pretty regular, so by rights it should have been due around the 12th July. The coup started on 15th and from then on our normal world began to fall apart. So my period was the last thing on my mind.

Since then, I knew I hadn't had one and now it was 16th August. That's just over two months!

I remember I started feeling depressed and tearful about the time I got to the mountains. I'd also felt aches and pains but I'd put them down to stiffness from no exercise and sitting around reading for so many hours. My emotional behaviour could have been a logical explanation for the fact I was frantic and frightened about what might be happening Alecos!

Being a rational person, I'd never been prone to tears and hysterics. Yet, for the last three weeks, I'd felt completely out of control even to the extent of being sick. This was something I hadn't done since I was a child.

Thinking back to the almost constant crying and depressions, then waking most mornings feeling flushed, achy and sick, I realised what an idiot I'd been. I ran my hands over my body. My breasts felt fuller and tender to the touch. My fingers ran over my stomach. It used to be hollow but now it felt fuller and more solid but not in the same way it did when I'd eaten too much.

My body was just doing what it was meant to do when one was pregnant.

I couldn't believe it. I was...pregnant.

My legs gave way and once again I collapsed onto the settee in absolute surprise and elation. I couldn't take it in. I had never felt so connected and yet so in awe of my body. Waves of emotion washed over me. First, disbelief, then happiness and joy, expressed in a great feeling of accomplishment and relief at my fertility as a woman and my ability, at last, to grow and nurture life. I was bursting with euphoria and wanted to run upstairs and shout it from the rooftop.

Alecos would be so excited and proud of me. He'd be overflowing with love and relief that at long last his dream of being a father would be realised.

Then my skin turned clammy and tears of despair tumbled down my cheeks.

This should be one of the greatest events that could happened to me in my life, but Alecos, the love of my life wasn't here to share in the happiness and joy of this precious moment. Loneliness and regret wrapped round me as I realised that we might not be seeing this child together.

I sat for ages on the settee in a state of shock. I couldn't believe that life would give me the treasure of a child with one hand and take Alecos away with the other.

How could it be so harsh and unfair?

Eventually I struggled to my feet and went to the phone. Although I couldn't share my joy with Alecos, my parents would be overjoyed to know they were to become grandparents. But their joy, like mine, was tempered with their knowledge that since the attack on Morphou I had no idea if Alecos was alive or dead.

I wanted desperately to share my news with Ann but we'd parted in such a rush after our encounter with Spiros, I'd forgotten to take her telephone number. And I hadn't the energy to face the nightmare of having to go through all the numerous administrative channels to get to Karl at the military hospital at Akrotiri.

Today should have been one of the most special moments of my life, a day full of joy and happiness to be shared.

Instead, I was alone. The rest of the day passed in the mundane motions of just existing.

28

The final days

The next morning when I woke I felt sick again, but now that I knew the reason, I was happy. I smiled contentedly, pressing my tummy gently.

Fortunately, I'd bought some crackers at the supermarket yesterday. For breakfast, I nibbled a couple with some warm milk to take away the nausea.

The Commissioner arrived early as he'd promised

"You look very well, despite all your problems," he said, patting my arm like an indulgent uncle, as he sat down.

I hadn't intended to say anything, but my news bubbled out and I couldn't stop myself. I grinned happily but added that although I was thrilled by the pregnancy, it could be one more problem added to an already long list, the first and foremost being the absence of Alecos.

Bringing him up to date, beginning with the arrest of Alecos by the Greek officer on the beach in Kyrenia, I also told him about the treachery of Spiros and the attempted rape.

"Yes," he nodded. "We have him on record as being a violent henchman of Sampson but as yet we haven't been able to find him."

I didn't tell him what had happened at the church. When the body turned up, they could form their own opinion. I also told him my worries that Alecos might have been captured or killed by the Turkish advance on Morphou just a few days ago.

"No, I doubt that," he said, lighting a cigarette, then looking at me in concern. "Does it upset you now if I smoke?"

I laughed. "So far you are the first person who has smoked since I've realised I'm pregnant, so I don't know yet. But go ahead and we'll find out."

He continued. "My guess is that he was released at the very beginning when the Turks arrived in Kyrenia. We needed every able bodied men to help defend our lines."

"But he wasn't a soldier. I don't think he'd ever fired a gun in his life."

"No, my dear. They wouldn't put him on the front line without any combat experience. They'd use him in some other capacity. What could he do?"

"Well, he didn't have any medical training and he had no idea how to cook. He could sing though," I said, flippantly. "But I can't see how that would help anyone!"

The Commissioner smiled. "No, there's not much call for singing when one is fighting a war!"

He thought for a minute then said: "He could drive though. He drove a heavy Mercedes, so perhaps they used him to drive a troop carrier or heavy vehicle. As he was in Morphou he would have joined the local National Guard. He was probably still there when the Turkish army swept through two nights ago. Yesterday the last defences at Famagusta fell. Now they've advanced to their pre-determined 'Attila' line, the fighting will stop," he sighed in relief as his shoulders relaxed.

Then he continued: "It's not in their interest to acquire any more territory. It would be impossible to

defend. There aren't enough Turkish Cypriots to pop-
ulate the area they have acquired and those that are
there will be in for a very hard time. They are used to
a civilized standard of living. Turkey will have to
resettle the area they have acquired with people from
the mainland. The first settlers will be uneducated
peasant farmers and convicts; they won't even understand the Turkish Cypriot dialect. There will be no
end of trouble!"

"Yes," I agreed. "The Turkish Cypriots are good
people. Alecos had many Turkish Cypriot friends from
his childhood in Limassol and we have some working
in the company too. They are always friendly,
hospitable and charming. I feel sorry for them now;
they are the ones who will suffer the most, in the end."

He puffed at his cigarette. "Soon the soldiers who
have been fighting in the north will be returning home
but we'll also have thousands of displaced people
from the captured north to resettle on the territory we
have left. The logistics of such a task are enormous
and heartbreaking. It could take months or even years
to sort out," he said sorrowfully.

"Do you think that Alecos could come home
soon?" I asked hopefully.

"Yes, my dear. I think there is every possibility. Be
patient though. Don't give up hope. It could still be
some time before everyone is able to return. But now,
on a happier note, do you have a doctor you can visit
to get help with the pregnancy?"

"Yes, if he's still in Nicosia."

"Well, if you can't reach him, here's the number of
our doctor, who I know is nearby. He can reassure you
about the baby. That will be one problem less on your
list of worries! Now I have to be off. I have more
work piled up than I can handle. But, if you need any

more help just phone and I'll see what I can do."

The Commissioner's visit had reassured me to some extent. Now I just had to wait and hope for Alecos to come home, unless the very worst had happened. But I couldn't and wouldn't consider the possibility. It left too much aching space that didn't have Alecos in it. I was sure the baby had been the result of our visit to Aphrodite's Baths during our wonderful weekend in Paphos. The Goddess of Love would never allow one of her children to be born without a father!

Although I considered myself as realistic and practical, I still harboured some romantic superstition deep down, and my belief in Aphrodite was it. I firmly believed in her protection. This whimsical notion helped me through the darker moments.

The rest of the day was spent shuffling through old issues of woman's magazines, looking for articles about babies and pregnancy. As I'd already discovered, both tea and coffee made me nauseous. Instead, I stuck to warm milk with crackers or dry toast. Reading the pregnancy articles about food and feelings gave me a good idea of what to expect and helped me through the day by keeping my mind off my other worries.

I was woken from a deep contented sleep, as the dawn light was filtering through the shutters. There was a violent banging at the front door.

I was petrified. I was completely alone. I jumped out of bed, my eyes darting round the room for something to defend myself with. I heard the front door splinter and shatter, followed by a savage roar and a drunken Spiros yelled "you bitch" as he barged through.

Oh my God, my mind screamed. We didn't kill him after all. Now he's here to have his revenge.

I looked around for somewhere to hide. Thoughts of how to escape rushed through my mind. Screaming for help was useless; there was no one in the building to hear me. Locking the bedroom door was useless too, he'd just smash through it like he'd done to the front door. I couldn't jump out of the window, we were too high up.

I was hyperventilating in panic. What could I do? Now he really would kill me. There would be no escape this time. The flat was too small. There was nowhere to run. I was trapped and I was absolutely terrified. What else could I do?

I dashed over to the French windows. Sliding the doors open I stepped out onto the balcony. Unlike the spacious terrace in front of the main living area, the bedroom balconies were narrow, designed only with room enough to stand outside in the fresh air. I grabbed a heavy long necked crystal vase from the dressing table as I went. Maybe I could knock him out again if he came through these doors.

Perhaps I could climb over the balcony rail and hoist myself across to the next door balcony? No, it was impossible, the gap was too wide, my arms weren't long enough to grab the opposite rail and I'd fall.

As I stood in the dark shadow beside the open door, shivering with fear and not daring to breath, Spiros burst like a crazed animal into the bedroom.

Switching on the light, he roared in a frenzy finding the room empty. Then seeing the balcony door open he yelled triumphantly and charged violently across the room thrusting himself drunkenly through the narrow doors. In his unsteady state his toe caught the raised metal guide runner of the sliding door and he tripped.

In one movement, the speed and force of his weight threw him forward, crashing directly on to the low balcony rail. Unable to stop his forward movement, he lost his balance and fell headlong over the rail, hurtling to the ground, three floors below.

Shocked and horrified, I didn't know what to do. I stood rooted to the spot, trembling in a cold sweat. The whole episode was like a dreadful nightmare. I couldn't believe it had happened. Slowly coming to my senses, I knew the only person who would really know what to do was Commissioner Marcos, the top policeman for the whole of Cyprus.

"I'll be over right away," he said. "Don't touch anything. I'll get the body removed. Don't worry, we'll sort it all out," the Commissioner said briskly.

He and his team arrived within a short time. After the body was taken away, the Commissioner, once again, sat down in my living room to question me.

He had seen the smashed front door, and knowing the violent reputation of Spiros wasn't surprised at what had taken place.

"Now I have to ask you a delicate question. Did he trip, as you say, or did you push him?"

I stared at him aghast. How could he not believe me?

"It happened exactly as I told you," I said desperately. "He tripped on the metal door runner. He must have left a dent in it. Have a look," I said jumping up and running in to the bedroom to point it out.

Sure enough, to my immense relief, there was a slight outward facing indent on the runner and the balcony rail was buckled as though something heavy had pushed on it. He nodded, satisfied.

"Is there anyone who could have heard the door being smashed?"

"No, the whole block is empty. No one would have heard or seen anything. I said worriedly.

"So there is no witness to vouch for you?"

"No," I shook my head in panic, sweat creeping onto my brow. "But wait a minute. Mrs Panayiotis, in the block opposite," I said, pointing to her window. "She's deaf and in a wheelchair, but she can see alright. She always waves to me when I'm on the balcony. She sits there day and night. She must have seen it happen."

"Yes, I can see someone there," he said, staring across. "Could she see anything in the dark though?"

"I don't suppose so, but Spiros switched the light on as he came into the bedroom. So both the bedroom and the balcony were illuminated. She would have been able to see everything."

"Good. I'll send a sergeant over to her flat to see what she has to say. Someone will come here to record the damage to the balcony. He'll patch up the door too, so you can close it till you get a new one fitted."

Looking around, he seemed satisfied. "You'd better get dressed, as you'll have to come to the police station to make a statement. But don't worry, there is enough evidence to show exactly what happened so it's just a formality."

He stood up to leave.

"We've been steadily rounding up Sampson's band of thugs. There won't be an inquiry into Spiros death," he said. "He has a history of rape and violence. What happened here was just one more charge to add to his record. So, ending as it did, IT closes the book neatly. We've got far more important things to deal with, without worrying about the death of this particular villain!"

29

The ending

After going through the formalities at the police station and the fixing of the front door, I was still in shock. The joy and excitement of the pregnancy was tempered by the terrible happenings of the morning, but I kept my mind busy with plans for the baby.

The Commissioners assessment of the war situation, had proved right, as later in the day came the announcement that the ceasefire line had been drawn by Turkey and the fighting had stopped.

I now felt there was hope that sooner or later Alecos would return.

Feeling elated at the news of the ceasefire. I got hold of the Commissioner's doctor and he agreed to see me later in the week.

That night I went to bed, safe in the knowledge that Spiros would never be able to harm me, or Alecos, again. His evil life had ended, but for us, our baby's life was just beginning. I fell asleep smiling and content.

Several days later, sitting in the kitchen, enjoying my early morning milk and toast, my mind full of happy thoughts of babies, I heard a scraping noise at the hastily put together front door. Then a loud creaking as it was slowly pushed open.

I jumped up in panic, sure that Spiros had, yet

again, returned from the dead.

Hovering in the doorway was a spectre from one of my worst nightmares. I screamed in horror as the tall figure, with a filthy face and blood stained bandages unravelling round its head and legs, shuffled slowly towards me.

The long straggly hair and beard were matted with blood. Ragged tatters hung from the emaciated body and torn strips of leather barely covered the dirt-encrusted feet.

I stepped back sickened by the sight and smell.

The figure raised its skinny arms towards me, the nails on its fingers like blackened claws. A gurgling sound came from its throat, and in a hoarse whisper it gasped: "Sally mou," as it collapsed into my arms.

The horror evaporated and tears of joy cascaded down my cheeks onto his swollen filthy face.

Lowering him gently to the floor, I removed his dirty, tattered clothing. Then, filling a bowl with warm water, I carefully clean the dirt off his wounds and soothed his bruised and battered body with a gentle application of antiseptic cream.

He stirred and murmured in his unconscious delirium but then lay still.

I covered him with a blanket and propped his head on a pillow. Sitting down on the floor next to him, I murmured reassuring words while stroking his hand, hoping my presence would penetrate his subconscious and he'd feel safe.

I sat with him for a long time. Despite his terrible condition, I felt then that even though we had both gone through terrifying experiences, we could overcome our ordeals now we were together again at last. We could help each other mend!

Eventually he stirred, twitching and crying out, as

though he was fighting to get away from something.

"Shh! Shh!" I whispered. "Don't worry, Alecos, my love. You're safe now. I'm here, I'll look after you." He seemed to understand and quietened down, then slowly his eyes opened. Looking up at me, his dry, cracked lips moved into a weak smile.

"Sally mou, is it really you?" he croaked.

I smiled and nodded. "Yes, it's me, my love. You're not dreaming. You're home now and you're safe. Just lay still for a few moments while I fix you something to eat."

He gave a slight nod and closed his eyes.

After I'd fed him some warm soup, I applied more medication and bandages to his wounds. Wrapping him in a soft towel to make him as comfortable as possible on the hard floor, I gave him a couple of Aspirins in warm milk. Moving painfully, he settled himself on the pillow and fell asleep immediately. I pulled up an easy chair and spent the night next to him. Once during the night he cried out but I soothed him, holding him close stroking away his fears. His breathing became regular and he slept calmly again. When he woke, his eyes darted round in fear but then, realising he was in his own home, tears of relief trickled from his eyes.

The doctor arrived the next day. He cleaned and dressed Alecos wounds and assured me there was nothing very wrong that plenty of sleep and good food would not mend.

The next day though still very weak, he held tightly on to me. I slowly helped him into the shower. The warm water soothed his wounds and cleaned off the last of the encrusted dirt from his body. Then we moved slowly into the bedroom and he managed to get into bed where he fell asleep again almost at once.

I kissed him gently and let him sleep till he was ready to move.

The next few days became a routine of feeding him small meals, dressing his wounds and letting him sleep till he woke. Time passed slowly, but soon he was able to eat more and his wounds healed. He didn't speak much but his eyes spoke of love and relief that we were together again. The rest and recuperation of the previous days had done their job. By the end of the week he began to sit up in bed, calling out for warm drinks and biscuits. Soon he was ready to sit at the table for lunch.

He gobbled up his scrambled eggs and finished off a bowl of fresh figs with yogurt and honey. Then he asked for more. He was definitely on the mend!

Some days after the cease fire, while my thought were involved entirely on the wounded Alecos, the leader of the Turkish Cypriots had proclaimed the establishment of an autonomous administration in the newly acquired territory in the North of Cyprus. Their longed-for ambition had finally been realised.

During his convalescence, Alecos hadn't talked about what he'd gone through. I didn't press him, as I knew he would tell me about his experiences when he was ready to face the horrors of the war.

He wasn't the type to lock things away inside himself. They would come out sooner or later and I hoped by letting them go, he'd recover completely.

"Would you like a cup of tea?" I asked him one afternoon as he shuffled into the kitchen to be near me.

"No, I don't want anything. Whenever there was a lull in the fighting, I would think about you and your 'four o'clock tea'. I missed you so much Sally mou. But you go ahead and have your tea. I'll watch you while you drink it and I'll know I'm home."

"No, I don't drink tea anymore!"

He looked at me in utter amazement." You don't drink tea? What's happened to you?"

"It makes me sick. I'm pregnant," I told him gently.

His mouth dropped open and his legs gave way. He howled in agony as his wounded body dropped onto the hard wooden kitchen chair. His face registered shock, but quickly turned into delight as my words sunk in.

"Are you sure? How do you know?"

"Yes, it's true. I saw the doctor and he confirmed it. He said everything was progressing as it should at this stage of the pregnancy."

"How many months are you?"

"He said around two months when I saw him. I think it could have happened when we went to Paphos after you came home from Germany. I knew it was a good idea to go to Aphrodite's Baths, but you wouldn't believe me."

Alecos shook his head in wonder.

"The baby should be born around March or April time so you'll have plenty of time to get used to the idea of having a family."

"Oh, Sally mou, apart from the joy of coming home to you, to become a father is the next best thing that could happen to me. I'm so happy. I feel I could go out and defeat the whole Turkish army with my bare hands."

I laughed, but then said seriously: "That won't be possible anymore. They agreed a ceasefire and drawn a line right across from Morphou and its orange plantations, across the fertile Mesoria plain, through Nicosia and right across to Famagusta's beaches and tourist hotels. The line goes across the whole of the north of the island so you couldn't get near them now even if you wanted to. And now they've proclaimed an autonomous state."

"I didn't know that. It must have happened while I was trying to get home. I can't believe it. That's terrible. So much land has been lost and so many lives have been wasted. I can't tell you how awful it was," he said with tears in his eyes and a lump in his throat.

"Don't talk about it now. Just think happy thoughts about the baby. That's what I did to stop me worrying about what was happening to you. My parents know about the baby, of course. They are thrilled that they will be grandparents. Now I can tell them the good news that you are much better too," I said putting my arms around him and kissing the tip of his nose.

"The Commissioner knows as well," I said. 'No one else was here in Nicosia so the Commissioner was the only person I could ask for help. He was the one who recommended the doctor."

"I'm so glad he was around to help you," he said, taking my hand.

"Yes, it was hard and frightening but I got through it. I only realised I was pregnant when I got back here from the mountains. After the capture of Morphou, I thought I'd lost you forever. I'd been depressed and crying for ages worrying about you. Then on top of everything, I started being sick as well. Eventually I put two-and-two together."

"My poor Sally. What a terrible time you must have had. I thought I was the one who was in trouble!"

That comment opened the floodgates for me and

everything that had happened came pouring out, in a torrent of words.

I started with the good thing. How kind the Fletchers and the Rixs had been to me. I told him about Princess the cat and then the wonderful news about Ann and Karl.

That lead to the attack by Spiros at the church when we thought we'd killed him.

Alecos blanched with horror and disbelief. By then I was in tears and he held me in his arms trying to sooth me out of my misery. I remember Mrs F saying we would mend in each other's arms. She was so right.

Of course, there was worse to come. I sobbed as I told him how Spiros had broken in to the flat, drunk and hungry for revenge, and the ghastly ending.

Alecos was in shock. But once he got over his rage and disgust on hearing what I'd been through at the hands of Spiros, he realised he needed to talk to the Commissioner about the consequences.

As he still wasn't well enough to go out, I called the Commissioner who came early the next day to the apartment.

He had been delighted to learn that Alecos had returned and had many questions to ask him about his part in the war. It was easier for Alecos to talk frankly man-to-man about his terrible experiences. I knew he had been reluctant to upset me with the horrors he'd been through, so I was glad that he could open up to the Commissioner to clear them out of his system before they started to fester.

They talked together for a long time, but after the Commissioner's assurances that there would be no repercussions about Spiros' death, Alecos healed quickly both in spirit and in body.

Now his worries were about the business. The newly built offices were almost out of bounds. However, he still had the original small store and office in Limassol. He decided that with a bit of effort, he could start again from there. But to get the business back on its feet, Alecos would have to spend long hours of each day and into the night at the Limassol base.

The big problem was that the Turks had captured Lourogina, a small village, a short distance from the main Limassol-Nicosia arterial road.

It had now become a strategic position and their bargaining tool. From there they could cut the main highway at any moment they wished, making communication and commerce virtually impossible for the daily life of the Greek Cypriot community in the south.

It would be impossible for me being pregnant to be with Alecos all the time. If we stayed in Nicosia, I would have to go back and forth to Limassol each day with Alecos, because we could be separated permanently if the Turkish army blocked the main road.

And with so many refugees already flocking into the Limassol area there was no chance of finding somewhere to live there.

We talked and talked, trying to find an acceptable solution. Eventually, we both agreed that as the airport had been virtually destroyed and the shipping lines were still in chaos, it would be safer for me with the baby on the way to go back to England to my parents.

As a British passport holder I was still eligible to be evacuated as a refugee, but now the airlift was virtually at the end, I had to leave immediately to be on the last flight out.

Once the decision was made, I packed my passport and a few necessities into a small case and we left for Akrotiri with no time to lose.

Alecos drove me to the checkpoint at the base. It was hard to tear myself away from him. These last days together, loving and nursing him back to strength, had compensated for all the anguish and heartbreak of thinking I'd lost him. Now it was happening again. I could hardly bear it, but I knew this time it was not forever so for all our sakes, I must leave.

Sitting on the huge noisy Hercules plane taking me away from my husband and home, I gazed down at the beautiful island of Aphrodite, the paradise island that was now in ruins and cried for all the people that were left behind to pick up the pieces of their shattered lives.

From the beginning of time, these island people had lived through wars and conquests. This latest war had torn the island apart, but the people were resilient and stoic and would once again weather the unhappiness and hardships, just as they had done for centuries.

Epilogue

On Monday 15th July 1974 a coup was staged against the Makarios government by the National Guard led by Greek army officers. The Cyprus President narrowly escaped assassination and sought refuge abroad.

On Saturday 20th July at dawn, Turkish troops equipped with the most modern weapons supplied to them by NATO, for the protection of their own boarders, invaded the island of Cyprus alleging a breach of the Treaty of Guarantee. By the 16th August 1974 they had occupied 40 per cent of the territory of the Republic.

The Turkish Government called the invasion force a 'peace keeping' force to protect the Turkish community. Instead it turned 200,000 Greek Cypriots into refugees - 40 per cent of the population - and occupying a large part of the richest and most productive area in the Republic, dislocating the economic structure of the country for generations.

The northern part of the island was depopulated by 75 per cent. The twin towns of Karavas and Lapithos which had a joint population of 7,000, was occupied for several months after the invasion, solely by a British couple determined to protect their home against looters.

The jet-set holiday destination for tourists was the

town of Famagusta, which was the last place to fall to the Turkish advance on the 14th of August, and its population fled in terror.

The Varosha district of Famagusta, where the high-rise luxury hotels set along the golden sands, is still today, 44 years later, like a ghost town. The skeletons of bombed hotels and looted shops and properties are now grown over with weeds, and are still heavily guarded by Turkish soldiers patrolling along the rusty barbed wire fence surrounding the area.

Tens of thousands of Turkish Cypriots living in the south were uprooted from their homes to be resettled in the North in the homes of the Greek Cypriots who had been driven out.

Turks from Turkey were sent to the North to repopulate the land. The area was vast and Greek properties were considerable.

This became an early example of ethnic cleansing.

The Turkish air force burnt hundreds of acres of cedar and pine trees in the Troodos mountains which were far from the fighting. The orange groves and fruit orchards in the Turkish held area were left unwatered and hundreds of thousands of livestock died before the area was eventually reoccupied.

Both Communities on this small Mediterranean island had their dreams. The Greek Cypriots' dream of Enosis, union with Greece. The Turkish Cypriots wanted Taxim, the partition of the island. Neither dream took into account the feelings of the other community and in the end, due to the wider political dreams of the Great Powers, it was the Turkish dream that became fact.

Eleanor Michael

About The Author

Eleanor Michael was born during the war years in London to an Austrian mother and a Greek Cypriot father. She was educated and worked in England until 1967 when she moved to Cyprus and subsequently married a Greek Cypriot businessman.

While in Cyprus, she accidently discovered the HQ of the terrorist faction intent on destabilising the government and killing the President. This event led to a military coup which provoked the invasion of the country by Turkish forces in the summer of 1974, who then captured over a third of the Island.

She was eventually evacuated but returned at the end of hostilities to the upheaval of starting up a once thriving business in the chaotic environment of a post-war torn Island. On the death of her husband, some time later, she returned to England.

Eleanor remarried and moved to the Algarve in Portugal where she has now lived for over 30 years. During those years, she was inspired by an authoress friend to write a novel about her experiences in Cyprus during that dramatic period of its history.

Eleanor has always loved books and has been an avid reader from a very early age. She never imagined that so many years later she would actually write her story as a novel that would be read by friends and strangers too. **www.EleanorMichael.com**

Printed in Great Britain
by Amazon